The Seduction of
Miranda Prosper

The Seduction of
Miranda Prosper

MARISSA DAY

HEAT | NEW YORK

THE BERKLEY PUBLISHING GROUP
Published by the Penguin Group
Penguin Group (USA) Inc.
375 Hudson Street, New York, New York 10014, USA
Penguin Group (Canada), 90 Eglinton Avenue East, Suite 700, Toronto, Ontario M4P 2Y3, Canada
(a division of Pearson Penguin Canada Inc.)
Penguin Books Ltd., 80 Strand, London WC2R 0RL, England
Penguin Group Ireland, 25 St. Stephen's Green, Dublin 2, Ireland (a division of Penguin Books Ltd.)
Penguin Group (Australia), 250 Camberwell Road, Camberwell, Victoria 3124, Australia
(a division of Pearson Australia Group Pty. Ltd.)
Penguin Books India Pvt. Ltd., 11 Community Centre, Panchsheel Park, New Delhi—110 017, India
Penguin Group (NZ), 67 Apollo Drive, Rosedale, North Shore 0632, New Zealand
(a division of Pearson New Zealand Ltd.)
Penguin Books (South Africa) (Pty.) Ltd., 24 Sturdee Avenue, Rosebank, Johannesburg 2196,
South Africa

Penguin Books Ltd., Registered Offices: 80 Strand, London WC2R 0RL, England

This book is an original publication of The Berkley Publishing Group.

This is a work of fiction. Names, characters, places, and incidents either are the product of the author's imagination or are used fictitiously, and any resemblance to actual persons, living or dead, business establishments, events, or locales is entirely coincidental. The publisher does not have any control over and does not assume any responsibility for author or third-party websites or their content.

PRINTING HISTORY
Heat trade paperback edition / January 2011

Library of Congress Cataloging-in-Publication Data
Day, Marissa.
   The seduction of Miranda Prosper / Marissa Day.—Heat trade pbk. ed.
      p. cm.
   ISBN 978-0-425-23865-3
   1. Magicians—Fiction. 2. London (England)—18th century—Fiction. I. Title.
   PS3576.E77S43 2011
   813'.6—dc22
                                                                    2010023004

PRINTED IN THE UNITED STATES OF AMERICA

10 9 8 7 6 5 4 3 2 1

This book is dedicated to
my loving husband and happily ever after,
Timothy B. Smith

Acknowledgments

The author would very much like to thank the authors of the Untitled Writers Group, the Excelsior critique group and the SF-FFWs newslist who actively supported the writing of this book. She'd also like to thank her agent, Shawna, for all her continuing hard work, and her editor, Wendy, who made this a better book.

One

Corwin Rathe knew he was in the presence of a Catalyst as soon as he entered the house, or rather his cock did.

Corwin paused in the threshold to admire the glittering private ballroom. As he inhaled the richly mingled scents of perfume and humanity, his cock began to swell, hot and eager. There was most certainly a Catalyst amid the sparkling throng. It was summer, and most of London society was making ready to retire to the country to escape the heat and stink of town. For Lady Viola Thayer, this was the perfect excuse for a party. She had thrown open the doors of her Mayfair home for approximately two hundred of society's finest. They moved about the room, dancing, chattering and, no doubt, intriguing. Despite the seriousness of his errand, and despite the fact that he suddenly had to resist the strong urge to stroke himself, Corwin grinned. With any luck the evening would prove productive, and very pleasant.

A liveried servant hastened toward Corwin, ready to eject him as an interloper. Corwin met the man's gaze directly.

"I have an invitation," he said in a tone that was firm yet conversational. "You will announce Mr. Corwin Rathe."

The footman's eyes unfocused briefly under the force of Corwin's bespelling gaze. "Yes, sir." He bowed, turned and did precisely as he was instructed.

"Mr. Corwin Rathe!"

Curious heads turned. Curious eyes narrowed. Corwin stood in place, giving the assembly sufficient time to look him over. He was a tall man with a form that was the result of an active and dangerous life: broad in the shoulder and narrow in the hip, with strong legs. His hair was midnight black, and his eyes nearly as dark. Tonight, he dressed in a burgundy coat cut away to show his patterned waistcoat, a spotless linen shirt and tight fawn breeches—a choice he was beginning to regret, due to the fullness of his erection.

As the company took his measure, Corwin returned the favor. He surveyed the ballroom, his gaze lingering on the delightful variety of women present (although any number of the men looked as if they also would be intriguing company, were they so inclined). It would surely take a while to select the Catalyst from so many fine flowers, but he was quite prepared . . .

Then he saw her.

Her hair was as black has his own, piled high on top of her head and crowned in the style *a la minute* with glittering gems and a trio of pale ostrich feathers. Her skin was tawny rather than pale cream. It went well with her black hair and her rich brown eyes. Her high-waisted gown was a bold, emerald green silk trimmed with pure white lace. It had been cut low, allowing him the delectable sight of her ample breasts. More feathers decorated the fan held to her gloved wrist by a slender chain. Her skirts were somewhat fuller than those of most of the other ladies in the room, done in an utterly mistaken—and futile— attempt to disguise the luscious curves of her hips and thighs.

But despite all these enticing attributes, she sat alone on a little gilt chair at the edge of the room.

As Corwin gazed at her, a quick pulse of blood to his cock told him she was indeed the Catalyst. He breathed a silent prayer of thanks to all the gods and goddesses. Not only was he in time; she was surely one of the most beautiful women he had ever seen.

Corwin's cock pulsed again, its urgency bordering on pain, but that only made him grin harder.

Soon, he told his eager member. *Very soon.*

Like everyone else in Lady Thayer's ballroom, Miranda Prosper turned to look at the stranger. Despite rumors of an indiscreet past, Lady Thayer now gave the most exclusive, elaborate and dullest parties on record. To Miranda's way of thinking, that was a very long record indeed. For her end-of-season party, Lady Viola Thayer had spared no expense. Each of the three chandeliers was fully lit, flooding the room with rich, warm light. Draperies of gold and ivory silk glimmered on the walls and festooned the high-arched windows. The parquet floor had been polished mirror bright. As for the guests, they were all the cream of London society, arrayed in their summer finery; a human garden of silks, laces and jewels.

But Miranda had been staring at them all for several hours now and was bored to tears by their glamour. A stranger might provide something new to speculate about, if only for a few minutes.

She was, however, utterly unprepared for what she saw, or for what that sight did to her.

Mr. Corwin Rathe was tall and broad. His supple fawn breeches showed off magnificently muscled legs. His face was chiseled, with high cheekbones, a long, straight nose, a strong jaw, and eyes like midnight.

It was those eyes that did Miranda in. Although Mr. Rathe bowed to the whole of the company, it seemed as if those deep, black eyes gazed only at her. She felt hot. She felt cold. No, she wasn't cold; she was fevered. That was the only explanation for the tremors running down her spine, and the flush rising to her cheeks. But there was no explanation at all for the sudden yearning that rose up from deep within her at the sight of the stranger. It was as if she had been starving for years, but had discovered the fact only at this moment.

No. Please, don't. Please stop, she begged her traitorous body. *It's pointless.* Miranda closed her eyes, and willed the sensation to go away.

At twenty-five years of age, Miranda knew with remorseless certainty that she was not the sort who attracted men. She was too short, too plump, her hair too coarse and dark, her eyes too bold, her nature too . . . discontent. She could not master the arts of flirtation and general coquetry that would snare her a husband and get her out of her mother's house. This, she knew, was very much due to the fact that she could not convince herself marriage would do anything but move her from one kind of cage into another.

So, she had become an "aging spinster," and as her mother was not quite prepared to let her sit home with a book, Miranda instead sat alone on the little gilt chair at the edge of the ballroom making polite conversation with the maiden aunts, or—more often—saying nothing at all, because sometimes it was all she could do not to scream.

Mother, of course, was not with her. Having despaired of anyone ever making an advance, proper or improper, to Miranda, Mother was on the other side of the ballroom. Every now and then the sound of her perfectly calculated laugh would rise above the music and more sedate conversation from where she made the glowing center for a gathering of wealthy widowers and titled married men. Miranda's mouth quirked itself up tightly and she wondered which of those wealthy, fascinated men was being selected as Mrs. Rowe-Prosper-Lester-Quicke's next husband.

Miranda looked away, not even bothering to hide her "so unattractive" frown. That proved to be a mistake, however, because now she could see Corwin Rathe making his way through the ballroom. He moved like a slash of night through the bright rainbow around him; smiling, bowing and being introduced. The more Miranda looked at him, the more intensely the heat flared inside her. Something else began as well, some loosening at her very center, and a tingling that reached up to her lips and down to the ends of her fingers. Unaccountably, an image flashed in Miranda's mind, of a man and woman in the darkness, naked bodies pressed tight together while their mouths fastened against each other in deep, passionate kisses.

Don't let this be love, she prayed, looking down at her hands clenched around her fan. *Don't do this to me.*

When Miranda at last looked up again, she saw Mr. Corwin Rathe standing not three feet from her. This time there was no mistaking the fact that his burning, black gaze focused on her entirely. The sight of him this close was so stunning and unaccountable that Miranda at first didn't notice that her mother stood with him, her hand resting lightly on his sleeve.

"Miranda, dear, this is Mr. Corwin Rathe," said Mother, smiling brilliantly. She wore her gold dress and light widow's cap the way a queen would wear her regalia and carried herself with an ease Miranda had never come close to matching. "Mr. Rathe, permit me to introduce my daughter, Miranda Prosper."

Mr. Rathe took Miranda's hand. The moment his fingers clasped hers, another picture flashed through Miranda's mind, clearer and more intense than the first. *She* was naked in the darkness, and so was he. His arms wrapped tight around her as he kissed her. His hands splayed across the curve of her buttocks, pulling her close as he bent to kiss her throat, her breasts.

Miranda's nipples tightened under her chemise, and she realized she hadn't answered him at all.

"Delighted to meet you, Mr. Rathe," she managed to croak.

"Charmed, Miss Prosper." His voice was soft, like velvet. It seemed to stroke her skin, and Miranda could not stop herself from shivering.

Mother raised her brows. "Mr. Rathe was asking if I knew you to be engaged for the waltz. I don't believe that's so?" More than a hint of impatience colored Mother's voice.

How is it we are even having this conversation? This stunning man was of mature years, Miranda could now see. *Why aren't you taking him for yourself?* It would not, after all, be the first time.

"No, I am not engaged at present," Miranda managed to reply, more clearly this time.

"Then, Miss Prosper"—Mr. Rathe extended his arm—"will you do me the very great honor of claiming you as mine?"

He meant for the dance, of course. But it didn't sound that way. It sounded like so much more. Miranda felt the flush creep down from her face to her breasts.

No! Don't! part of her screamed. There was danger here, as great as it was inexplicable. Where her certainty came from was yet another unknown, but it was real and she did not doubt it for an instant. Just as she did not doubt that this man was the cause of the fire that burned within her. If he left, that fire would die, possibly for all time.

Miranda found she did not want the fire to go out.

"Thank you, Mr. Rathe. I would be delighted." Miranda laid her hand on his silk-clad arm, and permitted him to lead her to the center of the dance floor. She was proud of how well she walked, holding herself calm and steady, keeping her shawl neatly looped across her arms, and her fan tidily folded in her free hand, even though the whole room was openly staring at the inconceivable sight of Daphne Quicke's unmarriageable daughter on the arm of this oh-so-intriguing stranger.

It's a mercy dance, thought Miranda. *Mother has persuaded him to this, and he has agreed in order to gain her favor.*

This thought thoroughly doused Miranda's spirits, and the mysterious fires inside her guttered hard. She stood passively while Mr. Rathe took her right hand to extend their arms and placed his left hand on her back. Even through the layers of their gloves, she could feel the warmth where he touched her, and another shiver that had nothing to do with cold crept across her skin.

"Now, then, Miss Prosper, will you be kind enough to tell me what has turned you so suddenly sad?" Mr. Rathe asked softly.

Miranda lifted her chin. "I thank you for the dance, sir," she answered. "But you need not cater to my feelings. My mother cares not one whit for them."

"Ah. I believe I understand." Behind them, the music lifted. A lovely Viennese creation wrapped the room in bright, rhythmic strains. Mr. Rathe began the steps at once. He was strong and graceful, leading Miranda into the turns without forcing her to follow. Each move was expert and fluid. Miranda found it unusually easy to fall into step with him. His well-formed arm beneath her gloved hand was a comfort, but his hand on her back . . . She felt the unnamed heat rising at her center again.

Mr. Rathe dipped his head close to whisper in her ear. "What would you say, Miss Prosper, if I told you it was for your sake alone I asked you to dance?"

Miranda parted her lips in reply, but no words came. In that instant, another vision washed over her. She was naked again and Corwin Rathe knelt before her. His broad, brown hands gripped her thighs, and his mouth pressed against her pussy. She felt his hot tongue lapping between her folds and his eager mouth sucking the soft flesh there. Pleasure flared up Miranda's spine, too strong to resist, and she gripped his arms, lost to desire.

In the vision she knotted her fingers in his thick hair and pressed him closer.

"For your sake alone." She heard his voice in her ear, cutting through the lustful dream. But even as he spoke to her in the ballroom, there in that other world she watched and felt his tongue thrust deep into her slit. "For the sake of your beauty and the satisfaction of your desire."

He licked strongly; one stroke, two.

"What are you doing to me?" She didn't know where she was, or what was happening. There was only this indescribable dream. In it, he was again standing, thrusting his tongue into her mouth as he had thrust it into her slit. She opened to that kiss, willingly, eagerly. Corwin pulled her close to rub her wet and swollen pussy against his gorgeously erect cock while with his right hand he firmly massaged her taut breast. Pleasure and need made her moan.

Then she saw they were not alone.

Another man walked from the shadows, watching them. He stepped up behind Miranda and put his hands on her waist, holding her firmly in place to receive Corwin's delightful attentions.

The fire that blazed through her at the touch of that second phantom man must kill her. She must die from this searing madness.

"Don't be afraid," Corwin murmured. "I have you safe. You see it, don't you? You feel it."

"Yes," she gasped. In the vision Corwin smiled at her and stroked her face. The second man was as tall as Corwin, but whereas Corwin was dark as midnight, this other man was all red-gold like the dawn. That golden man slid his hands up her curving sides to cup her breasts. He pulled her back against him to press his rigid cock into the split between her buttocks.

"I feel it too, Miranda." Corwin's hands slid down, stroking her thighs. In the dream or in reality? She couldn't tell anymore. "The need, the desire. It's real for me as well."

The vision melted away, and there was nothing but the music and the rhythm of the dance. They moved together through the ballroom that was magnificent and crowded, and as mundane as it could be. There was, however, nothing mundane about the riot inside Miranda as she looked up into Corwin Rathe's black eyes.

"What are you doing to me?" She should pull away. No. She should *run* away now, at once, but she couldn't bear the thought of separating herself from the touch of his hands. Her breasts felt full and heavy, and her pussy was a space of pure, liquid heat. As frightened as she was, she also felt more alive than she ever had before, and she could not stand to let go of all these new, oh-so-mesmerizing sensations.

"Say my name," he whispered harshly. "I want to hear you say my name."

She could not refuse. "Corwin," she murmured.

"Yes." He sighed, sending a fresh shiver through her. He brushed his thumb across her cheek. "I want you, Miranda," he said simply. "Do you want me?"

All the breath in Miranda's body seized tight. It was impossible, what he was suggesting. It must be impossible. Such things as she was seeing, as she was feeling, could not ever be.

"I can't . . ."

But he did not let her finish. "Miranda, that is not what I asked." He pulled her closer so that she could feel the brush of his hard chest against her ruched nipples, and the smile of his mouth against her ear. "I asked if you want me. Like this."

Two of them again, two of them, and they were naked and glorious, one in front of her and one behind. The dawn-light man lifted her breast with one hand so Corwin could suckle her, even while he himself slid his hand between her legs.

"And this."

She sprawled on her back. The dawn-light man stroked her breasts with his masterful hands while Corwin slid between her thighs, stroking her, plunging his fingers into her, preparing the way for his immense, erect cock.

"Yes." The sound that escaped her was more a moan than it was speech. "Yes, I want you."

"That's it, Miranda. Do not fear to speak the truth to me." Corwin turned them again. His hand stroked the curve of her back. The whole world was filled with light and his heady scent and the fevered desire that flowed through her. "Do not fear what you feel now."

"How can I? How could we . . . ?"

His smile broadened and a light that promised mischief sparked in the depths of his dark eyes. "Walk with me."

"But . . ." she began again.

"Shhh." He laid his long finger against her lips. "I told you, I have you safe. Come with me."

He gave her his arm, and to her dismay she leaned heavily against it. Desire had robbed her of her strength and she staggered, almost falling. Corwin caught her, wrapping his other arm around her and pulling her close, so that her thigh pressed against his.

Everyone will stare. I will create a complete scandal.

But not one head turned. Not one conversation faltered as Corwin led her through the knots and crowds of Lady Thayer's guests.

"How . . . ?" She gasped.

In answer, he turned her back toward the dance floor.

There she saw herself, and she waltzed with the very dignified Mr. Rathe. They both moved with perfect, polite decorum while a good four inches of light showed between them.

"What is this?"

"Magic," Corwin murmured. "For the next three hours, all these people here will see us together, dancing and conversing. It will seem to them that we behave naturally and politely as we move through the evening. I could take you here and now in their midst, and they would know nothing. Would you like that, Miranda?" His hand slipped down her back to cup her buttocks, and that illicit touch sent a heated flash of need between her thighs. "If I laid you down now in all this music and light?"

"I can't stand it," she gasped. "It is too much!"

"Then we must hurry." With those words, Corwin Rathe swept Miranda into his arms and strode out the terrace doors.

Two

*G*ods all, why did I say that about taking her right there in the ballroom? It's difficult enough to walk as it is. Corwin's first idea had been to ghostwalk them both out of there, but that would leave him too weak for the delightful exercise to come.

What a creature this Miranda Prosper was! When he drew her into the glamour with him, her passion had flared so brightly, he'd just about spilled himself right there, and that coupling was merest illusion. He had lain with dozens of Catalysts, with Darius and on his own, but never had the response to his presence been so swift and so intense, and when he had introduced Darius into the vision, her desire had only soared that much higher.

Oh, precious and brilliant Miranda. What have you to teach us about passion?

She wrapped her arms around his neck. Her flesh was warm, her scent divine. He could not resist any longer and dropped his head to claim a kiss. Her mouth was more than ready for him. He pressed his tongue between her parted lips, tasting and stroking.

Oh, yes, so very ready. Is your pussy this ready for my cock?

Corwin held her closer, carrying her down the steps and out into the blessed, all-embracing darkness. The Mayfair neighborhood where Lord Thayer kept his town house allowed room for large gardens, and Lady Thayer had used it to full advantage, creating a refuge of formal paths, thick hedges and flower beds within the high brick walls. Corwin navigated the edges of the garden to avoid the other guests strolling about in the sultry summer night. All the while, he savored the rounded shape of Miranda's thighs against his arm. The side of her magnificent breast brushed against his chest with each step. That soft, involuntary caress was a fair way to driving him mad. But he had to get her out the back gate. He'd left enough of a trail inside these walls for those with eyes to follow. Only on the other side could they both have what they so desperately craved.

And then, of course, there was the fact he had promised her Darius as well as himself. It would be ungentlemanly not to keep his word with so rare and wonderful a lady.

The back wall of Lady Thayer's garden was red brick covered with old ivy. The gate in the corner was entirely wooden, but the lock and chain holding it closed had proved surprisingly complex. It had taken hours of patient work on Darius's part to get them open. Corwin set his back to the door, eased it open, and spun, ducking through the archway. Miranda giggled and clung more tightly to his neck, which just made him have to kiss her again as he kicked the gate closed behind them. This next garden belonged Viscount Stokley, who had already vacated his house for the summer—thanks to a precisely timed and entirely forged note from his estate manager. It was quite dark here except for the light that shone over the wall, but Corwin did not have to slow down. His night-strengthened instincts guided him, as did the deepening awareness of Darius's presence.

Miranda laid her head against his shoulder, lost in a daze created by desire and her dreamlike journey in his arms. He wondered if she could hear how his heart hammered in his chest—not from exertion, for this little walk was nothing to a man of his kind—but with a lust that was profound and simple at the same time. He wanted the woman in his arms. He wanted her naked beneath him, or on top of him; he wasn't feeling particular. He simply and urgently wanted to plant his cock deep in her sheath and he wanted to hear her scream his name.

All the hells, Corwin, calm yourself! Darius's impatient voice sounded in his mind.

Corwin bared his teeth in the darkness. *You wait, Darius, until you meet our Catalyst. You'll roar like a lion.*

The quality of the other Sorcerer's silence was skeptical. Corwin snickered.

'Tis not so funny. There've been lights hanging about and someone tried the gate while you were gone.

This got Corwin's attention. *A Sorcerer?*

I sensed no magic, admitted Darius.

Just some sneak thief seeing the dark house and trying their luck, then. Nothing for us to worry about. Corwin lowered his head to breathe in the scents of lavender and desire that perfumed Miranda's hair.

This, of course, made her lift her face toward his, and he could not resist a third hot, open kiss from her delicious mouth. And even as he tasted her there, opening himself to the tentative explorations of her tongue, he wondered what this mouth would feel like around his shaft. His cock throbbed and his balls tightened.

"No more, no more, dear one." Corwin pulled back and smiled gently at the confusion in her eyes. "We're almost to the place prepared for us. There, I promise you shall have all that you desire."

All that you desire. Corwin's words robbed Miranda of her remaining strength and her head dropped back against his shoulder. Her mouth tingled from his kiss. Her thighs burned from his promise, and from the visions he had shown her.

Magic, he had said. Magic was impossible. Her father had been a man of the Enlightenment. He taught her that magic and superstition belonged to the distant Dark Ages. But how else could she explain what she had seen, much less what she now experienced?

Unless I am more fully my mother's daughter than I realized. The thought sent a chill wind through her, threatening the flames Corwin had raised with such ease. The tension between desire and sudden fear tore at her and she moaned again.

"What is it, Miranda?" Corwin cradled her close and pressed a kiss to the top of her head. "What's the matter?"

"I'm afraid." To her shame, she pressed her face against his shoulder. Probably this was a mistake, for she could now inhale his intoxicating scent and feel the soft brush of silk against her cheeks.

With exquisite care, Corwin set her on her feet. They stood on a gravel path. Behind him, Miranda could see the bulk of a large town house. Beside it stood a small trellised bower hung with grapevines. Blankets had been laid on the ground and cushions piled about to make a lover's nest. Miranda turned her face away, because she did not want Corwin to see the doubt in her, after she had come so far, had said such things . . .

But Corwin touched her cheek, turning her face toward him and tipping up her chin so she had to meet his gaze.

"Listen to me, Miranda," he said. "I swear by all that is holy, you will take no harm from what we do in this place. Nothing happens here but what you desire, and nothing will be taken that you do not freely give. Here, there will be only pleasure, and all that will return home with you is the dream of pleasure."

Moonlight shone in the depths of his eyes, and his warm fingers were gentle beneath her chin. He'd drawn back somehow, damping the flames of desire, giving her space to breathe and to think. She could pull away if she wanted. She could run back through the gate to Lady Thayer's.

It was understanding she was free that removed the last of her fears. Miranda threw herself into Corwin's embrace. His arms closed around her, crushing her against his chest. She could feel him against the whole length of her, but most especially she could feel the rock-hard swelling of his cock as it stroked the softness of her belly.

Miranda was a virgin, but she was not naive. She knew about the act, the bare physicality of it at least. What she had not known before this moment was that it was possible to want it so much.

"So, Corwin," a man's deep voice growled from the darkness. "Let us see this extraordinary woman you have brought us."

Miranda turned in the shelter of Corwin's arms. A man emerged from behind the grape arbor. Miranda sucked in her breath. It was him—the man of red-gold dawn-light from the visions she had been granted in the ballroom. And he was completely and magnificently naked.

"This is Darius," said Corwin, running his fingertips down the length of Miranda's throat and kissing the tip of her ear. "He also is here to answer your desire."

Memory of her sensual visions assailed her: of one man in front of her, and one behind, of hands and mouths and her caught in the middle, helpless in a storm of pleasure.

Miranda trembled. Her heart hammered within her chest as if seeking escape, yet she could not tear her eyes away from the man in front of her. Her previous visions had not conveyed to her the power of this second man, the command with which he carried himself, naked as he was. He was stronger than Corwin, more controlled, and much more dangerous. Like Corwin, Darius was tall. As she had seen in her visions, he was fair. Even in the moonlight, she could see his hair's reddish glint and the golden dusting of stubble on his chin. That same gold glinted on his chest, and made a tangled nest for the thick, dark cock that hung indolently between his thighs. Miranda forced her gaze back up to his face. His eyes were deep and smoky blue. They bored into her, seeing, she was certain, every spark of desire she carried inside.

"Run away, little girl," Darius purred. "If you do not want this, want us, run away now."

But Miranda did not move. She could not move. She was too swollen with want. Her lips parted, already yearning toward this man's kisses, and whatever else he might bring to her.

"You see?" Corwin lifted Miranda's unresisting hand and kissed her gloved fingertips. He ran his hand across the back of hers, up to the hem of her long glove, tucking one finger underneath to touch her skin there. "There is no fear in her. She wants what we have to offer."

Darius lifted one golden brow, his gaze burning her as it raked up from the hem of her gown, and lingered on the flushed swell of her breasts. "More than that, I'll be bound. I do believe she needs it."

"Yes," Miranda whispered. She barely knew what was to come, and yet she knew for certain if she did not take it, something inside her would snap in two.

Darius stalked forward, and Miranda let him come. Each movement he made seemed more graceful and intriguing than any dance. Corwin was a sheltering wall at her back now, his hands resting on the curve of her hips, spreading warmth across her belly up and to her breasts. Miranda tilted her face up for Darius, knowing he would kiss her, impatient for him to do so.

But Darius was in no hurry. Like Corwin, he lifted her hand, gliding his fingertips across her satin glove. He took her feathered fan from her wrist and opened it. Softly, he drew the feathers across her lips, and across her bosom where it swelled above her low neckline. The soft, teasing touch made her shudder back against Corwin.

Darius tossed the fan aside. He caressed her throat with his fingertips as he dipped his head down to finally claim his kiss. His lips were smooth and strong, and more yielding than she had anticipated. His scent was lighter than Corwin's, yet sharp, like the smoke that warns of hidden embers. His heated touch went straight through to her veins, loosening her, opening her mouth so he could slide his tongue more deeply inside. She moaned as the pleasure of Darius's invasion took her, and she pressed closer and opened wider. She wrapped her hands about his neck as he cupped the back of her head, holding her still so he could slide his tongue against hers, stroking firmly and confidently. Corwin's broad hands moved against Miranda's hips and sides, caressing, almost as if he meant to soothe her, but the dizzying warmth of their sensual attentions blossomed through the whole of her body.

"By the gods!" Darius gasped, breaking the kiss and looking over Miranda's head to Corwin. "What have you brought us?"

"A dream," Corwin replied, turning Miranda to face him once more. "A perfect dream of Miranda."

Corwin kissed her again, hot and deep, and she opened fully to him. He cupped one hand under her ass, drawing her to him. With the fingers of his other hand, he traced her skin at the plunging neckline of her dress, dipping beneath it to draw his fingertips against her breast.

She moaned and writhed against him. He chuckled into their

kiss and closed his hand around her breast. The sensation made her gasp, and then made her melt against him.

"You are not one for subtlety, are you, Miranda?" Darius said as he moved close behind her. "I think we can dispense with these trappings right away."

His strong, broad hands glided up her back and pressed her against Corwin, driving her breast into the darker man's palm. Corwin massaged her there expertly, all the while continuing his searing kisses. Darius speared his fingers into Miranda's hair, lifting away her feathers and her jeweled pins so that her curls tumbled down around her shoulders. Then he drew his hands down to the tapes that held her gown, opening them one at a time.

Corwin's mouth moved from hers, and he kissed his way down her cheek to her throat. Miranda's head fell back against Darius's bare chest and he growled again. Her skin brushed his, the crisp hairs rasping deliciously against her cheek. With one hand, Darius pushed down the shoulder of her dress. With the other, he traced her lips, parting them with two fingers and sliding those fingers into her mouth.

Miranda's mouth seized eagerly on this new treat. Her tongue swirled around Darius's hard fingers and she sucked strongly, hardly knowing what she was doing, only that it felt wickedly good. Darius's third finger pressed next to the other two, and she took that one as well. He tasted of salt and wine, and the way he filled her mouth made her sheath feel hollow.

Cold air touched her breast, causing her nipple to harden abruptly. Miranda moaned again. Corwin seized her in his hot hand and plumped her breast, letting her ruched nipple slide between his fingers and squeezing it between them.

"Yes, you like it hard, don't you, Miranda?" said Darius. He drew his fingers out of her mouth, and then plunged them in again so that she could continue sucking them. "You want it hard and deep." He pulled his fingers out all the way this time, and slid his hand down to her other breast, seizing her nipple in his dampened fingertips. "Say that you want it hard."

But before she could speak, Corwin took her breast into his mouth, and sucked it deep. His teeth grazed her; his tongue teased her. None of which made Darius cease his attentions on her other breast with his hard, wet fingers. The twin sensations poured liquid heat into her veins and she bit back a moan.

"Oh, no." Darius slapped her breast lightly. "None of that. Let us hear you, Miranda. Or we might have to stop."

Miranda let out a shriek at the suggestion—half in fear, half in anger—and jerked backward, grinding her hips against Darius, who was now as fully hard as Corwin. Corwin grasped her hips, pinning her in place, so that he could catch the tip of her breast with his tongue and lap at it. Miranda writhed, caught between their bodies, one cock pressing against her belly, the other at her back, each movement heightening the burn of her pleasure. She moaned again—this time holding nothing of the sound back—twisted again, rubbing harder, seeking something she did not comprehend, but knew she must find.

"Ah, yes, Miranda," said Corwin, his lips and hot breath brushing her nipple with each word. "You must show your lovers how well they please you. You must tell them how you want them."

"Yes. Yes. I want you."

"Yes." Darius took hold of her arm and reached for her loosened gown. He drew down one lace-edged sleeve, then the other, first of the dress, then of the chemise beneath, so that she stood bare-breasted in the moonlight.

"Beautiful," murmured Corwin reverently

Darius slid his hands under her breasts and lifted them, offering them up to Corwin. Corwin did not hesitate, but took her in both his hands, claiming her mouth once more while he stroked her, rolling her nipples between his fingers, caressing her, massaging her. She gasped and sighed and arched against him. Darius pushed her dress down farther: to her waist, to her hips, to her thighs, and finally let it fall. She wrapped her arms around Corwin, rubbing her body, naked except for her gloves, stockings and shoes, against his buckskin-clad thighs.

Darius closed his hands around the halves of her ass, squeezing and caressing her there with rhythms as confident and masterful as those Corwin used on her breasts. She dug her fingers into Corwin's shoulders, wanting nothing more than for him, for them both, to be naked against her.

By some unspoken signal, they began to lower her down to the satin quilts spread upon the arbor's floor. Darius pulled Miranda to him, and Corwin pushed her back so that she leaned against Darius's chest while he lay against the pile of cushions. From behind, Darius ran his hands over her hips, to her thighs, pulling them apart until she sprawled wide-open on top of him. Corwin knelt in front of her, and pulled off her gloves, drinking her in with his eyes as Darius stroked her belly and her inner thighs.

"Now, Corwin," said Darius. "I think you should strip for our lady."

Corwin's smile was dark and wicked. Slowly, he stood. Darius's hands stroked Miranda's thighs, rising higher and higher until he brushed her dark, damp curls with his palm. He cupped her and she gasped, her eyes falling closed.

"Watch," Darius commanded, squeezing her there, sending a fresh jolt of pleasure through her. "Watch your lover, Miranda, as he readies himself for you."

Miranda's eyes flew open. Corwin towered over her, dark and tall and magnificent. The moon's shadows outlined the bulge of his erection. He stroked himself, once, and again. With his free hand, he opened the buttons of his waistcoat, revealing the shining white linen shirt underneath. He undid the buttons of his fly, one after another. She stared, hungry, fascinated at his unabashed display, as he stripped off both coat and cravat. At the same time, Darius's finger touched the very tip of her slit, and then slid down between her folds. Shameless, searing pleasure flooded her and she groaned, pressing back against Darius's hot, hard cock.

"You're so wet, Miranda," said Darius, stroking her with the same two fingers he had given her to suck. "So wet and so ready. I could make you come right now. Do you want me to make you come?"

She didn't know what he was talking about, but all her internal muscles clenched at the promise in his voice, and at the sure touch of his hand as he slid his fingers down to the entrance of her sheath. Darius's skin was fever-hot beneath her, and the hairs on his chest and thighs created strangely delectable sensations against the sensitive skin on her back and legs. But best of all was his hot cock pulsing against her ass and back. She struggled to keep her eyes open, to watch Corwin as he pulled his white shirt off, revealing the expanse of his chest. Miranda cried out at its loveliness, leaning forward to reach for him, which plunged Darius's fingers deeper into her, even as he pressed down with his forearm to hold her in place straddling his thighs and hard cock.

"Not yet, not yet," Corwin said, with a dark glee in his voice. "Not until you ask nicely." Darius pulled her back against him, stroking her pussy with one hand, plumping her breast with the other.

"Please," she whispered. The fingers in her pussy stroked up, and down again, and up higher and more firmly, coming to the tight nubbin of flesh that throbbed at the tip of her slit. Darius pressed there, and the sensation was so intense, she saw stars, and when her vision cleared, Corwin had removed his boots, and kicked his trousers away.

He was magnificent. His cock was huge and hard and beautiful. She wanted it. She wanted it in her hands and in her pussy and now she knew why she had sucked so eagerly on Darius's fingers—because she wanted it in her mouth too.

"He's going to suck you, Miranda," said Darius, his fingers circling her nub in time to his words. "He's going to suck you until you learn what I mean when I speak of you coming for us. And when that is done, he's going to fuck you just to make sure you have learned your lesson properly."

And Corwin knelt in front of her, in front of them, and slid his hands up her thighs, spreading them wider, pressing her back farther so that Darius's hot cock nestled itself deep between the halves of her ass. Darius shifted his hands to her breasts, rolling her nipples between his fingertips, wringing another moan of delight from her.

"Say you want it, Miranda," Darius ordered. "Say you want us."

"Yes!" she cried out. "Oh, God, yes! Please!"

"Yes, Miranda," whispered Corwin, and she could feel his soft, heated breath against her pussy. "Now."

There was nothing soft about his coming down to her. His tongue plunged into her slit, strong and sure, licking up all the way to her nub, and down to her entrance, plunging inside, pulling out and thrusting in again. Miranda screamed as the pleasure took her. As in the vision, she knotted her fingers into Corwin's hair to hold him in place. He lapped at her slit, each wicked stroke driving her further from sanity. He lifted her right leg and then her left over his shoulders so he could nuzzle closer. She would die if he continued. She would die if he stopped. Darius's hands closed tightly around her breasts, playing unceasingly with her nipples as Corwin grabbed her hips, bracing her against Darius so he could thrust his tongue more deeply into her. Darius's cock rubbed hard between the halves of her ass, heightening her delirium.

"Come for us, Miranda," panted Darius in her ear, lowering one hand to stroke her belly, to hold her more firmly against his cock as she writhed in pleasure from Corwin's thrusting, teasing tongue. "Show us how good it is for you. Come now!"

And Corwin ran his tongue over her nub, licking and sucking hard as Darius rolled her nipples once more. Her pleasure spiked, impossible to contain a heartbeat longer. Miranda screamed as her body—so wonderfully confined between her two lovers—erupted into frantic spasms of ecstasy that set her slippered heels drumming against Corwin's back.

Slowly, the spasms eased, leaving her suffused with a delightful, silken lassitude.

"Oh, Miranda," murmured Corwin, lifting his head from her pussy. "You are so very sweet." He gathered her, limp and dazed, into his arms, and pulled her down to the ground with him, cradling her on top of his body, kissing her softly. She smelled her own scent on him, and tasted salt and musk like the sea.

Miranda stretched out on top of Corwin. His hands wandered up and down her, stroking her back, her ass and her thighs. All the while he kissed her gently, the tenderness of his lips and the very tip of his tongue soothing her, drawing her back from the deep place into which she had fallen. He was hard. She was aware of the press of his cock against her thigh, but she could muster no urgency at the awareness. It was merely one more pleasant fact in a haze of sensual enjoyment.

At last, Corwin rolled them onto their sides, deepening his kisses. She did not resist. She lay lax and content, letting him take what he wanted from her. But slowly, a kind of restlessness rose up in her, a sense that this thing, as fine as it was, remained incomplete. She had thought her strength gone, but the more he caressed her, the more she wanted to touch him. She ran her hands up his sides, across the hard planes of his chest, down

27

his well-muscled thighs, enjoying the warmth of his smooth skin against her palms and losing herself in the exploration of the strange new landscape of his body. Her hands knew neither shame nor hesitation. He was open to her, nothing forbidden. She gripped his wonderfully hard ass and squeezed, delighting as it made him kiss her more deeply yet.

Her hand stroked up his thigh, and brushed the side of his hard cock. For the first time she felt the velvet softness of it against her fingers, and suddenly it became vitally important that she touch him there again. She wrapped her fingers around the thickness of his shaft, marveling how it was both soft and hard, and how she could feel his heart beating against her hand. She squeezed slowly, as if testing the sensitivity of his flesh.

"Oh, yes, Miranda," Corwin groaned. "Oh, gods, yes."

Excitement sparked afresh in her. She could undo him too. She ran her palm up his length, cupping his blunt tip, stroking down, drawing her fingers around the hilt of his shaft. His balls were high and tight. She hefted them against her right palm even while she continued stroking his shaft with her left. Corwin groaned aloud and she rewarded him, stroking and squeezing until his eyes fell closed and his fingers dug hard into the softness of her ass.

It was sweet. It was mesmerizing. It was power of a sort she had never imagined.

"Enough!" Darius's voice grated harshly behind her. Miranda started. She'd all but forgotten he was there, watching everything she did with, did to, Corwin. The fresh awareness of it shot fire into her veins and she felt her pussy begin once more to swell and strain. Without taking her hands from Corwin's cock, she turned her head to look at Darius.

Darius crouched in the darkness, his blue eyes blazing with reflected moonlight. His member jutted out of the darkness between his thighs. He was not a man. He was an incubus, a daemon lover come from the shadows to take her.

She should have been terrified, but she wasn't. Desire, as hot and sweet as mulled wine, poured through her. She was alive with need now, with one man's hard cock in her hands, and another displayed so blatantly for her.

"Take him," ordered Darius. "Now!"

Miranda knew what he meant, but she hesitated, caught between the flames of desire and an abrupt remembrance of how little she knew of these matters, even between one woman and one man.

But Darius growled and crawled forward. Corwin, panting, watched the approach of the other man with wide eyes. His hands quickened their rhythm on Miranda's breasts, and his cock throbbed hot in her hands.

Darius crawled behind her. Miranda sucked in her breath, both afraid and thrilled as he grabbed her hips. He ground his cock against her ass, forcing her pussy against Corwin's velvet length. She gulped and cried out, and pressed Corwin against her again. Nothing had ever felt so good. Nothing could feel so good. Corwin was calling her name, and Darius's, and together, the men's hands were raising her up until she straddled Corwin's thighs.

For a moment she felt the broad head of Corwin's cock at her entrance. For a heartbeat she knew fear.

Then Darius pressed her down, and Corwin pulled her down, and his cock plunged full length into her sheath. Shock and anticipation made her cry out. Pain blazed for an instant and was gone, and he was inside her, embedded to the hilt in her satin heat.

Glorious.

"That's it, Miranda." Corwin stroked her thighs lovingly, firmly. "Feel it. Feel how good it is."

"Yes." Miranda stretched herself, leaning forward to deepen the press of him in her, lost in this new sensation. She ran her hands up Corwin's chest. Her fingertips found his nipples, and she played with them as he had played with hers. To her amazement, he laughed. She had not imagined people *laughed* during the act, and a new, gentler warmth surged through her.

"Now, Miranda Prosper," said Darius roughly. "We will teach you to ride."

From behind, Darius pulled her to him until she could feel his cock pressed against the small of her back and his balls rubbed her ass. Mischief overtook her and Miranda shimmied her hips. A wave of pleasure almost drowned her as Corwin's cock slid against her inner skin and Darius's against her outer.

"So eager." Darius drew his hands hard across her belly, moving his left up to grasp her breast, and his right down to plunge his fingertips into her slit. "So sure she is ready. Let us see how well you take to this kind of ride, Miranda."

Beneath her, Corwin thrust up, and behind her Darius pressed down, and she gasped again. Darius's thighs and hands worked together, bringing her down to meet Corwin's thrusts, then lifting her up and bringing her down again. Corwin's fingers dug into her thighs. His shaft stroked her slick sheath, hard and harder, and Darius's fingers in her slit matched the rhythm. Miranda caught that rhythm, and her own thighs began to work, began to move, driving Corwin deep into her, stroking Darius against her, against her ass and slit, breast and nub. It was too much. It was not enough. Corwin called her name. She cried out in answer.

"Harder!"

"Beg us," ordered Darius, circling her nub with two fingertips.

"Please!" she moaned, grinding down on Corwin's cock. "Please! Harder!"

Corwin thrust up and Darius drove her, drove them, down. His cock and his balls slid against her as he bent her forward, forcing her pussy to press against his fingers, moving Corwin's shaft deeper into her. Corwin surged forward, grasping Miranda's breast and guiding it into his mouth. He suckled her, hard and fast. Together her lovers thrust, and she struggled with them and against them, trying to escape, trying to force them deeper and closer. Her mind was gone. The whole world was gone. There was only the sensation of their hands and mouths and cocks, only the harsh sounds of their breathing, as they all of them thrust together again and again.

Then Corwin shouted and his hips arced up, driving his cock hard into her until his balls crushed her pussy and slammed her nub against Darius's fingertip. They hung like that for a timeless moment and Miranda felt herself flying free, her spirit stretched against the moonlit night, open wide to draw in all the pleasures of the world.

Corwin bucked wildly beneath her and Darius shouted and pumped his cock uncontrollably against her ass, his fluids hot against her back, and his fingers driving into her. Their twinned ecstasy poured into Miranda, raising her higher and higher still. She was beyond her own body, beyond the dull Earth. She was a being of air and golden light and wild power separate now from her earthly flesh. Her body, strained past its limits to endure its delight, rode her lovers hard, until it had to shudder and buck and cry out. She was aware of all this, and yet it was almost a trivial matter. The other, soaring pleasure that enveloped her spirit was so much greater and more absorbing.

Once more, her body's delectable spasms slowed and soothed. Now Miranda looked down at Corwin beneath her, and saw he looked strangely pale. Corwin's eyes, wide with astonishment and something very close to fear, met hers.

"What . . . ?" said Darius thickly. He pulled away, falling sideways onto the blankets. But beneath her, Corwin couldn't move.

Miranda reached out and stroked Corwin's brow. *Poor creature. It was too much for him, this wild pleasure.* She felt his cock begin to soften in her.

"Sleep," she whispered. Slowly, Corwin's eyes closed and his head lolled back. She climbed off him and stood, stretching her arms overhead toward the shining moon. It was all so beautiful. The night air was soft against her skin. The moonlight thrummed through her veins, stroking each nerve ending—sensitized by the passion her lovers had shown her—into fresh life. She was strong. She was free.

Darius struggled to push himself back onto his knees. "What have you done to him!"

Miranda looked down at Corwin, huddled unconscious at her feet. Some part of her mind was aware she should be concerned at his pallor, and at how shallow his breathing was, but she could not make it matter. So, she simply bent to reclaim her shift and gown.

"Stop!" Darius flung out an arm to intercept her. Miranda turned and struck out in one fierce movement. Darius flew backward, hitting the trellis hard enough to shudder the entire arbor before he slid to the ground. Miranda regarded him with her cool gaze for a moment, then turned. Shrugging casually into her clothes, she walked away and left her lovers lying on the ground behind her.

Three

Darius's first thought was to charge past the bounds of the protective circle and drag Miranda back to them, but one glance at Corwin's pale form lying amid the scattered cushions stopped him cold. On hands and knees, he crawled across to the other man.

"Corwin?" Darius shook with fear and with rage as he laid his hand on Corwin's sculpted chest. After an agonizing moment in which he could sense nothing but the pounding of his own heart, Darius felt Corwin's breath rise and fall. The movement was far too slow, but at least it was steady.

Darius had to grit his teeth together to keep from roaring into the darkness. There was no time for such gestures. Corwin was cold and damp to the touch. If nothing else, he was in danger of taking a severe chill.

Darius looked to Viscount Stokley's house. They had not wanted to use it except in case of emergency, but this certainly qualified. Swiftly, he gathered Corwin and the quilts into his arms and carried him to the kitchen door. Darius murmured a spell and kicked hard. The door opened, and he didn't really care to which force it had yielded.

He carried Corwin down the steps into the dark kitchen. The fire was dead in the hearth and there was no fuel, but at least they were out of the damp. Darius laid Corwin by the hearth, bunching the quilts underneath his head for a pillow.

Corwin did not stir.

Darius sat back, rubbing his palms against his thighs. If Corwin died . . .

I will not let it happen. By all the gods in Heaven and all the daemons in Hell, I will not lose you!

Slowly, Darius gathered up his broken composure. He needed to be still. He needed his mind to be clear. He breathed the cooling night air deep into his lungs. He was weak. He too had been robbed by Miranda Prosper. Not nearly so much as Corwin, who had placed himself inside her, but more than enough to dim his inner focus. Darius forced himself to concentrate. He closed his mind off from worry, from fear, seeking the place deep within, the reservoir of power at the center of his being.

Normally, Darius had Corwin to help control the opening of that inner door, as he helped Corwin. To do it by himself was difficult, but not impossible. Darius stretched, he strained, and slowly, oh, so slowly, his inner barriers fell and he felt his power rise.

Like starlight.

Like fire.

Like sunrise breaking over the world.

It filled him. It buoyed him, pouring wild joy and reckless-ness into him, lifting him high above the cold clay earth.

Darius opened his eyes and looked down at Corwin, so still and pale and beautiful. His black hair shimmered against the pillow's pale silk. Darius laid his hand over Corwin's heart, bent close and kissed him fully and openly on the mouth.

At first, there was only the sweetness of the kiss. As far gone as Darius was in the wash of his own power, he cared for nothing else. Slowly, however, Darius realized Corwin did not respond. Darius's heart pounded. His muscles trembled. He deepened the kiss, focused his power and forced his breath and power into Corwin's still form.

Softly, Corwin stirred and groaned against Darius's mouth. His hand lifted, and dropped back.

"Corwin?" Darius pulled away and grasped Corwin's wrist, feeling for the pulse. "Corwin Rathe, open your eyes! Look at me!"

Corwin drew in a sharp breath. He coughed. Darius gripped his hand hard, and Corwin's eyes fluttered open.

"Gods and goddesses," Corwin breathed. "What happened?"

Darius dropped back onto his haunches. He pressed Cor-win's warming hand to his forehead, and for a moment could do nothing but breathe. When finally he could speak, Darius told Corwin what he had seen and done.

"I'm going to kill her," Darius grated.

"Stop it, Darius." Corwin's hand tightened around his, but with none of his usual strength.

"She almost killed you!" Darius cried.

"Whatever happened, it was not her fault. She was an innocent."

"How can you be sure?"

Corwin coughed and swallowed, and his head dropped back. Darius barely had time to catch him and lower him to the quilts. "It's been a while, but I know when I'm with a virgin."

"There are other ways to make use of a Catalyst."

"Name me a Sorcerer who leaves his Catalyst untested," Corwin panted. "Darius, you must take me to her. Then, one way or another, we'll know."

Darius's jaw clenched until he felt the muscles in his cheek twitch. But Corwin was right. If Miranda truly was ignorant of her own nature, at this moment her life was in danger. He thought of her tender, shadowed beauty burning away from the force she now carried within her, and his guts turned over.

"But what if she is one of theirs?" Darius laid his hand on Corwin's brow. It was dry now, though he was scarcely any warmer.

"Then you get away and warn the captain."

Fear lanced through Darius, reigniting his harsh anger. "I won't leave you."

"Darius . . ."

"Never," he declared flatly. "There must be a way other than to put you in such danger. I'll summon help."

Corwin winced, but managed to prop himself up on his elbows. "No time, no time. If she is innocent, she's dying right now. She's not going to know what to do with any of the power she's absorbed."

"You keep saying so, but an untried Catalyst would not have been able to drain you, not like this. If it wasn't Miranda Prosper who did this to you, who was it?"

"I don't know," Corwin panted. "Did you check the circle?"

Darius pulled back. It was not possible. He'd been on watch.

Except he'd heard a noise, like someone trying to get in at the garden gate, and he'd gone to check. No. It couldn't be . . .

Darius leapt to his feet and ran back out into the night air. The moon was still high enough to show him the way back to the arbor. There on the ground he could still see the smudged remains of the protective circle he'd traced, and he could still make out some of the runes he'd laid.

Enough to tell where they'd been scratched out and retraced. Darius's blood ran cold.

No. No. My fault. Mine. He'd been taken in by a trick so old and so simple he hadn't even thought of looking for it.

Darius scrambled to his feet and ran back to Corwin's side, not caring what noise he made, not caring that he left the door flapping on its hinges behind him. He didn't need to say anything to Corwin, who was still up on his elbows; Darius's stunned and crestfallen expression told the whole story.

Corwin awkwardly pushed himself up into a sitting position. "There's much more going on than we knew." He rested his forearms on his knees. "We have to find her, before she is beyond help."

Before you both are. But Darius said nothing, only helped Corwin to his feet. "Where do we begin?"

"I think we must do a little more housebreaking." Corwin took two steps forward and staggered.

But Darius was right beside him. "Lean on me."

"Who else is there, Darius?" said Corwin as he laid his arm across Darius's shoulders. "Who else?"

Four

There had never been such a beautiful night. Miranda glided through the arched gateway between the two gardens. Moonlight turned the formal hedges and flower beds into silver sculptures and towers from some fairyland. She tilted up her chin and gazed at the stars as if they were long-lost sisters. It was not possible she should feel so strong, so vital and alive.

And from such forbidden pleasures.

But a more unforgiving flame spread beneath her skin. It crept up from the damp soles of her feet inside her ruined stockings and slippers. At first it was easy to ignore, but the closer she came to the house, the more insistent and less wholesome it grew, until it became a terrible itch under her skin. The delight warming her began to melt away in the face of the growing discomfort. Her toe caught on a stone, and Miranda stumbled.

What is happening to me? Miranda lifted her eyes toward Lady Thayer's house, and the light seared her eyes.

She was aware now that there were other people on the garden paths, strolling here and there, couples come out from the party to enjoy the rare, clear London night. Faces she could not quite make out turned toward her as she stumbled again. The stars seemed so distant now, cold and pitiless. Her head felt light, but all her limbs were far too heavy and the itching inside her was quickly turning into real pain.

"Miranda!"

Miranda stumbled again, lurched and would have fallen, if her outstretched hand hadn't found a stone bench. She sat down heavily.

"Miranda, where on Earth have you been!"

A silhouette strode purposefully across the sloping lawn. This one she could not mistake. Her mother bore down on her like some dark angel of fury.

Daphne Quicke stopped in front of her daughter, hands on her hips. Miranda lifted her head to look at her but had to drop her gaze a moment later—which caused her to miss seeing her mother's disapproving frown waver, for just an instant.

"Did he hurt you?" Mother asked flatly.

It took Miranda a moment to understand the sort of question her mother asked. The ballroom, the dance with Corwin Rathe, belonged to a different world from the place of fire and pain she had entered. He might have hurt her, but she didn't know how, because she didn't understand what was happening.

"Honestly, Miranda, it's not that I mind you finally attracting men, but you might have had the sense to be discreet!" Mother took one step closer, and laid a cool hand on Miranda's forehead.

"You're fevered. Thank heavens. It will provide an acceptable explanation for your appearance."

Mother seized Miranda's wrist and dragged her to her feet. "We'll go in the side door. I always knew you never listened to me, and now I have my proof. I despair. If I wasn't there at your birth, I'd wonder if you really are my daughter . . ."

Continuing on this theme, Mother dragged Miranda around the side of the house, her hand clamped on Miranda's wrist like a manacle. Miranda staggered along in her mother's wake because she could not do anything else. The light lanced into her eyes and the fire burned through her bones, robbing her of any ability to think.

"Oh, Perkins, thank heavens!" Mother wrapped her arms around Miranda's shoulders. "My daughter has taken ill. Send for my carriage at once."

"Yes, madame. Mellon, help the lady. Lace, send for Miss Prosper's maid."

Those were the last words she understood for some time. Miranda felt as if she had been removed into a private space of pain. There was no time, barely any sensation of movement, only the endless fire in her sinews and skin. She had just enough awareness to feel herself lifted into the carriage. Sometime later, she recognized rocking and jouncing as the conveyance rolled over the London streets' ruts and cobbles.

Miranda's lungs began to burn, and she could not catch her breath. Other hands raised her up, supporting her. She wheezed and shivered as they helped her climb the stairs. Conversation went on around her, but she could make little sense of it.

"Will madame wish to send for the doctor?"

"Oh, I don't think there will be any need at present. A warm bed, a night's rest, and I am sure she will be right as rain."

"Yes, madame."

The door closed and Miranda shivered beneath her blankets. The silk nightgown in which she had been dressed provided no comfort. The cold gave way once more to fire, and with the fire came a vision like a flash of lightning. She saw two men staggering through the dark streets, leaning together, struggling even as she struggled.

Miranda.

Miranda twisted her head sideways, trying to bury her face in the pillows to shut out the visions and the voice.

Miranda, can you hear me?

"Stop it," she begged. Her throat burned; her vitals burned; her very soul burned. "Please, make it stop!"

I want to, Miranda, but I can't find you. Say my name, Miranda. Say it!

"Corwin," she croaked. *Corwin!*

Another vision lanced through her. She saw him, saw them, standing in the mews behind the house, staring up at her window. Darius had his arms wrapped around Corwin. Corwin dug his hand into his side, like a man trying to stop the pain of his own wound.

"You'll kill yourself trying to ghostwalk up there," Darius muttered.

Corwin shook his head hard. "There's no other way fast enough."

Miranda heard other voices, these much closer.

"Miss Prosper! Oh, do wake up, Miss Prosper!"

"I don't like this. She's in a real delirium now."

"Should we fetch her mother?"

"Madame Bitch? Not likely. Get round to Dr. Harrington's. Sharp, now!"

"Madame won't like it."

"I'll take the blame if it comes to that. Go!"

"Yes, ma'am."

A rough hand touched Miranda's forehead. Miranda recognized it as belonging to Louise, her maid. But Louise was not whom Miranda needed, and Miranda tried to shake her off, but she could scarcely move. The terrible light was devouring her from the inside.

"What on Earth!" cried Louise.

A cold wind wafted over Miranda's face. She shivered violently and struggled to lift her head. The burning within blurred her eyesight, but she saw two tall men being faced down by stout Louise.

Corwin? Darius?

Yes, Miranda. We are here.

"Get out of here!" cried Louise. "Get out of here at once, you shameless things, or I'll rouse the house!"

Faintly, beyond the fire, Miranda felt a prickling across her skin that was both new and intimately familiar.

One of the shadowed forms moved closer. "Get away from her!" snapped Louise, and she darted forward, but the other man—Darius, Miranda was now sure—blocked her path.

"You will find the girl and tell her there's no need for the doctor. The fever has broken, and Miss Prosper has asked to be left to rest. You will check in on her again in the morning. Go now."

Louise swayed on her feet. "Yes, sir," she said, her words slurring badly.

"You will be saving her life. This is the only way to save her life."

"Yes, sir." Louise's tone had changed, growing brisk and efficient. She bustled out the door and shut it firmly behind herself.

Miranda dropped back onto the pillow. The tide of pain dragged her under, threatening to drown her.

"Corwin," she whispered. "I'm burning alive."

"Shhh, shhh, Miranda." She felt the mattress dip and she was aware of a warmth and human presence beside her. "It's all right. You've just drunk a wine that is too strong for you." A man's hand stroked her cheek. Corwin! But there was something wrong. His hand was cold and weak. Miranda forced open her eyes, but she could see nothing of him but shadow.

"Are you here to help me die?" she whispered.

"No, dearest." He was panting now. "We are here to help you live."

"Save your strength, Corwin," said Darius gruffly. The mattress dipped again as Darius sat on her other side.

"You have taken something Corwin needs, Miranda Prosper," Darius said. "You must give it back."

"I don't understand."

"You must touch him, Miranda."

The thought made her stomach clench, and for a moment she

thought she would vomit. "No. I can't." She squeezed her eyes shut and tried to turn her face away.

The mattress shifted again, and Miranda was aware of Darius lying down behind her.

"Look at him," commanded Darius, reaching around to cup her chin and lift it so her face was angled toward Corwin in front of her. Darius's breath was warm and strangely gentle against her ear and his hand firm and strong as he held her. "Look at him with me, Miranda."

Darius pressed himself behind her. Her nightgown made only the thinnest of barriers between them. She could feel every inch of his naked body against her: his chest, his thighs, his cock. She felt his heart hammering. His hand glided down her arm, making the cloth slide against her skin, and slowly, his living warmth began to seep into her. All these sensations seemed to cause Miranda's internal strength to stir. She found she could bear her pain more easily. She could open her eyes to look at Corwin.

Corwin sprawled on the bed, as pale as marble and almost as still. She could take in all of him with her freshly cleared gaze, as if he were a sculptor's masterpiece—so beautiful, so perfectly masculine, and at the same time so weakened that it was plainly all he could do to raise his eyes toward her.

"Touch him, Miranda," whispered Darius in her ear.

"I can't." Fire burned beneath Miranda's skin, seeking exit through her pores. "I'll hurt him."

"No. Not this time. I'll help you."

Gently but irresistibly, Darius lifted her hand. He laid Miranda's palm against Corwin's and folded their fingers together.

Miranda shook as their skin made contact, but Darius held her—held them—in place, his strong hand covering their two weak ones, and the burning tide within her ebbed further yet.

"That's it," murmured Darius. "Open yourself to him, Miranda. To us. Let the fire inside you flow free."

"It will kill him."

"No, Miranda. It will heal him. Trust me."

Darius lifted her palm away from Corwin's and glided it up Corwin's arm, making her stroke the sick man's chilled flesh. Something ethereal reached from Darius into her, nestling itself inside her. She could feel Darius's strength, not just in his grip, or in his cock—which was growing hard where it pressed against the small of her silk-clad back—but in spirit somehow. Where Darius's strength entered, the fire Miranda had imbibed drained away from her heart. It flowed into her veins, down her arms to her hands, to her palms and fingertips.

Darius took her other hand and laid it on Corwin's right arm. Embracing her with his hard-muscled arms, Darius sat himself and her up and leaned her over Corwin's pale form. His chest pressed against her back, his hands continued to move hers, showing her how to touch Corwin; how she should caress his shoulders and stroke his chest, gently chafing his nipples with her palms. Darius breathed deeply and slowly, and the rhythm of his breathing crept into Miranda, until she found her breath matching with his. With each intake of air, she felt the fire leave her, to be replaced with the twined scents of the men—scents of night air, sweat, musk and something more.

Darius moved their hands lower, stroking Corwin's hard, flat abdomen. Corwin sighed. He stretched and he shifted. Darius moved her hands up to stroke Corwin's shoulders again, then down once more to rest her palm over Corwin's heart.

Corwin was still pale, but the terrible haunted look had left his eyes, replaced by the bright spark she had seen there before. She could feel both of their rhythms now—Darius's breath and his heart at her back, Corwin's heart beneath her hands. It seemed that those unique rhythms synchronized and merged with her own, becoming one pulsation strong enough to surround the flames, to seize them and change them.

Darius lifted both her hands away from Corwin's chest. Miranda whimpered; she could not help it. She did not want to leave off touching Corwin. She felt Darius's mouth smile against her cheek as he lowered her hands to Corwin's cock.

A sigh escaped Miranda as the velvet softness filled her hands. She tried to stroke Corwin herself, but Darius would not permit it. His hands commanded hers, running them up and down Corwin's cock. It began to swell under their attentions, and Miranda felt her heart leap. Darius's breathing grew ragged. His own cock pressed urgently against her hip as he controlled her hands, forcing her to go slowly, to caress Corwin's shaft, to cup his balls and finger the blunt tip.

To make Corwin sigh again. To make him say, "Yes. Oh, yes."

Miranda felt her spirit open wider, and the remaining fire— dangerous no longer—reached out. She knew instinctively she wanted to bring this inner flame to Corwin. She wanted that as much as she wanted to bring his cock inside her, but she didn't know how it could be done.

"Kiss him, Miranda," said Darius, as if he read her thoughts. "Lie down with him."

Miranda needed no further urging. She kissed Corwin, strongly, and openly. She felt Darius move away, but in no way was his strength gone from her. Corwin caught her in his arms and rolled her onto the bed beneath him. He pinned her against the mattress and thrust his tongue deeply into her mouth. Miranda laced her fingers through his hair and kissed back hungrily. At the same time, she spread her thighs so his hardening cock could press more closely against her pussy. Her nipples tightened and strained as he moved on top of her. The slick coolness of her thin nightdress grew hot from their fevered skins. She stroked his back, all the way to his taut ass, and dug her fingers in, making him gasp, making him rub his cock harder against her.

"Now." Darius positioned himself so he could lift Miranda's head and pillow it against his strong thighs. He reached down and slid his hands between Miranda and Corwin, cupping her breasts in his palms and massaging them. Where before his touch had eased the fires, now it brightened them, joyfully. She arched her back, thrusting up with her breasts to seek Darius's hands and her hips to meet Corwin's cock. Corwin stretched over her, taking his weight on his elbows, as he ground his hips against hers, making his hard cock circle against her straining nub. She felt something brush her cheek, and realized it was Darius's tight balls and erect cock caressing her face as he rolled and teased her nipples with rough fingers. Miranda gasped. She moaned. Fire, all was fire, but now it was beautiful, and if she should turn to ashes from it, it was all she desired.

Corwin shoved her nightdress up around her waist, and Darius drew it over her head and cast it aside. Cold air washed across her, making her skin prickle deliciously. Corwin ran his hands up her thighs, lifting first one leg, then the other, and wrapping them around his waist so he could move into the embrace of her thighs.

"Yes," she groaned, rubbing his hips with her thighs' sensitive inner flesh. "Yes, now!"

"Yes, now," said Darius.

Obedient to her, to them both, Corwin thrust deep inside her. She gasped with the pleasure of it, instinctively reaching out with hands and spirit to caress him. Darius's masterful hands on her breasts and the wicked caress of his hard cock against her cheek urged her on, opening her spirit yet further. The bright fire flowed from her to Corwin. Their heartbeats surrounded her, capturing her with their rhythm, as Corwin thrust again, and again.

Darius lowered her head down onto the pillows, which freed Miranda to grip Corwin's thighs with her hands and force him down into her, harder and deeper. She felt Darius move beside her. He captured her right hand and wrapped her fingers firmly around the thick, velvet heat of his shaft. Delight assailed her as Darius made her hand move on him in time with Corwin's thrusts, using her shamelessly for his pleasure even as she drank in the pleasure that flowed from them both. She opened herself wide so she could return that ecstasy, that nameless strength, to them both.

Miranda rocked her hips, again and again, drawing Corwin's

cock into her until it could go no deeper, digging the fingers of her left hand into his ass. She pumped Darius's swelling cock furiously, loving the sensation of his hand holding hers as she did. It was too good. She could not contain the fire, the delight, anymore, and her climax rolled over her, delirium and delight, fire and passion, sending her into spasm after spasm.

Corwin cried out and she had just enough control left to raise her bucking hips to meet his as his climax racked him. Then Darius thrust into her palm, his wordless lion's roar washing over them all and his seed spilling hot over their hands.

Five

Lady Viola Thayer surveyed her ballroom. It was far enough into the morning that the older guests and married couples had retired, with or without their legally allowed partners. The younger and the unattached remained. They flirted, gossiped and enjoyed the freedom of the dance floor while their chaperones drowsed in the corners or drank strong tea at the refreshment table.

With a minor exception, it had been a most satisfactory evening. Most satisfactory. Already, Viola had identified four men and two women with influential positions or considerable fortunes who were ripe for temptation and seduction. She would be able to work on them over the course of the summer. By the time the haut ton reassembled in London for the next season, they would be firmly in her pocket.

Viola smiled and waved her ostrich-feather fan to hide it. *Now, where has my lord Thayer gotten himself off to?*

A strolling tour of the ballroom—with frequent stops to chat with her well-content and somewhat drunken guests—did not turn him up. Neither did perusal of the card room, or the smoking room.

Which leaves only one possibility.

Lady Thayer left her company. At this late stage of the party, no one would remark, or indeed even care, if their hostess absented herself. She headed to the hushed library and closed the door softly before crossing to the hearth. Her nimble fingers traced the decorations on the mantel until they found the correct plaster rose and pressed. A section of wall swung back, revealing a dusty passage beyond.

In most Mayfair houses the supposed "secret" passages were simply servants' hallways, allowing maids and butlers to discreetly exit a room before their masters entered it.

In the Thayer's town house, however, there was a genuinely secret stair, and it went down deep, below the kitchens and past the wine cellar. Beyond where a scream or any other fuss could be heard by the people above. They'd modeled it after a similar arrangement in Lord Thayer's country estate and had it installed by discreet workmen shortly after they took possession of the residence.

At the end of a dirt-floored corridor waited a single door made of rough planks and bound with black iron. Lady Viola extracted a heavy key from her reticule and let herself in.

The room beyond would not have seemed comfortable to many. The thick crimson draperies brought no warmth to the stone walls they covered. chains dangled from the support beams and the posts had thick bolts screwed into them. Those bolts allowed the room's master to use the ropes and chains hanging on the far wall to secure an individual in any number of positions. Water, and other fluids, stained the carpets.

My lord was not feeling terribly experimental tonight, thought Viola as she sauntered into the room past the splintered bed frame. A young woman lay there, spread-eagled on her back, chained by her wrists and ankles to the square corner posts. The remnants of rough clothing were the only cushioning underneath her, and red welts showed how she had struggled. She was not struggling now, however. She lolled on the bed, her breathing hard and ragged and punctuated by low moans.

Lord Sinjohn Thayer lounged in a wing-backed chair, his shirt open, his breeches only partially buttoned and his booted feet propped up on a large ottoman shaped like a man and a woman. They were rendered in incredible detail; both blindfolded and tightly gagged and both on their knees, so that they bore the velvet cushion on their backs.

As Viola entered, Sinjohn raised his glass of wine to her.

"Madame!" He held out his empty hand and she gave him hers to kiss, which he did quite thoroughly, lighting sparks of desire deep within her. As a young woman, she had been to the court of the Prince of Wales and savored many of the exotic pleasures on offer there. But nothing had compared to the pleasures taught to her by the Sorcerer who claimed her as his Catalyst. "Is all well?"

Viola took a deep breath. She hated to disappoint him, but she hated to admit she might have made a mistake even worse. "Not entirely, my lord."

Sinjohn set his glass down on a table. "What is it?"

Viola looked at the table. Its pedestal had the shape of a naked woman with her bound hands stretched over her head to support the top.

"I saw Rathe and Marlowe leaving our neighbor's house. They were not well, but neither were they dead."

Lord Thayer licked his lips. "And the girl?"

"Gone home with her mother, a sudden fever, apparently."

"So." Sinjohn sipped his wine meditatively. "They were stronger than we thought."

"They might not survive until morning," she said hopefully.

Sinjohn pursed his mouth. "It is possible," he agreed. "But I think we cannot count on it."

"What do we do?" Viola paced to the door and back again. "They'll know . . ."

"Calmly, my dear. They already knew Smith and his merry men were going to sneak into our party. It was to lure them in that we invited Mrs. Quicke and her daughter at all."

"Yes, but . . ."

"I said calmly." A hint of steel touched Lord Thayer's voice. Viola closed her mouth at once and dropped her gaze. "Now," he went on. "Supposing they do survive, and that they now have little Miranda Prosper to play with and protect, our goal is unchanged. Rathe and Marlowe have proved themselves too dangerous to be permitted to live, and Miss Prosper too strong to waste."

"They'll be checking the guest list," said Viola, endeavoring to keep her voice cool. "To try to discover the Sorcerer among the invited attendees."

"Which will bring them to you and me in short order." He sighed. "The question is, what will they do then?"

Viola forced herself to think. In all their years together, her husband had seldom been wrong. It was his gifts for manipulation as much as her own that had brought them this close to gaining the favor of the Fae court. If they fulfilled their task, they would take their place among Their Glorious Majesties' most trusted agents in the mortal world.

"They dare not risk an open confrontation," she said slowly.

Sinjohn nodded in agreement. "And their resources are so thin, I doubt they'll commit to a full-scale battle without hard evidence." He gazed meditatively at his fingertips. "So, they will be on the hunt for that evidence. Where will they look to find it?"

Viola smiled. "Well, in three more days, they'll be able to look in the conveniently empty town house of their chief suspects. But"—she tapped her chin—"at the risk of degenerating into circular reasoning, they know that we know their identities and so will be on guard, because . . ."

"Exactly." Sinjohn kissed her hand again. After a moment's thought, he dabbled her fingertips in his wine and then laid them in his mouth. He licked and sucked until she could feel a delicious tightening at her center. A quick glance showed her his cock stirring beneath the loose fly of his breeches.

"So in need, my lord?" Viola murmured, leaning down to run her hand along his growing erection. "Is there nothing left of the tidbit I sent you?"

The both looked over to the young woman on the bed frame. Her eyes were open and still.

"Not a thing," murmured Lord Thayer with a smile.

"Greedy." Lady Viola squeezed him, letting her nails dig in ever so slightly in the way she knew he liked. "Perhaps I should send you to Miranda Prosper."

"Perhaps you should." Sinjohn's smile curled up, cruel and masterful. Viola's breath caught in her throat to see it and she felt her pussy grow damp. "I admit I find myself quite curious to know what kind of woman needs two men to slake her thirsts."

Viola settled herself onto her husband's lap and wriggled her ass against his cock. She wrapped her hand around Sinjohn's throat, stroking him and claiming him at the same time. "Then, my dear, I shall have to make a gift of her to you."

"So generous, my wife." He fondled the mounded flesh of her breasts where it showed above the scooped neckline of her gown. "But as you so rightly point out, Rathe and Marlowe will be wary, so we must be exceedingly careful in our preparations."

"I believe I shall enjoy that." She ran her palm over his chest.

"I'll make sure of it, my dear." He chuckled deep in his throat and bent to close his teeth around her nipple, causing her to hiss with the sweet pain. Too soon he released her. "But, alas, the party is not yet over."

Lady Thayer sighed. "Yes, and Lord Dunmore is losing so badly at cards. He will shortly be in need of a loan. If we provide it, I am sure he'll be willing to do any number of little favors in return."

"So." Sinjohn set her on her feet again, but not without a hint of regret in his eyes. "Each of us to our duty, then. But fear not—enough of pleasure will follow, very soon."

She smiled, and knew her eyes shone with all her simmering expectations as she curtsied to him. He stroked her cheek briefly before she straightened and began to make her way back upstairs.

Six

"Sweet Miranda," Corwin murmured as he softly stroked her back. "How are you now?"

How am I? She had no words. Her bones had melted away, leaving only a delicious liquid inside her. She could not move; she could not think. She could only lie on the feather bed beneath the linen sheets and enjoy.

As the last echoes of their climaxes had faded, Corwin had rolled away, stretching himself out full length beside her on the bed. He slid one arm around her shoulders to cradle her, and Miranda gazed up into his dark eyes. Her body was at peace, as was her mind. She was herself again.

Except not quite. It seemed impossible that Miranda Prosper had done so many things that she could scarcely give name to, let alone receive such pleasure from.

"And you, Corwin?" asked Darius. Darius sat upright on the

other side of the bed, one leg tucked under him and one foot on the floor. His spent cock lolled against his thigh.

"As you see." Corwin sighed contentedly, running his free hand down the side of Miranda's breast. She snuggled closer, enjoying the feel of his warm chest against her. "Lie down, Darius. Rest awhile. No one will be stirring for a good hour yet."

Darius growled, but he did lie down at Miranda's left side. He did not, however, relax at all, and he eyed Corwin over Miranda's head. What passed between them, she did not know, but slowly, with a hesitation that was either reluctance or a misplaced bashfulness, Darius stroked her cheek with the calloused tip of one finger. It was a tender and intimate touch, and it made her reach out in return, to trace a line from Darius's jaw down his throat to his shoulder. She wondered at the strength of him, at how his form could be so beautiful to her eyes and even more so to her hands.

Corwin dipped his head close and kissed the tip of her ear. "He is magnificent, isn't he?"

"Stop it," grumbled Darius, but he didn't pull away from Miranda's curious fingers.

"Ticklish too," went on Corwin. "Shall I tell you where?"

Miranda could not have said why, but it was that comment that brought her once more back to reality. Here she was, in her own bedchamber, naked in bed with two equally naked men. Two men who had not only been boldly, shockingly intimate with her, but who also obviously shared an equally bold, and even more shockingly intimate, relationship with each other.

It was as if cold water had been dashed in her face. Miranda sat up abruptly, crossing her arms over her breasts and looking around frantically for something to cover herself with.

Darius slid a sideways glance to Corwin, who simply got up and went into her dressing room. She heard the rush of fabric and a moment later he returned with her turquoise night-robe, which he handed to her. Reluctantly unfolding one arm from her breasts, Miranda took it. As swiftly as she was able, she stood and wrapped the robe around herself, cinching the belt tight before double knotting it.

Darius picked himself off the bed and crossed to the window. He leaned his forearm against the wall, staring out at the waning night.

"P-Perhaps you should go," stammered Miranda, her gaze darting from one man to the other.

"Not before we talk," said Corwin. "You need to know what has happened here tonight, and why."

Miranda clutched the satin lapels of her robe beneath her chin. "Is there really any need? It was simply one of those things that happen between men and women . . ."

Darius gave a most ungentleman-like snort. "Put on a pair of breeches, Corwin. In this state, you'll only make things more difficult for her."

Corwin nodded. "Good idea."

Miranda was willing to swear she did not even blink. One moment, Corwin was stark naked in front of her, and the next he was clad in a dressing gown of burgundy velvet trimmed with black satin. She could see a white shirt underneath the robe. A pair of furred slippers covered his feet.

Miranda staggered backward. "How . . ."

"Stop it," said Darius sternly behind her. "You knew well before this there was magic happening around you. Don't turn fainting fool on us now."

His words stung her pride and Miranda straightened her shoulders. "I am not a fool; neither am I prone to fainting," she said, even though seeing Darius now dressed in a fashion similar to Corwin did nothing for her composure.

Darius nodded once. "Good."

Corwin looked from one of them to the other, with something perilously close to amusement coloring his expression. Miranda frowned hard at him, and his face at once became a mask of perfect sobriety.

"Explain yourself," she ordered.

Corwin raised his eyebrow a trifle, and the smile that played about his expressive mouth threatened to turn charmingly boyish. But Miranda refused to be moved by it, and continued to level at him the glare she had honed through years of public balls and supper dances.

Corwin bowed neatly from the waist, as if acknowledging her point. "The term most commonly applied to ones such as Darius and myself is 'Sorcerer.' "

Miranda did not permit her glare to soften one bit. "And what exactly does that mean?"

"It means we are born with the capability of shaping and wielding the power of magic."

A fresh wave of uncertainty swept through her, but Miranda forced herself to stand against it. "I would say there is no such thing, but that would contradict the evidence of my senses. So, I must accept it. You . . . both of you"—she glanced at Darius, who was still staring out the window at the darkened lawn—"are Sorcerers. You are working magic spells. What has that to do with me, and what happened to me tonight?"

Darius opened his mouth, but Corwin raised his hand to cut him off.

"Are you familiar with the theory of electricity?" asked Corwin.

Miranda inclined her head. "My father was a man of science. He read me Dr. Franklin's papers on the subject."

Corwin's brows shot up in genuine surprise this time. "Excellent. Then you are perhaps aware that the electricity may be both generated and stored."

"I have heard something of it, yes."

"It is rather the same with the power of magic. Like electricity, magic is a natural occurrence. A Sorcerer carries a store of it inside himself on which he may draw to work his art. But that store is small, and can be quickly depleted. Much larger supplies of magic exist in the natural world. Some places, indeed, are huge reservoirs of power."

"Then why does not the Sorcerer draw on those?" Miranda asked.

"They do," replied Corwin. "But tapping nature's reservoirs can be difficult, and time-consuming. It takes great skill and sometimes many years to create the tools necessary to reach it."

"You're talking of magic wands and so forth?"

"I am." Corwin nodded. "And such tools are not always reliable. They can channel too much magic into the wielder, or not enough, or the shape and nature of their making can warp the spell. So, most Sorcerers prefer to rely on their own inner stores of magic, or on a Catalyst."

"And what, pray, is that?"

"A Catalyst is a person who can naturally attract and channel the magic of the world around them, as one of Dr. Franklin's lightning rods channels the lightning.

"You, Miranda Prosper, are a Catalyst."

Miranda hesitated, uncertain she could trust her voice. "Are you attempting to tell me I am not human?"

"No. You are as human as we ourselves."

"You should perhaps have chosen a better example."

Corwin glanced over to Darius with something like a plea for help. Darius just shrugged and waved his hand, both gestures plainly saying, "You got yourself into this; you can get yourself out."

Corwin sighed with exaggerated patience. "You are perfectly human, Miranda. You are simply blessed with a particular talent. If you had been a born opera singer, or mathematician, it would be the same."

"No, I don't think it would." Miranda knotted her fingers together. "Is that why you . . . came to me? Because I am this thing, this . . . Catalyst?"

For the first time since they had begun this strange conversation, Corwin stepped toward her. "I came to you, Miranda, because I was in need." He reached out and took her hand, threading his fingers gently through hers. "I needed the strength I knew you could give me."

His voice was soft, and all humor gone from it. His hand against hers reminded her of all the other touches, the ones that had awakened and inflamed her. She swallowed and made herself meet his dark gaze.

"Was the . . . the . . . sexual act . . . necessary?"

"Not strictly," Corwin admitted. "But it is the swiftest and surest means for the Catalyst to channel power to the Sorcerer. It is also, by far, the most pleasurable."

His smile and touch remained gentle, but Miranda saw the fresh spark deep in his black eyes. He was remembering too—the way he had touched her and suckled her. Was he thinking of his cock thrusting inside her? She was, and of how very much she had enjoyed it.

She pulled her hand out of his.

"Why both of you?"

Corwin glanced at Darius, who lifted one eyebrow.

"Darius and I have been comrades in battle for a long time. He needed strength as much as I did." Corwin smiled again. "And, I am not ashamed to admit, it was also because I enjoy it that way."

"You do?" Miranda kept her gaze on Corwin. She did not think she could stand looking at Darius at that moment.

"Yes, very much. And I believe that you did as well."

Two of them, their hands exploring her, arousing her, mouths against her lips, tongues teasing her hard nipples, her hot pussy. Their hard cocks, in her sheath and in her hand . . . Oh, yes, she had enjoyed every moment of it.

Miranda gripped the lapels of her dressing gown again.

"Which is neither here nor there," interjected Darius sharply. "What you need to know, Miranda Prosper, is that you are an unusually powerful Catalyst."

Corwin cut in. "When you were with us the first time, you should have drawn the magic from the blossoming plants, from the trees, and from the Earth even, and it should have channeled through you into Darius and myself. That is not what happened. Instead, you drew magic out of me, and you held it inside you."

"Nearly killing yourself and him in the process," finished Darius.

Miranda stared at the both of them. "Is that true?" she demanded of Corwin.

Corwin shot Darius a warning look. "It is true," he said. "The fire you felt in you, the pain and illness and all the rest of it . . . That was the effect of drinking down my magic. Because you did not know how to disperse it, it stayed in you, raw and uncontrolled, and yes, it would have killed you had we not found you."

"And that I almost killed you? Is that true as well?"

"What nearly killed me was my own folly," said Corwin. "I was too eager to make love with you to check the precautions I had made against such an eventuality, as rare as I believed it to be. I behaved like a reckless boy, and for that, I am sorry."

Some of Miranda's anger and fear subsided at this, but Darius folded both arms and resumed his pensive staring out the window.

"So, you are telling me I am some sort of succubus, then?"

"No. A succubus is a daemon. She drinks a man's sexual energy to feed herself, and that will eventually kill him. What happened between us was an innocent mistake on your part, and a foolish one on ours."

He said these last words to Darius, and Miranda turned to see Darius's reaction. For a long moment, Darius stood still, his face grim. Then he nodded stiffly.

Miranda wrapped her arms across her breasts, hugging herself. She must think clearly. She must set aside her shock and disbelief, and all words like "perversion" and "insanity." They would not serve her. She must analyze what Corwin and Darius said, and come to an understanding of it.

She took a deep breath. "You said you were in a battle. Against whom?"

"Ah." Corwin sat down on the plush bench at the foot of the bed. "Now we come to the difficult matter."

A laugh bubbled up inside Miranda and she pressed her fingertips to her mouth. "After all you have told me, *this* is difficult?"

"It is," Corwin replied. "Because now I have to ask you—the daughter of a man of letters—to believe in fairies."

"Fairies?" repeated Miranda. "Little winged girls that flit about the bottom of the garden?"

"Hardly," said Darius. "Neither are they in the habit of granting wishes or riding cows dry or any other such trifling bits of mischief."

"The Fae are a race of powerful magical beings," continued Corwin. "They live in a world of their own, but in ancient times there were gates opened between our world and theirs."

"Another world," she said slowly. "How is that possible?"

Corwin spread his hands. "How is it possible that our world

is here? Shakespeare was right, Miranda. There are more things in Heaven and Earth than are dreamt of in any one philosophy."

Miranda found her mouth had gone dry. She moved to the washstand and poured herself a cup of water from the pitcher. Corwin and Darius watched her in silence as she drank. "Go on," she murmured.

"Much of this history has been lost," said Corwin. "But those who have studied it believe the gates were opened naively, by ancient Sorcerers who sought wisdom, and perhaps beauty, for the Fae can be astoundingly beautiful. By the time they realized their mistake, the whole Isle of Britain was in jeopardy, and they rushed to close the gates. But it is difficult to shut something that was never meant to be opened. Ever since that day, at times of great change, the gates shudder open again, and the Fae can slip through.

"The first great invasion came in the time of Camelot. It was Queen Guinevere who put an end to it, though it cost her dearly. She was not able to speak of the reasons for her actions, and so was cried out against as a traitor to her royal husband, though he himself never turned from her.

"The second came in the time of Queen Elizabeth. She and her Sorcerer, John Dee, were able to put paid to it then. He gathered to him the Sorcerers from all the nations of our island and they shut the gates again, it was thought for all time."

"But they were wrong," said Darius heavily. "And we are paying now for their mistake."

"So . . . you've been fighting an invasion? A . . . a . . . fairy army?" The words sounded ludicrous, but Miranda forced herself to squash her doubt. She had said and done so many impossible things since sunset, surely this was not too much more.

"I wish it was an army," Darius muttered. "An army we might be able to beat, depleted as our numbers are. This is worse."

It seemed to Miranda the room grew cold. All humor had vanished from the two men and their faces had both turned hard.

"The right king of the country has gone mad," whispered Corwin. "The prince, his son, is prisoner to lust and dissipation. Invention, machinery and riot are changing the whole nation. How could so much chaos fail to breech the gates once more? We thought we were ready, but our enemy has grown clever, and cautious. This time, they have come through in ones and twos. They whisper promises into the ears of greedy, mortal Sorcerers, corrupting our already paltry numbers and turning us against one another. This time instead of an army, we are fighting assassins who can strike quickly and fade away. We are fighting men and women who know all our strengths and our weaknesses because they share them."

"But why is it happening? What do these . . . Fae want from us?"

"Our lives," said Darius. "That spark of ourselves that is the soul. They have none themselves, so ours calls to them. They long to warm themselves by it, but end up only smothering it, and increasing their own hunger for it. They bring us glamour, power and beauty beyond description, and they kill us with it."

Miranda looked to Corwin for confirmation and he nodded. "It is that simple, and that complex."

"And there are people who are aiding them in this?"

Again, Corwin nodded. "Sorcerers are not immune to the promises made under glamour. If anything, we are more susceptible."

"Why is that?"

"Power corrupts," said Darius flatly. "And we are already powerful. Some of us believe we know what is best for 'ordinary' men and women. It is but a small step from there to convincing us we should rule, and that the lives of a few of those ordinary men and women are a small sacrifice for perfect peace and stability."

"And for power," added Corwin. "For ever more power."

Miranda shuddered. "I find that difficult to comprehend."

"Do you?" The corner of Darius's mouth curled up. "So, what did it feel like when you held Corwin's magic inside you?"

Miranda opened her mouth to say it had been hellish, but she stopped herself. That was not entirely true. At first, it had been amazing. She had been filled with strength and life. She was as great as the sky overhead, burning like a hundred stars. Nothing could touch or harm her, not her body, not her spirit. To feel so again, to feel so always . . . that would be a true temptation.

"What happens now?" she asked. "You have what you need and you will go?" She tried to speak the words calmly but a tremor crept unbidden into her voice.

Corwin exchanged another long glance with Darius and once again Miranda had the unaccountable feeling of much more passing between them.

"Ordinarily that is what would happen, yes," said Corwin.

Miranda tightened her jaw to keep it from trembling. "But this is not, even by our standards, an ordinary situation."

"You are powerful, Miranda," he went on. "The most powerful Catalyst I've ever encountered. If you want . . . it is possible for us to teach you to how to use your gift. To draw and channel magic safely."

"To become our Catalyst," said Darius gruffly. "He is asking you become our Catalyst for the duration of this fight."

Miranda felt her eyes bulge in their sockets. She was being invited to join them? To stay with them, learn more about . . . about magic, about sex, about these two powerful, magnetic men who stood with her now. Her mind reeled at the thought.

"What if I say no?" she asked. "What if it's too much and I do not want this?"

"We can take it away," said Corwin. "I fear we cannot heal your maidenhead, but we can . . . gentle the memories of how you lost it; give you a more ordinary and acceptable encounter with a more ordinary and acceptable man to hold on to. All memories of magic and . . . us, will leave you and you will be free to carry on with your life as normal."

Normal. Miranda looked down at her own hands, which her mother called unalterably coarse. Her normal life was sitting on hard chairs in ballrooms watching her mother lay siege to every man who was available—and quite a few who weren't— then going home to listen to Mother carp and snipe about Miranda's inadequacies. To leaven this, there would be the perpetual round of calls and shopping and teas, with no purpose to any of it beyond filling the endless, gray London days.

She looked at Corwin, and at Darius. What they revealed to her was exciting and enticing, true, but they also spoke of danger beyond her ability to imagine. If she said yes now, she would not later be able to turn back. She might be giving up her life and her sanity to escape from nothing worse than the boredom accepted by thousands of her sister spinsters.

But if she said no, she would not see Corwin again. Or Darius. She would never know the feelings and sensations she had discovered with them during the night. She would never again take part in the wonder that she had been shown—neither the magic nor the sex. A whole world had opened before her, and she wanted to know more, to do more. She did not want to run back into that smothering place her life had always been.

I will not.

If it cost her life, then so be it. A short and purposed life would be far better than the longest life in her mother's house could ever be.

Miranda squared her shoulders and faced the two Sorcerers. "I am with you."

Seven

Dawn was just breaking over the roofs of Mayfair as Corwin and Darius walked down the empty street. They had clothed themselves again in their evening wear, so that they appeared to be nothing more than two gentlemen strolling casually home from a late night out.

Not that there was anything casual about Darius's long stride. Darius had not once looked at him, let alone spoken to him, since they had snuck out of Miranda's house, and Corwin could feel his comrade's anger in every pore.

Corwin sighed and glanced around the empty street. "So," he said, pitching his voice low, just in case. "Are you going to tell me what the problem is?"

This actually caused Darius to break stride and swing around to stare at him. "You cannot be serious."

Corwin shrugged. "Let's say that I am."

"You *lied* to her, Corwin."

"You would prefer I had told her that she was endangered because we failed to keep a decent watch."

Darius waved his words away impatiently. "I'm not talking about that. You *used* her. You let her believe you took her for love and need, and didn't bother to tell her we'd come to this place to find her, and bind her if we could." His fists clenched. "Neither did you see fit to tell her that the reason we were sent to find her was that Catalysts in London have begun to vanish."

Corwin found himself uncomfortably taken aback. "Oh, yes, and if I'd phrased it so tactfully, she would have fled."

"That is not the point," snapped Darius.

"It is the point. Stop and think, Darius. She was already ter- rified, and halfway to believing that she is something inhuman as it was . . ."

"She is. We are."

Oh, not again. "Stop it, Darius."

But Darius had already turned away. "What human being does as we do?"

"Do you mean the magic, or something else, Darius?" Cor- win asked impatiently, and instantly regretted it. "Darius?"

Darius shook his head. "That does not change the fact that you lied to her. She now believes that we, that you, care for her."

"What makes you believe that I don't?" Corwin sighed. *We really are going to hash it out all over again.*

"Corwin, you were only at that ridiculous ball because we are under orders to protect the Catalysts we find and discover why they are vanishing."

Corwin shrugged. "These are not mutually exclusive things.

We have found her. We will protect her. It so happens this woman we are bound to protect is lovely, brave and passionate. How could I see her and not care for her? How could you?"

Darius made no answer and Corwin knew his words had struck home.

"Admit it, Darius. She roused you just as thoroughly as she did me."

"It was the Catalyst I responded to," he muttered. "Nothing more."

Corwin sighed. Darius had never come to terms with the . . . breadth of his own affections, and Corwin did not have the energy to revisit that old argument now. He was tired. It had been a long night and there was absolutely no prospect of bed until they reported to their captain.

If Darius wants to deny his own feelings for another day, fine. Let him.

"There's a carriage house in the King's Road," Corwin said, looking up and down the street to get his bearings. "We can get a bite and hire a hack to take us to the captain."

Darius drew in a deep breath. "Very well," he said and they walked on in strained silence.

The carriage house was a clean, well-run affair. The man and wife who kept it were already up and bustling about when Corwin and Darius arrived. While the hack was readied, they were able to dine on bread fresh from the oven spread thickly with butter and marmalade, as well as cold ham and boiled eggs washed down with pots of good beer. The driver was pleased to see their ready money and took them into the city without complaint, weaving the carriage expertly through the morning traffic of rattling carts, vans and wagons. They got out at the mouth of a nameless, narrow street overshadowed by the gleaming dome of St. Paul's.

Corwin paid the man off, and he and Darius entered an unmarked door halfway down the dim street. It might have been anything from a counting house to a solicitor's to a tailor. They removed their hats and walked into the neatly appointed sitting room. A fresh fire blazed in the hearth, for the morning had turned chilly.

"Come through, gentlemen, come through."

Darius glanced at Corwin, and Corwin smiled. They were expected, and neither was surprised.

Down a short corridor, they came to a room that was more a library than anything else. Bookshelves stuffed with fat, leatherbound tomes lined the walls from floor to ceiling. Only one in three was actually in English and more than one were written in a language that had died out a thousand years ago. In the middle of this literary wealth sprawled a broad desk, crowded with stacks of paper, inkwells and pens, as well as scrolls rolled up tightly and tied with ribbons of various colors.

Behind the desk sat their captain, a man Corwin and Darius knew only as Captain Smith.

Smith was a small man with a ring of grizzled gray hair around a bronzed and mottled scalp. He wore a long, unfashionable black coat over white breeches and stockings, and Corwin had the feeling he was older—perhaps far older—than he appeared.

The cognomen "captain" was purely a formality. Smith had no connection with the military that Corwin knew of. But then, Corwin knew next to nothing about the man himself, and that was as it was supposed to be.

"Sit down, gentlemen, sit down." Smith waved them to the two chairs waiting in front of the desk. "You have eaten? Good," he said when they nodded. "Now, tell me about your night."

Smith listened silently while Corwin and Darius recounted the events of the previous evening. Naturally, they left out the details of exactly what had passed between them and Miranda Prosper. Darius's face remained stony and his voice almost monotone when he described being lured away from the protective circle by a series of strange noises and the movement of light that could have been a lantern.

Corwin had not heard the full story and held his peace as he listened. Clearly, whoever had distracted Darius had done everything but shout his name.

At last, they finished, and Smith sat back in his wide chair.

"Your priorities were correct," their captain said. "The most important thing was to remove Miss Prosper from the Thayers' house to a place of relative safety."

Darius folded his arms and looked away.

"To a place of relative safety," repeated Smith firmly. "You were there not just to protect any Catalyst at the gathering, but to let the traitor know you were aware of their presence and activities. You have clearly accomplished both."

"At what cost?" muttered Darius. "We almost got killed."

Smith smiled thinly. "'Almost' can be a very large margin,

especially in the realms in which we move. What interests me more is the method of the deception." Smith fingered the chain holding his quizzing glass. "They knew where you'd be. They could have simply lain in wait and attacked physically at an . . . inconvenient moment and stood a much better chance of killing all three of you." He spoke calmly, as if their deaths were no more than an obscure intellectual exercise. "Your wards would have done nothing against a pistol shot or knife. So, why did they not avail themselves of that opportunity?"

"They didn't want us dead?" suggested Corwin. The quip earned him a long and hard look through Smith's quizzing glass.

"They wanted to make our deaths look like an accident, or to throw suspicion for them onto Miss Prosper," put in Darius.

Smith nodded. "Just so. One or the other. We sent you there to smoke out the traitor, but we must consider the possibility that the traitor brought Miss Prosper to the party to lure us there."

"Miranda had nothing to do with this," snapped Corwin.

Smith's shaggy brows lifted. "I did not suggest she did, Mr. Rathe. A Judas goat does not need to understand its job in order to do it."

Corwin found he did not much care to hear Miranda characterized as a Judas goat, but held his tongue.

"An elegant plan all around," Smith mused, tapping his glass against his weathered palm. "If it had worked, our two finest men would be drained and dead, and all our suspicions would be pointed toward the unprotected Miss Prosper. Were she to disappear shortly thereafter, we would only think that her masters had spirited her out of reach. Very elegant indeed."

"Three birds with one stone," whispered Corwin.

"The question then becomes why Miss Prosper?" Smith went on as if Corwin had not spoken. "A Catalyst who is also a daughter of the haut ton. Was she simply convenient, or did they have some particular reason for choosing her from a list of candidates?" His eyes narrowed. "Our traitor does not seem to do things in a random fashion."

"Either way, she is going to need protection," said Corwin.

Smith nodded. "And training. We must make sure she is secure in her abilities and in her loyalties before our traitor has the opportunity to advance whatever designs he, or she, may have on Miss Prosper. So, Mr. Rathe, Mr. Marlowe, your mission remains unchanged. You must secure Miss Prosper to our cause and find our traitor."

"What if the traitor's plan is to bring us close to her?" asked Darius.

"That sort of supposition, Mr. Marlowe, leads very quickly to paralysis." Smith tucked his glass into his waistcoat pocket, only to pull it out again a moment later. "It is not impossible that I am sending two good men further into a trap, and failing to rescue an innocent young woman from it. It would not be the first time I've made a hideous mistake." His blue eyes clouded over for a moment, and Corwin hoped to never know what could cause such sorrow to crease a man's face. "If it is a trap, you must find the trigger before it springs or die trying."

It was a cold-blooded statement, and yet Corwin couldn't fault the old man. This was war, and they were all soldiers.

"Our traitor was probably in attendance at Lady Thayer's

party," said Corwin, shifting the subject to an area where he could take action.

"That is indeed probable," agreed Smith. "So, you would do well in beginning your investigations with her guest list. Most of them, unfortunately, will be following tradition and scattering themselves to the four winds over the next week."

"The better to search their town houses," said Darius.

Smith looked at him, his brows raised. "Excellent thought, Mr. Marlowe. Mr. Rathe will take charge of Miss Prosper's training with your assistance, but you will lead the active investigations of Lady Thayer's party guests. If that is satisfactory?" Smith waited for a moment, but they were all aware neither Darius nor Corwin was going to contradict his direct instructions. "Very good. Thank you, gentlemen."

Dismissed, Corwin and Darius got to their feet and made their bows. Corwin saw that Darius was not pleased, and he was not bothering to hide it. Despite what had passed between them in the arbor and her bedchamber, Darius clearly still did not trust Miranda. He certainly did not welcome her presence. Corwin bit back a sigh.

I've got to talk to him.

But as Corwin turned to follow Darius out of the study, Smith spoke.

"Mr. Rathe, a word."

Darius eyed Corwin, but continued out into the front room. Corwin faced Smith and folded his hands behind his back.

"Sir?"

Smith raised his glass and looked at Corwin through it for a long, silent moment. Beneath that piercing gaze, Corwin had to work to remind himself he was a grown man, not a schoolboy in the headmaster's office. He was only partly successful.

"Mr. Rathe, you are a talented Sorcerer, and a courageous man," said Smith at last.

"Thank you, sir."

"But you have a cavalier streak about you, particularly in matters of human relationships. If you do not guard against this, it will land you in significant trouble one day."

Corwin felt his brow begin to furrow, but quickly smoothed his expression out. "I will do my best, sir."

"I am not offering you fatherly advice, Mr. Rathe." Smith's voice turned cold. "I am warning you as your superior. I am well aware of your tastes and habits, and of your ongoing liaison with Mr. Marlowe." Smith waved his glass toward the door. "I do not judge. In fact, I do not particularly care. But if you permit those tastes and habits to jeopardize your mission, I will personally make sure you are never able to jeopardize anything again. Do I make myself clear?"

In those last words Corwin felt the full weight of Smith's years, intellect and power leveled at him. Corwin had convinced himself that his personal life was not part of the struggle for the existence of the Isle of Britain. Smith clearly did not share this conviction, and he would not tolerate carelessness on the part of his subordinates.

"Yes, sir," said Corwin

"Very good, Mr. Rathe," said Smith more softly. "You may go."

Corwin walked to the door and laid his hand on the knob. "I will not let you down, sir."

"It is not me, Mr. Rathe. It is nothing less than the human race."

"Yes, sir." Corwin opened the door, but as he stepped through, he heard, very softly:

"Good luck, Mr. Rathe."

Corwin closed the door without looking back.

Darius stood near the hearth and looked up as Corwin emerged from the corridor.

"Well? What did he say?"

Corwin took his hat off the hook where he'd hung it. The encounter had rattled him far more than he cared to admit, even to himself. He took refuge from the fact by making light of it. "He warned me not to make a fool of myself over a pretty face."

Darius snorted. "I could have given you the same advice. Are you going to listen to him?"

Which is really too much coming from you. He faced Darius and waited until he was sure the other man was looking him fully in the eye.

"Do you trust me, Darius?"

Darius neither blinked nor flinched. "You know that I do."

"And yourself?"

At that, Darius looked away, and that told Corwin all he needed to know. "I trust you, Darius," Corwin said.

But Darius had taken himself out onto the street, and gave no sign that he had heard.

Eight

After Corwin and Darius left her, Miranda lay in her bed a full two hours, just staring at the canopy, trying to quell the surging tides of emotion inside her. Fear, excitement, confusion, desire; she felt them all, separately and in infinite combination. At last, she'd sunk into a shallow, restless sleep where dreams both bright and dark chased themselves through her mind.

When she woke, warm sunlight seeped in around the edges of the heavy curtains. She had sat up certain of one thing and one thing only. She was desperately in need of a wash.

Even so, it had taken all her courage to ring for Louise. Miranda felt certain some shimmering trace of Corwin and Darius must linger in the air, or that she somehow had been visibly changed by her encounter. This was foolish and she knew it, and yet the sensation would not leave her. She was not afraid, not exactly. What she had learned, about the nature of the world, about herself—it was so huge that it would have been unnatural not to feel dizzy.

Perhaps I should leave words like "unnatural" alone for a while longer.

If Louise noticed anything was amiss, she gave no sign. Still, Miranda decided to confine herself to her chamber for the day. As little as she liked to admit it, she was not ready to face her mother, who—although she did not know the details—knew all was not as it should be. Elated, exhausted and bewildered by all that had happened, Miranda spent much of her time sleeping, and when she was awake, she tried again and again to come to terms with all that had happened.

It was eleven o'clock the following morning before Miranda could make herself prepare to walk downstairs. To delay any longer seemed like rank cowardice. A new life had begun for her two nights ago. She would have to live it, and live with it, from this day forward. She had Louise help her into a morning gown of pale blue muslin sprigged and sashed with lavender. More lavender ribbons went into her hair, which Louise coiled, curled and braided to a fare-thee-well, and took so long about it that Miranda had to force herself not to squirm. But when it was completed, she had to admit she did look very well indeed.

Why, Mother might even approve.

Chin high, Miranda Prosper descended the stairs to the sun-washed breakfast room.

The sideboard was crowded with covered silver dishes. Mother believed that a real lady did not eat in front of other people if it could be avoided, or, if it could not, she ate as sparingly as possible. This meant that on any given day breakfast at home might be her only full meal, so she made sure it was a generous one.

Miranda's stomach made several unladylike noises as she helped herself to coddled eggs and fresh trout, some lovely raspberries and cream, and two fresh muffins. Tea did not seem strong enough this morning, so she drew a cup of coffee from the urn. She sat down with her heavily laden plate and began to tuck in. It all tasted delicious.

It must be true what the French say. Hunger is the best sauce. But there was something else to it. Despite her fears and misgivings, Miranda felt alive, and ready to enjoy life. It was as if Corwin and Darius had awakened more than simple desire in her.

Not that there was really anything simple about that desire. Miranda remembered their hands on her, their mouths everywhere. She flushed hot as the thought and memory of hands and mouths led to that of hard cocks, in her pussy and pressing between the halves of her ass . . .

Stop that, Miranda ordered herself sternly as she sliced into her fillet of trout. But then she paused. *But why should I? Why should I not enjoy this too?*

Revelation bloomed slowly. Now that she knew it was not a pointless emotion, that softly simmering desire *was* enjoyable. Its warmth was teasing, and just the tiniest bit distracting, but it gave her a sense of nothing so much as anticipation.

And Corwin promised they would return.

This made Miranda frown. Certainly Corwin *had* promised

to return, but would he? Perhaps he had just said that so she wouldn't make a fuss when they left. Perhaps they were planning the conquest of some other young woman right now . . .

"Well, Miranda, there you are."

Miranda froze and her heart thudded hard against her ribs. Mother had entered the dining room, looking like the cat that had drunk the cream, only to find it had gone off. "I must say, I am pleased you had the good sense to stay in bed yesterday. Otherwise, if anyone had come calling, they would have ceased to believe the story of your having a fever."

Miranda sighed. Another morning she would have quailed and shrunk back. But everything was different now, including this. "Mother, everyone at Lady Thayer's was too busy with their own affairs to worry about mine."

"If you had been with anyone other than the new and fascinating Mr. Rathe, that might be true." Now it was Mother's turn to sigh. "I must say, it never really occurred to me that I might have to hush up a scandal about you, Miranda."

"Does this mean you are disappointed or the contrary?"

Mother frowned, a perfect and depressingly familiar little moue. Miranda's spirit flagged, but only for a heartbeat. She boldly met her mother's gaze, and something inside her loosened, a fetter she had never before been able to undo.

"Did he give any sign of his intentions?" Mother asked sharply. "Or even promise to come calling?"

Miranda set down her fork and blotted her lips, trying to remain calm while her mind raced furiously in search of a suitable reply.

Mother's eyes narrowed. "Well, Miranda?"

At that moment the doors at the far end of the room opened and the footman, Halloway, entered. Miranda turned toward him and hoped the wash of relief flooding through her did not show in her eyes.

"A gentleman to see you, madame." Halloway stepped up to Mother and held out a silver tray on which lay a single calling card.

It took all of Miranda's strength not to lunge for the card. Mother picked it up, read it. Her eyebrows arched. "It seems we are honored with a visit from Mr. Corwin Rathe," she said. "I trust, Miranda, you are ready to receive him?"

Miranda's heart hammered against her ribs. As calmly as possible, she laid her napkin aside. "Of course."

"Tell Mr. Rathe we shall meet him in the morning room, Halloway."

"Very good, madame."

The footman left to perform his duty and Miranda found herself once again under Mother's silent scrutiny. The knowledge that Corwin was only yards away both buoyed Miranda up and brought all her fears rushing back to her. How would she face him? How would she face him in front of *Mother*? And how would he behave toward her? He'd been gentleman enough in the ballroom, and he clearly understood discretion, but still . . .

Mother stood. "Shall we go find out if we are still going to be able to make something of you?"

I should have expected you to say something of the kind. But even so, as Miranda got to her feet to follow her mother, she had to pinch the bridge of her nose in an attempt to stop the prickling behind her eyes.

The morning room was small but comfortable. The bay windows opened onto the well-groomed gardens and admitted a wealth of summer sun. Mother had decorated the place with her usual excellent taste, and the creams, pinks and yellows of the furniture and hangings were cheerful without being too dainty or overly fussy.

In the middle of all this stood Corwin. He appeared to Miranda as he had the moment he first stepped into the ballroom: composed, elegant and devastatingly handsome. This morning his spotless breeches and linen were topped by a plain buff waistcoat and blue coat that—in Miranda's opinion—set off his strongly formed shoulders and arms to perfection. His cravat was simply tied and did nothing to distract from his wonderfully masculine features.

"Good morning, Mrs. Quicke. Miss Prosper." Corwin bowed to Mother and to Miranda with the same expression of cheerful politeness on his face, but Miranda did not miss the mischievous gleam in his dark eyes.

"Good morning, Mr. Rathe." Mother briefly gave Corwin her hand.

"Good morning, Mr. Rathe." Miranda made herself speak politely as she dropped her curtsy.

Mother looked from her to Mr. Rathe. Miranda could tell she was performing one of her rapid internal calculations. Despite her misgivings about Miranda's own conduct, that calculation evidently came down on the side of accepting the man she believed—not incorrectly—to have already compromised her daughter. He was, after all, handsome and, to judge by his clothes and comportment, clearly well-off.

"Won't you sit down?" Mother flashed one of her dazzling smiles and gestured to the overstuffed chair by the window. "The girl will be in directly with coffee."

"Thank you, madame." Corwin bowed again before he took the seat offered. "I trust I find you ladies well this morning?" He spoke to them both, but Miranda caught his eyes lingering on her for an extra heartbeat.

"Perfectly well, thank you, Mr. Rathe," she murmured, and did her best to make herself mean it. The truth was her heart was beating like a drum and had not slowed at all since she'd heard mother read his card.

"We are both enjoying excellent health, thank you," said Mother. "It must be the wonderful weather we're having this summer. I don't believe I can remember so many pleasant days."

Miranda felt she had moved into some kind of strange otherworld, listening to the man she had made such passionate and dangerous love with calmly discussing the weather with Mother, while Mellon came in bearing a tray of coffee and muffins. All was as it should be, but at the same time, it was on some level utterly unbelievable.

After Mother had allowed an interval for Corwin to butter his muffin and comment on the excellence of the coffee, she got down to business. "Do tell me something about yourself, Mr. Rathe."

Miranda felt something close to panic rising in her and she shot Corwin a nervous glance. He met her eyes easily.

Don't worry, she thought she heard him say. *I have this in hand.*

Oblivious to this exchange, Mother prattled on. "I'm sure I spoke to my entire acquaintance at Lady Thayer's last night, and no one seemed to know a thing about you."

"I'm not surprised at all," returned Corwin pleasantly. "You see, Mrs. Quicke, I'm not the sort of character many people of standing choose to associate with."

"Oh?" Mother rested her chin on her hand. "And why on Earth should that be?"

"First of all"—Corwin looked carefully about the room, then set down his cup and saucer so he could lean in closer to her—"I am actively employed."

"No." Mother laid a hand on her bosom while Miranda struggled to keep a straight face.

"Yes." Corwin nodded solemnly. "My father owned several large tracts of land in the Canadian territories, and after I left Eton, I was sent out to manage his properties there."

"Goodness!" This time Mother was genuinely surprised, and intrigued. "Mr. Rathe, you do not mean to tell us you're a—what is the term?—a . . . a . . . cowboy?"

Miranda tried to picture Corwin on horseback, in a leather coat with a wide-brimmed hat pulled low over his long hair. In her imagination he rode a white stallion across a flowering meadow with forests and mountains rising up to either side. She had to stop. The image made it next to impossible to breathe.

Corwin caught her eye and raised his brow just a fraction,

as if to say, "I know what you're thinking." A deep blush burned across Miranda's cheeks.

"My father made his money in the fur trade," Corwin went on to Mother. "He was one of the original investors in the Hudson's Bay Company, but afterward he turned to raising horses and cutting timber."

Corwin paused for another sip of coffee. "My time in the wilderness was reason enough for the . . . fastidious to keep away from me, but there is worse to come."

"You fascinate me, Mr. Rathe," said Mother, and she sounded as though she meant it. "Please, do go on."

"When my father died, I sold out his shares in the land and the ships, and instead took a government position. So, you see, I am now that lowest of creatures, the civil servant."

"How perfectly scandalous!" Mother clasped her hands together delightedly. "But the sale of your properties must have left you the possibility of a gentleman's life?"

Corwin slid another glance toward Miranda. This time she found herself perfectly calm. She had no idea whether Corwin was telling Mother the truth or a complete fabrication, but whichever it was, it struck exactly the right chord, and Miranda did not see any reason to interfere.

"Actually, it was the sale of horses to His Majesty's government for use in the late wars that finally settled my fortunes," said Corwin. "But I found a life of idleness did not suit me. My mind is of a restless nature and requires employment."

"You must find England terribly dull after life in the wilds."

"I assure you, madame, my life there instilled in me a deep

appreciation for a sound roof, a dry bed, an absolute lack of wolves and bears, and"—he held up his muffin—"good, solid English cookery."

They all laughed at that. Corwin finished the muffin, wiped his mouth with his napkin and stood. "Miss Prosper, the morning is very fine. I was wondering if you might consent to take a turn in the park? With your permission, of course, Mrs. Quicke."

Mother bowed her head regally, and turned shining eyes toward Miranda. Miranda found she suddenly had to deal with the unexpected sight of her mother for once *not* being disappointed in her.

Miranda got to her feet. "I'd be delighted, Mr. Rathe. Thank you."

Corwin offered her his arm, and she laid her hand on it lightly. With an additional bow toward her beaming mother, he led her away.

Nine

"You have both charmed and amazed my mother."

"Have I?" returned Corwin innocently. "Good. That will make any number of things easier."

The morning was gorgeous, and it was not only Miranda's elevated spirits that made her think so. The summer sun shone down from a rare, clear blue sky. Around them, the park's flowers all seemed determined to show off their best and the air was filled with the scents of roses and greenery. It was lovely to be strolling through this space of ordered perfection with her hand on Corwin's steady arm.

It was still a little early in the day for the majority of the ton to be out, so they had the park's rolling greens almost to themselves. Louise, who was supposed to be chaperoning them, had discreetly and most improperly asked if she might be permitted to visit the greenhouses, and Miranda gratefully gave her consent.

Miranda's bonnet dangled down her back on its loosely tied ribbons while she braved the possibility of freckles to let the sun's rays touch her face and the summer breeze play through her elaborately arranged tresses. The day was too beautiful to hide from.

Besides, Corwin was smiling at her.

"Was it true, what you told her?" asked Miranda curiously.

"About my background? Every word."

"It seems so strange, knowing what you are . . ." She faltered, but Corwin only smiled and drew her hand a little closer around his arm.

"Sorcerers are not creatures apart, Miranda. Unless I want to try to keep myself entirely by magic—a feat which is intensely difficult and prone to many dangers—I require money, shelter and companionship." He smiled meaningfully and laid his hand across hers. Although they both wore gloves, she felt his unmistakable warmth against her. "Just like any other man."

It would have been so easy to let herself drown in the deep gaze he turned toward her, but Miranda was determined not to be distracted. She wanted so much and yet knew so little. It was time to rectify that. "And Darius?"

"Darius had a rougher time of it," said Corwin. "His family was less . . . tolerant than mine of a son who did not fit the mold. My father decided to send me somewhere I could . . . 'run it off' was his phrase, if I recall correctly. Darius's father, on the other hand, kept him on a shorter and shorter leash."

She remembered the danger and the power in Darius's manner. "What happened?"

Corwin's jaw hardened. "Darius did what bored and overly controlled young men frequently do; he turned to drink and gambling. These were pursuits his family could at least understand, so they did nothing to check them, nor did they recognize that they were, for Darius, a form of slow self-murder."

He was not speaking to her now, but gazing down the gravel path in front of them. She could feel the suppressed anger coursing through his veins, and she understood it. The thought of Darius, who was so strong and magnificent, falling into dissipation was almost too much to consider.

"What happened?" she asked.

Corwin gave a wry chuckle. "He tried to cheat me at cards."

Miranda felt her eyes almost start out of her head. Of all the offenses one gentleman could commit against another, cheating at cards was ranked among the worst, almost demanding a duel.

"He was very drunk at the time," Corwin went on. "So much so that when I accused him, he took a swing at me, and what began as a personal matter quickly dissolved into a street brawl." He laid a hand on his ribs. "I carry the ache of it to this day."

Miranda made a face. "Now you are having fun with me."

"Perhaps a little." Corwin winked. "But I wasn't having any fun then. Darius was drunk enough to start a fight, but not so drunk that he was going to lose easily. I was hard put to defend myself, and when I did at last get hold of him, I realized several things in a startling hurry. The first of these was that I was facing another Sorcerer."

"You could tell he was a Sorcerer by touching him?"

"He was leaking magic like a sieve. Not his fault. He had no idea who or what he was, and none of us know how to control ourselves without proper training."

"What else did you realize?"

Corwin turned his face toward her. "Do you want me to say it aloud, Miranda?"

She blushed and looked straight ahead of her. "This path leads to the lake," she remarked.

He followed her gaze. "So it does," he replied coolly. "Shall we go that way?"

"Yes, I'd like that."

They strolled on in silence for a time. Miranda was grateful, as it gave her time to absorb this new information. It also gave her time to chide herself for her continuing bouts of bashful and missish behavior.

Still, I cannot reasonably be expected to change the habits of a lifetime in one day.

This led her to thoughts of two nights before, to the ballroom, and seeing Corwin for the first time.

"How did you come to be at Lady Thayer's party?" she asked.

His eyebrows shot up. "Could I not have been simply invited?"

"You could, but I don't believe you were. Mother could not find anyone there who admitted to knowing you."

"Ah." His smile was indulgent. "Miranda, you see through me already. No. I crashed the gate, by magic."

"In what way did you use magic?" They were coming to the shady edge of a little wood. Ferns nodded beneath the trees, filling the air with their sharp, green scent.

"One of the most basic powers of the Sorcerer is Persuasion,"

Corwin said. "Most people believe what they see, and remember what they choose. Persuasion works with this natural tendency. I Persuaded Lady Thayer's butler that I was invited."

The idea that he might be capable of something of that kind had been stirring uneasily in the back of Miranda's mind. It gave rise to another question, one she didn't want to ask, but knew she must. "Can you Persuade anyone to . . . anything?"

Corwin caught the hitch in her voice and faced her, taking both of her hands in his. "Are you asking if that was why you came with me?" he said.

"Yes." Corwin's touch was gentle, and would shortly become distracting. *I must remain focused. I must watch his eyes.*

But his eyes remained clear, and he nodded, accepting both her honesty and her concern. "The answer is no. I could not, for instance, Persuade the butler who let me in to run naked across the lawn yelling, 'The king is a bloody bastard.' Not only because he had absolutely no inclination or desire to do so, but because it would run precisely counter to his personal, moral feelings. He was, however, inclined to admit people to her ladyship's party and had no deeply held moral objections to doing so."

"So what did you do to me . . . ?" There. She'd said it, the real issue that had nagged at the back of her mind even while she had so enjoyed his company in the summer sun.

Corwin's smile grew warm and highly mischievous. "Really, Miranda, do you think it proper do discuss here?"

Her cheeks heated. "You know to what I refer," she replied primly.

"Yes, I do, more's the pity."

He kissed her gloved hand and Miranda felt the heat spread down her throat to her breasts. She became suddenly aware of the brush of cambric and muslin against her skin, of how closely and smoothly her silk stockings encased her legs. She almost didn't dare look at Corwin, because the sight of his smiling mouth made her long to lean forward and capture his lips in a heated kiss. If she did that much, she knew she would only long to do much more.

"What are you thinking, Miranda?" Corwin whispered.

"I am thinking you are a long time answering me."

A smile lit Corwin's face. "I shall have to remember that when I make an inquiry of you, I will get a most direct answer." But even as he spoke, a gleam in his eye said he did not believe that she had told him all that was on her mind. He knew she was thinking of kissing him, of touching him, of stroking his cock until it grew hard in her hands, and he himself was having similar thoughts.

A deep blush rose in her cheeks.

"Please answer me." She had meant to speak the words with frosty politeness, but all she could manage was a kind of breathy whisper.

Corwin bowed but did not release her hands. "Are you familiar with the idea of glamour?"

"From fairy tales. It's a form of magical disguise, is it not? A way to make someone think a ruin is a luxurious castle, and so on."

"Yes. The Fae do it easy as breathing. We human Sorcerers can work a version of it, outwardly or internally. I can make a vision for the whole world—of the two of us dancing politely, for instance. Or I can make a vision just for you . . . a most particular, most private vision." His smile grew sharper, and slier, and Miranda could not help but remember that first vision, that premonition of what was to come, of herself, naked between Darius and Corwin . . .

Her breath was coming fast and shallow. Corwin ran his thumb over her fingertips, and that tiny gesture was giving rise to the most remarkable level of heat.

"Miranda, you blush so beautifully." Corwin touched her cheek. "Truly, I think I shall find it impossible not to kiss you."

"Don't, Corwin," she whispered, even though her lips had parted the instant he said "kiss." "Someone might see."

"Miranda, Miranda, what were we just discussing? No one will see a thing if I do not wish them to."

Before she could protest again, he pulled her into his arms and his mouth covered hers. He ran his tongue around her lips, savoring them before pressing for entry. She opened eagerly, longing to feel even this much of him inside her. His tongue slid along side of hers, stroking dexterously, creating a delicious sensation that somehow reached all the way to the very center of her. It robbed her knees of any strength so that she was forced to lean against his hard chest, or fall backward.

One kiss was not enough. She'd known it wouldn't be. Of their own volition, her hands caressed his face, running up his jaw to his temples and finally knotting into his hair so she could prevent him from moving his enticing mouth from hers. He held her tight with one arm while his other hand glided down her back to stroke her hips and the curve of her ass. Miranda shivered and pressed against him, close enough to feel the ridge of his burgeoning erection beneath his breeches.

"Oh, Miranda," gasped Corwin. "I knew I would not be able to resist you."

He tipped her backward, kissing her mouth, licking, stroking nibbling, while with the back of one hand, he brushed the tip of her breast. Miranda's nipple tightened instantly. At once, he engulfed her breast with his whole hand, massaging and plumping, reveling in the feel of her.

He backed them both up slowly until she was pressed against a broad tree trunk. She was grateful for the support, because she could no longer stand on her own. She was dizzy with her own heat and his kisses. She was already wet and she wanted desperately to lay herself down entirely, right here on the green, so he could be on top of her and enter inside.

And yet, when he lifted his mouth from hers to draw breath, she asked, "What of Darius?"

This caused Corwin to smile, but his hand did not cease its maddening attention to her breast. "I am not sure I understand, Miranda." He lifted her breast upward and planted a silken kiss on the exposed skin right at her gown's neckline. As soon as his lips touched her there, Miranda could not remember what she'd asked.

But it was important. It was. "Should we . . . without him?"

Corwin drew back, his face a study in wounded pride. "Do you doubt my ability to satisfy you without Darius's assistance?" He leaned close again, his breath hot against her ear. His hand worked her breast, his ceaseless bold caresses filling her with the sweetest agony she had ever known. "Miranda, you have only begun to discover what I can do with you and to you." She tightened her thighs to try to stop her pussy's straining, but this proved to be a mistake. It only trapped her wet heat, and even that felt good.

"I will make you come with my mouth on your pussy; then I will make you come again with my fingers inside your sheath," Corwin whispered, and each word seemed to invoke the sensation it described. "I will teach you all the delights of servicing a man's cock, and I will drive you to the heights of pleasure while you have me in your mouth." Miranda moaned at his words and rubbed her thighs together. She could come like this, with just his words and breath burning against her skin. "Only then will I enter your sweet, sweet pussy. I will fuck you long and slow until you beg me to make you come again. Then, for doubting me, I will make you wait while I take my full pleasure of you, sheathed so tight inside you, stroking your ass and your clit . . ." A thought seemed to strike him. "Do you know what I mean by your clit, Miranda? It is just here . . ."

His hand thrust between her thighs and pressed the fabric of her skirt right into her slit, and his fingers found the sensitive nubbin of flesh there. Delight lanced through her and she moaned.

"Or perhaps I'll just tease you like this." Corwin circled his fingers, rubbing her own skirts against her. "Perhaps I'll show you I can make you come for me without even removing a stitch of clothing."

Miranda groaned, and Corwin laughed, a low, throaty, intensely exciting sound. He pressed his fingers closer, rubbing harder. She gasped and arched her hips, and he caught her ass with his other hand. Now she was trapped. He was rubbing her hard with both hands, one front and one back, a wicked, burning massage.

"Touch your breasts, Miranda," he urged. "Caress yourself. It will feel so good. You know it will."

She did know it. She ran her hands over her breasts, capturing her own nipples through the fabric of her demure day gown, pinching and rolling them as Darius and Corwin both had. She sighed with the pleasure flooding her, and this only made him rub her harder. The pleasure sharpened, stretching to fill her, raising her up toward her limits.

"Oh, yes!" she cried. "Oh, Corwin!"

"Tell me what you want, Miranda. Tell me what you need."

"I want to come! I want you to make me come!"

"As my lady commands."

He cupped her ass tight with one broad hand and pressed the heel of his other palm firmly and suddenly against her throbbing clit. Miranda squeezed her breasts and the pure hot pleasure burst through her, splintering her awareness and driving her body into spasms. It seemed an age before they faded, bringing her back down to the world of sunlit warmth and to Corwin cradling her against his strong chest.

"Miranda." He kissed her softly on her cheek, on her brow, as she wilted against him. "My beautiful Miranda. You will not, I trust, doubt me anymore?"

"No, oh, no. But . . . that wasn't why I was asking . . ."

"I know." She felt him smile wickedly against her temple. "But I could not resist." He kissed her throat. "Well, perhaps I could, but I did not wish to."

"But . . ." Guilt threatened. She had done so much that was beyond the pale in the last forty-eight hours—in the last forty-eight minutes—that she felt in danger of losing all sense of right and wrong, at least while this man was near her. "But, aren't you and Darius . . . together?"

"We are lovers, and have been for several years. You knew that, Miranda." He took her hands and backed into the woods, drawing her with him.

"Yes, I did. And that's why . . . if you and I . . . That is . . . if we continue . . ."

He arched his brows. "Are we betraying him? Specifically, am *I* betraying him with you?"

"Yes. You must be aware, this . . . situation . . . It is a little complex."

"And highly unorthodox." Corwin sat down in a nest of ferns with his back against an ancient oak and stretched his legs out in front of him. From this angle, Miranda could see the outline of his hard cock clearly, and it was a most distracting sight. "To answer you, no," said Corwin. "Being here with you is in no way a betrayal of my relationship with Darius."

"I don't understand." He still held both her hands, and now he was looking up at her with the most absurd lopsided smile on his face. Drat the man, this was *important*! Even now, with him so hard and her still so wantonly, wickedly hot.

"You don't understand wanting to make love with Darius? Really, Miranda, you certainly had me deceived . . ."

"Stop it."

"I'm sorry, but, my dear, you do turn such a wonderful shade of rose when you are teased." He let go of her hands, and began to take his gloves off, tugging at them one finger at a time. It was a simple thing, an everyday sight, but Miranda couldn't take her eyes from his hands. Her breath grew shallow and her dress felt far too tight across her breasts.

"I don't understand how you could be with him, and still want me," she said hoarsely.

"And I don't understand how anyone could see you and not want you," he replied frankly as he removed his hat, dropped his gloves into it and set it aside. "Or Darius either. You are both so strong, so passionate and so very beautiful." He took her hands again, drawing her down to him. She moved to sit beside him, but he guided her straight onto his lap, not astride, but what she could only think of as sidesaddle. "I do not deny I am unusual in that I have no preference in whether my bed partners are . . . crested or cloven, shall we say. I enjoy the delights of both men and women, and both at once if all parties are willing. It is not something that has always been easy."

"And Darius? Does he play this game because of you?"

"It is no game, Miranda." Corwin lifted her dangling—and somewhat squashed—bonnet off her shoulders and set it down beside with his hat. "Not to me, and I hope not to you." He raised her right hand and with his very capable fingers undid the buttons on her gloves. He was undressing her, and himself, in daylight. She should have been shocked, she should have been at least distracted, but as it was, she felt ever-so-slightly impatient.

"But what of Darius?" she pressed.

Corwin stopped what he was doing and looked up at her. "You care a great deal about what he thinks."

"I have no wish to hurt him, or to . . . come between you."

A new light shone in Corwin's dark eyes, something softer and gentler. It felt for a moment that she had seen through to something deeper than she had yet known from him. "You are a good woman, Miranda Prosper, and you have a good heart," he said with a true tenderness in his voice. "I cannot tell you all I know, because there are some things it is only right that Darius tell you himself. But I can tell you this much. Darius is like me, although he does not choose to admit it. He wants—he needs—both men and women. But he does not give himself as . . . lightly as I sometimes have. His heart has been broken in the past, and broken badly. Now he guards himself from harm by pushing those around him away." Corwin tilted his head to one side. "Again, in this I think you and he are very much alike."

Which was truer than she wanted to consider at this time. "But . . ." she began.

"Miranda." Corwin wrapped his arms firmly around her waist. "I have been most patient with these questions, but the time for talk is long past. I want you, my dear, and I will have you."

She had no idea what mischief made her raise her brows. "Will you indeed, sir?" She started to scramble to her feet.

The world spun. Miranda suddenly found herself flat on her

back amid the ferns. Corwin held her wrists pinned on either side of her head and he straddled her, his hard, muscular thighs trapping hers.

"Yes, I will."

His kiss was hard, hot and merciless. He gave no ground, gave her no chance to respond in kind; he simply took and took until breath and sense were gone and Miranda could only yield before his onslaught. It was wonderful. He was magnificent, and her surrender to his thrusting, stroking tongue sent a fresh wash of delight through her sensitized body. His weight should have overwhelmed her, but it didn't. She welcomed him, arching her hips against his, reveling in the tight press of his body. She wanted to touch him, to caress his ass and his thighs, but he held her helpless, intent on taking all he wanted of her mouth.

All at once his arms were around her shoulders and the world spun again. Now he was the one on his back, and Miranda was on top and astride him. His hands stroked her back, and lingered on her ass, cupping, massaging, wantonly enjoying the soft flesh there.

Miranda wriggled, rubbing her breasts against his chest, and her pussy against his cock. She sat up, which, she found, pressed her ass more firmly into his eager hands. She could see his face now, his wicked and delighted grin, his eyes made bright by passion.

Miranda ran her palms down his chest, feeling how hard he was breathing, and then she dragged them in slow circles over his bulging cock. She'd never get enough of touching him there. It was as exciting and fascinating as the feel of his hands on her, especially when he sighed as he did now, and arched himself underneath her.

All of which turned her mind toward their previous conversation. "You said you would teach me . . ."

Of course he knew instantly what she was talking about. "So I did, and so I will. But not now, my dear, we have not the time I wish to devote to that most-pleasant lesson. No, for now, we must take the road we have traveled before." He reached beneath her skirts, running his hot hands up her thighs. Miranda sighed and closed her eyes, the better to concentrate on his touch. His hands splayed across her thighs for a delectable moment before he found her curls and stroked, dexterously fondling her folds. Then, all at once, he thrust two fingers into her and she gasped and rocked forward, forcing him deeper.

"Naughty, naughty, Miranda." His fingers wriggled inside her, sending ripples of pleasure through her and at the same time making her giggle. "You are so eager to touch me, my dear, why don't you put my cock into this lovely, wet pussy?"

It was difficult to move with any kind of conscious volition while he stroked her, long and slow, as he'd promised. Only the understanding that his cock would feel even better inside than his hand gave her the ability to work the buttons on his breeches' fly, to reach inside with both hands to cup and caress his hard, thick cock.

"Oh, yes, Miranda." Corwin closed his eyes and his fingers thrust deep, showing so plainly what he wished to do. She ran her fingers up and down his shaft, delighting in the heated velvet of the skin there. "Yes."

He withdrew his fingers and with both hands roughly pushed her skirts up around her thighs. Miranda lifted herself onto her knees and with both hands guided him to her entrance. His hands gripped her ass and she felt him shudder, sensed he was restraining himself from slamming her down against him so he could bury himself to the hilt inside her. A sense of power surged into the pleasure and she lowered herself a bare inch, just enough so her folds enclosed the head of his cock.

"Oh, Miranda."

"'Oh, Miranda' what?" She reached behind herself and pulled his hands away, holding them out to the sides. She had no idea what made her so wicked and bold. She had no idea if such things were even done. But she wanted to do this. She wanted to see the way it made him drop his head back as she snuggled him inside her, just a little bit more.

"Oh, Miranda, *please.*" It was a game; they both knew it. He could break her hold in a second if he wanted to, but the sound of him begging her sent another rush of heat through her. She was strong, daring, free. She could do whatever she wanted to this beautiful, powerful man and he would only beg her for more.

"Please what?" she settled herself further. It was maddening to have him half-in, half-out like this, and yet she forced her knees to hold still.

"Please, take me deep," he groaned. "Please, take me all the way inside your gorgeous, hot pussy."

"As sir commands."

Miranda let her knees buckle and pressed down until he was fully seated inside her. She gasped and called his name and he wrapped both hands around her hips. She leaned forward, meaning to kiss him, but he lifted himself up and instead rubbed his face against her breasts.

"Wicked woman," he whispered, kissing her breasts, lapping at her nipples through the fabric of her gown while his hands stroked her thighs. "Ride me, Miranda. Ride my cock."

She began at once to move, rocking her hips back and forth. The sensations were maddening. But it was evidently not enough for Corwin. He shoved his hands back under her skirts and gripped the halves of her ass, lifted her up, and slammed her down.

"Ah!" she gasped as he filled her utterly. "Ah!"

He lifted her again, and again. It felt so good. She wanted it, wanted more, wanted faster. She raised herself, and fell on him, impaling herself on him over and again, aware of nothing except the honeyed delirium of his hands, his cock.

"Ride it hard!" he commanded.

"Yes!" She bucked against him, her body beyond her control, seeking only the pleasure of him, wanting him entirely inside her, wanting to hear him cry out, to command, to beg. His hands were on her ass, her hips, her breasts. His tongue was everywhere too, laving her breasts, lapping her throat and thrusting inside her mouth as his cock thrust into her pussy.

"Corwin!" she screamed against his mouth as she came undone. He gripped her hips ruthlessly, forcing her against him even as her climax rocked her so hard she could not see. There was nothing in the whole of the world save the ocean tide of ecstasy rolling her under, and then she felt him beneath her, thrusting up, wild uncontrolled, lost, completely undone by the pleasure of her body.

Ten

Viola Thayer waited while the footman announced her, then breezed into Daphne Quicke's sitting room. Mrs. Quicke stood as Viola entered, looking cool and collected, but Viola felt the excitement simmering just beneath the woman's skin. Daphne was at home, alone, on a fine afternoon in a sitting room that sported last year's colors. Viola also could not help but note the distinct absence of invitation cards on the mantel. Even with the season just about finished, there should have been one or two for the coming summer exodus.

Oh, dear, Mrs. Quicke, are the ladies of the ton finally tired of you chasing after their men?

"Lady Thayer." Mrs. Quicke made her curtsy. "How delightful! Won't you sit down? Halloway, send in Mellon with another cup."

"I am so glad I caught you at home, Mrs. Quicke." Viola smiled and settled on the chair offered, adjusting her skirts minutely. "What a charming room! So sunny, and such delightful colors."

"Why, thank you." Mrs. Quicke accepted the compliment without batting an eye. "And may I say what a wonderful time Miranda and I had at your party. Such charming society! I declare I feel ten years younger for it!"

The girl arrived with the fresh cup and saucer, and there was a pause in the mutual flattery while Mrs. Quicke ascertained how Viola took her tea—with lemon—and offered sandwiches—cucumber—and biscuits—declined. Viola watched Mrs. Quicke surreptitiously while she fixed the plate and cup. Daphne was aging as gracefully as a woman could, but the signs were there. Her hair was too bright from the dye. The skin around her throat was beginning to sag and the creases at the corners of her eyes were deepening and spreading. But it was the veins on the backs of Daphne Quicke's hands that truly gave her age away. No young woman had such hands. And it was not only the room that was wearing last year's colors. Mrs. Quicke's light blue afternoon gown had been made over at least once.

"Thank you." Viola accepted the cup and sandwich. "I am a little surprised to find you alone," she remarked. "Where is Miranda this afternoon?" She sipped her tea and had to acknowledge that it was very good. Daphne Quicke clearly was a mistress of the art of keeping up appearances.

"She has gone walking with that charming Mr. Rathe. You won't mind my saying, Lady Thayer"—Daphne Quicke dropped her voice into a confidential tone—"I had all but given up hope for Miranda. It pains a mother's heart to say it." Here Mrs.

Quicke laid a dramatic hand on her bosom. "But it is true. Now, though, I should be very much surprised if there was not something . . . beginning."

"As should I, Mrs. Quicke." Viola nodded, grateful her opportunity had come so soon. "That was why I particularly wished to have a word with you." She set the cup down and assumed a serious mien. "I wanted to put you on your guard."

"On my guard? Why, Lady Thayer, whatever do you mean?" It was a breathless protestation, but Lady Thayer saw the caution behind it. *You already suspect something, don't you? Perhaps that your little Miranda is not quite the innocent she was? If you only knew . . .*

Lady Thayer laid her hand on Mrs. Quicke's "I am afraid, my dear Daphne . . ." She paused. "I may call you Daphne, mayn't I?"

"Of course, of course."

"And you must call me Viola." Viola watched her flattering familiarity do its work before she scooted just a little closer. "I'm afraid, Daphne, that Mr. Rathe is not quite what he represents himself to be."

"No?" Daphne's eyes widened. A casual observer would have seen nothing but shock. The disappointment was entirely in the set of her sloping shoulders, and the dimming of the light in her expression.

Lady Thayer shook her head slowly and solemnly. "No. He is, in fact, not a gentleman."

"Oh, Viola, you had me most concerned." This time the hand pressed to Daphne's bosom was far less artful. She really was having difficulty catching her breath. "He told us about his background when he called this morning."

"Did he?" Lady Thayer frowned.

"Yes. And I can certainly understand the considerations for someone like yourself, but for Miranda I think a man of active profession, even a civil servant, will do very well. Indeed at her age, we simply cannot afford to be too particular."

Very neat, Mr. Rathe. Very nice, Lady Thayer thought toward her absent opponent. *But I am not prepared to let you have Miranda Prosper quite so easily.*

"So you would look with favor on such a match?" Viola rested her fingers against her lips. "Oh, dear."

"I'm sorry, Viola; have I said something wrong?"

"I certainly do not want to interfere, Daphne," Lady Thayer said primly. "Especially not with a mother's very proper concern for her daughter's welfare, but . . ." Viola paused just long enough to make sure she had Daphne's full attention. She needn't have worried. The woman was hanging on her every word. "You might not want to be too hasty in this matter."

Mrs. Quicke's eyes narrowed, and for a moment Daphne's mask slipped enough to allow Viola to see the mercenary calculations running through her mind. "Is there something I should know?"

"Yes. And that was the other matter I had hoped to mention. You know I will be having my house party next week, at Hallowgate?"

"Always quite the event of the summer," said Daphne. It was a polite nothing. They both knew she had never been to one of Lady Thayer's country parties. Viola suppressed a smile. It would be fun to draw this out, to play with this silly, shallow woman and see how many hoops she would jump through to get what she wanted. But, alas, there was no time for such a game. Later, perhaps. Mrs. Quicke was certainly ripe for all kinds of sport.

"I was hoping this year, if you're not otherwise engaged, you and Miranda might do me the favor of attending."

Greed, pure and simple, smoldered in Daphne Quicke's eyes. "Why, thank you, Viola. We do not have any other engagements for the week, so that would be delightful."

Time to move in for the kill. "Oh, I am glad. I have a most particular reason for asking." She favored Daphne with another confidential little smile. "A nephew of mine, the Honorable Robin Summerfields, will be there. Have you met him?"

"I don't believe I've had the honor."

"He has been at Oxford and has had very little time in London. A most serious scholar. But he was in town briefly last Christmas, and he saw your Miranda at Lady Featherstone's birthday party."

"Did he?" For the first time, Daphne Quicke evidenced genuine surprise.

"And he was most favorably impressed. So impressed, in fact, that he has been asking if you are going to be at my little get-together, and he practically begged to be introduced to her."

"To Miranda?" Mrs. Quicke did not bother to disguise her shock.

Lady Thayer nodded. "To Miranda."

"Well." Mrs. Quicke sat back, clearly trying to reshape her established outlook to fit this new intelligence. "That is most excellent news. I'm sure Miranda and I both will enjoy meeting your nephew very much."

"And Mr. Rathe?"

Daphne glanced out the window, past the garden toward the street, no doubt more concerned than previously about exactly where her daughter had gotten herself off to. "Well, as they have only just met, there has been no time for any real attachment to grow between them. Indeed, just between us, Viola, it may improve your nephew's impression of Miranda if there is another man paying his addresses. You know how nothing elevates a girl's charm like a rival in the background."

Lady Thayer let herself appear to consider this. "I had not looked at it quite that way, Daphne. You really are very clever." She stood and smiled. "Until next week, then?"

"Until next week, Viola."

Lady Thayer left, feeling quite satisfied with her afternoon's work.

Eleven

"Well." Darius leaned against the oak tree and folded his arms. "Here we all are, then."

This was the first time Miranda had seen Darius since he'd left her bedchamber. She had imagined his presence would be less intense in the daylight, and more like Corwin's. But she had been wrong. Nothing had eased at all about him. His blue eyes raked her from top to bottom where she sat next to Corwin, even though her appearance was completely proper. Corwin's magic had removed the grass stains from their clothing and she even had her bonnet on her head with its ribbons neatly tied. After Corwin and Miranda had . . . recovered from their lovemaking, Corwin told her about his appointment to meet Darius in an isolated section of the park near one of the groundskeeper's sheds. Miranda readily agreed to accompany him. Now they sat on a wooden bench beside the shed, holding hands, but nothing more than that. But Miranda felt certain Darius knew she had been making love with Corwin. A blush rose in her cheeks, but Miranda couldn't tell what contributed most strongly to it—that Darius knew what she had been doing, or that she very much wanted him to know. If he knew, he might become aroused at the thought, and if he became aroused . . .

Really, Miranda, you are becoming a thoroughgoing wanton!

"Hello, Darius." Corwin seemed completely unruffled by the other man's burning gaze. He motioned Darius to sit with them. "I was wondering when you'd find us."

"Were you?" Darius looked from Corwin to Miranda and raised one eyebrow. Miranda felt her cheeks burn.

"Good afternoon . . . Darius," said Miranda.

Darius bowed, but said nothing. Miranda's brow furrowed. She had trusted Corwin when he'd said Darius would find no insult or betrayal in their being together without him. But now, faced with Darius's clear disapproval, she was forced to wonder if Corwin had . . . not lied, perhaps, but exaggerated the extent of the openness of his relationship with Darius.

"Any news?" Corwin was asking.

"Not a damned thing." Darius dropped onto the bench. Miranda flinched at the oath. Which was ridiculous, but she could not help it.

Darius and Corwin exchanged one of their long looks and Miranda found she could not endure it anymore.

"*What* are you two doing?"

"I beg your pardon?" inquired Darius.

"When you do . . . *that*." She gestured at his eyes. "Something is going on. What is it?"

"Observant," Darius remarked over her head to Corwin.

"She is, isn't she?" Corwin squeezed her hand fondly, a condescension Miranda was in no mood to humor. She drew her fingers away his and slapped him across the knuckles, an action that widened Corwin's dark eyes and startled an expression that might almost have been a smile from Darius.

Miranda chose to ignore this. "As a matter of fact, I am observant," she replied coldly. "Now, will either of you deign to tell me what it is I am observing?"

"The formal name for it is 'empathetic communication,'" said Corwin.

"And, pray, what is that?"

Speaking mind-to-mind without words. Thus.

Miranda clapped her hands over her ears.

"Corwin," growled Darius. "Stop teasing her."

"How did you do that?" Miranda cried, staring from one of them to the other.

"It is one of the gifts held by Sorcerers," said Corwin simply.

Miranda lowered her hands. "Could I . . . ?"

"Speak to us?" Corwin considered for a moment. "You already have, although you were fevered at the time and probably do not remember. Do you want to attempt the experiment now?"

"Yes."

"Very good." He gestured to Darius. Both men got to their feet and walked about a yard away before turning to face her.

"Close your eyes," said Corwin. "And think of a phrase, something you know well. Now picture myself or Darius and in your mind, imagine speaking the phrase to us, just as you would naturally."

Trying not to feel silly, Miranda closed her eyes. She pictured Corwin first—smiling and charming as he had been in the morning room. But she quickly found she could not hold the image of him in her mind without Darius as well. Darius, brighter in complexion and yet so much darker in spirit, held himself distant and tried so hard to remain cold. Why was it Corwin was open with her and Darius was not? What had she done?

A vision touched her, sudden and bright like a lightning flash: a woman, of wealth and taste, pale-skinned and golden-haired, her face twisted in hopeless outrage. Her hand lashed out and Miranda felt the ringing slap as if on her own cheek.

Miranda gasped and opened her eyes.

"Well-done, Miranda," said Corwin softly. "Not quite the result intended, but very well-done indeed."

"I'm so sorry." She said it to Darius. Though she could not have said why, she was certain the vision had come from him. She was equally certain it had been a memory.

"It doesn't matter." He was lying. It did matter, and he was ashamed enough that he would not look at her. "I should have guarded my thoughts more carefully."

"Why don't you try again, Miranda?" suggested Corwin.

"No," she said slowly. "Not just now, I think."

She desperately wanted to know the story behind what she had inadvertently witnessed. But she feared if she attempted the empathetic communication again, she might not be able to resist reaching to try to find an answer that Darius was not ready to give. Such an invasion would make any relationship between them even harder to create.

"As you choose." Corwin nodded, but the look he cast toward Darius was silent and unfathomable. "It is important, however, we begin your training."

"My training?"

He smiled. "There is much a Catalyst should know, beyond the act of love, my dear."

"Oh."

"Disappointed?" inquired Darius archly.

"Now who's teasing her?" Corwin frowned at the other man. "Yes," he continued to Miranda. "You will recall I said that the act was only one way to create a channel for magic?" She nodded and he went on. "Because creating such a channel is for you an inborn ability, it is something you can do by wishing, if you concentrate closely enough. Now, if you would please stand up, and come here. Thank you." Feeling a bit as if she were in the schoolroom, Miranda moved to stand between the two men. "Now, I shall stand to your right, and take your hand. So. Darius, if you will take her left?" Darius did as Corwin instructed, but he did not look at Miranda. He kept his eyes straight ahead.

Between the two men, Miranda suddenly felt very small. Her head barely came up to their shoulders. Their gloved hands engulfed hers. With one small motion either of them could turn her, or turn toward her, brush their lips against her face, her throat, pull her close against their hard bodies to allow her to feel their swelling cocks against her . . .

"It will be more difficult to concentrate this way," she said, grateful her voice was still under her control, even though her thoughts did not seem to be.

Corwin smiled. "It is, I assure you, necessary. If you are successful in creating a conduit, the power you raise will need somewhere to go. We do not want a repetition of the other night."

Miranda shuddered, remembering the pain that had racked her. "No."

"Now, Miranda, I want you to close your eyes once more . . . Very good. And concentrate on the soles of your feet."

Miranda creased her brow. "I beg your pardon?"

"The greatest source of power is our Mother Earth, and the point that is in closest contact to Her is your feet. So, if you would please concentrate on the soles of your feet."

Miranda tried. It was not easy—shutting out the touch of their hands, the sun on her face, the wind brushing the back of her neck—to focus on a portion of herself she seldom considered. But slowly, she became very aware of her soles, the feel of her of silk stockings, and of the way her thin slippers curved over the irregularities in the ground.

Then, almost without meaning to, she became aware of the Earth: how it stretched out all around, dark and solid, yet teeming with rich, warm and infinitely complex life.

"Very good, very good, Miranda," murmured Corwin, and she realized she could now sense him with her mind as well as with her hand. He was a bright presence beside her, like pure light that was somehow as rich as honey. Darius was there too, compelling and complex, like bitter chocolate to her senses. It was strange to feel them thus, but it was wonderful at the same time. "Now, picture, if you can, a network of light that stretches into the soil."

As he spoke, Miranda found that she could see a glimmering web laced through the living Earth. It was not bright like sunlight, but a shimmering black, the color blood might be while still inside the vein, and like blood, this webwork pulsed with vitality.

"Excellent, Miranda. Imagine that vitality flowing upward into you, up through your legs, through your torso and out your hands, into us."

It was easy, almost disturbingly so. As she stretched her thoughts toward it, that web's strands wrapped softly around her. Her skin tingled, first cold, then hot, and she felt a pulsating tide rise within her, very like desire, but more delicate, a sense of hot and sweet together that seemed to nourish yet created a fresh hunger.

Now to us, Miranda.

At Corwin's gentle command something inside Miranda fell open like a blossom. The vitality she drew from the Earth flowed toward the men on either side of her. She sensed their thirst for it and felt them open to drink it in. A need to slake that thirst came to life in her. Her palms, her fingers, grew so warm she fancied that if she had opened her eyes, she would see them glowing, and yet she reached down deeper, seeking yet more of that darkly shining essence, to draw up and pour forth into the men who reached for it, for her.

Enough, Miranda. Enough, my dear. Come back into yourself.

It was difficult. A large portion of her wanted to stay open to this new awareness. But Corwin continued his gentle urging and

Miranda slowly began to pull back. She felt her body, blood and skin close around her and become solid again. She felt the whole of herself once more, the sun and the wind against her skin, the brush of her clothing, and the hands wrapped around hers.

"Open your eyes, Miranda. See what you have made possible."

Miranda did open her eyes, and she gasped.

When Miranda had closed her eyes, there had been nothing between them and the battered shed but a stretch of grass and stubble. Now there was a waist-high tangle of rambling roses in full bloom making a riot of color; scarlet, snow white, rich pink and vivid yellow.

Corwin smiled and plucked a deep scarlet blossom. "For the lady." He bowed as he presented it.

Miranda took it carefully.

"Beware the thorns, Miranda," said Darius harshly. "They too are real."

Miranda turned toward him. He was flushed, not with health as Corwin now seemed to be, but nearly fevered. His eyes shone with a fierce hunger. Miranda swallowed at the sight of it, for she knew it was directed at her. She could feel his heat radiating against her skin. He wanted her. He was hard, and she did not even have to look down to know this. Her body told her, raising a warmth inside her that was as real and as palpable as the magic had been—her desire answering his.

She took a step toward him, but Darius groaned, and moved away. Miranda froze, suddenly afraid.

"Darius," whispered Corwin. "Darius, there is no need for this."

The look Darius shot Corwin was so full of venom Miranda's hand flew to her mouth. Then Darius turned on his heel and strode—almost ran—away from them.

Corwin's jaw hardened. "Go find your maid, Miranda. And don't worry. We'll both be with you soon." With that, he loped after Darius.

Miranda stared until both men vanished into the wood. Her head was swimming. She was standing by a bed of roses she'd created—or one that the power she'd brought into the world had created—a kind of miracle she could have never believed. And yet the moment Darius turned from her, the achievement, the magic, seemed hollow and sour. She didn't know what to do. She didn't know what to think.

Slowly, reluctantly, Miranda began walking across the meadow toward the greenhouse.

Behind her, one by one, the roses withered and vanished.

Twelve

Darius heard Corwin coming after him, crashing through the bracken and cursing as he did, but the brooding man did not turn around. He did not want to face Corwin and hear his hectoring questions. He did not want to have to endure Corwin demanding to know *why* he couldn't just fuck Miranda Prosper behind the groundskeeper's shed, as if it were normal to burn with desire for a woman while his lover—his *male* lover—looked on, or even joined in enthusiastically. Corwin didn't truly know what it was to be rejected. No one ever turned Corwin down, or if they did, it never touched him. Nothing ever truly touched him.

Have I ever truly touched you?

Seeing the way Corwin looked at Miranda, a beautiful woman with whom he could live openly, Darius had to wonder. Duplicity did not come naturally to Corwin. What if he was tired of living all his life in the shadows? What if he yearned for simpler passion that he could be honest about?

Because it simply wasn't possible to truly want more than one kind of love. It wasn't natural. It couldn't be, not in the long run. Corwin would leave him. And the reason he would leave was Miranda Prosper.

Miranda, who was brave and beautiful and who lit a fire in Darius like no one else ever had, except Corwin himself.

Impossible. Unnatural.

Darius barely saw the lake when he came to the edge. He was out of breath and his fists were clenched so hard his knuckles had begun to ache. The silver-blue surface rippled in the pale daylight and for one terrible moment Darius wondered if it was deep enough in the center to drown a strong man if he dove in far enough.

"Darius."

Corwin. Darius could feel him. He could catch the scent of him even here on the fresh summer wind.

"Are you trying to hurt her, Darius?"

Of course you are thinking of Miranda.

Miranda. Darius remembered the feeling of her hand in his, so strong and yet delicate. She tried so hard not to be afraid as this new, strange world opened around her. He understood that. He wanted to reach out to her, to protect her as she made her journey into understanding, to hold her and tell her it would be all right.

But how can I, when I don't believe that myself?

"It's killing me," he whispered.

"What is?" Corwin moved closer, although he stayed behind Darius. Darius was glad. His erection had not yet gone down, and he felt ashamed of it as a schoolboy would.

"This. This need." He could have lied, could have pushed Corwin away as he had so many other times, and Corwin would have given up and gone, just as he always did. But he didn't.

"Darius . . ." began Corwin with that familiar impatience. This time, Darius snapped.

"No!" He rounded on the other man, his fists clenched hard at his sides. "It is not simple! If you don't care, I do. I care . . . I . . ."

Corwin stood stock-still. He met Darius's gaze without flinching. "What?" he asked simply.

"How can I love her when I love you?" demanded Darius. "How can that be right?"

He'd said it. He'd said it aloud, and it could not be undone. The force of this truth set his hands trembling.

"Do you love her, Darius?" asked Corwin softly.

"I don't know," Darius whispered, running his shaking hand through his hair. "I want her. I can't stop thinking about . . . about us, together."

"You and her, or all of us?"

Darius closed his eyes and swallowed hard. His throat had gone suddenly dry. "Both."

"Ah."

Fury snapped Darius's eyes open. "Don't mock me, Corwin!"

"No, Darius." Corwin met Darius's eyes and Darius saw his comrade and lover was both sorry and sad. Anger fled as abruptly as it had come. Darius wanted to take Corwin into his arms, to hold him and apologize, to say it was all right if Corwin left him, as long as he, Corwin, was happy.

But it isn't all right, because this isn't about whether Corwin wants her. It's about the fact that I want them both.

"Darius, I do not pretend what is happening is simple," said Corwin softly. "But I know this much—love is not water in a well. If it is real, it cannot be used up no matter how many partake of it."

"That is a fine platitude for jealous siblings, but this is different."

Darius waited for Corwin to say something teasing, as he had so often before, but while Corwin smiled softly, his dark eyes remained solemn. "Very different. But it is real, and because it is real it leaves us with only two choices—to face it or to run from it. You know as well as I we cannot run. If we do, we endanger our mission, our country, our very freedom, not to mention the lives of thousands, Miranda Prosper among them."

"So you're saying it's my duty to give in to this lust?"

Corwin's smile twisted. "Don't be thick." He slapped Darius's shoulder. "I am saying that if you are wasting your energies trying to deny your feelings, you will not have full use of your brain, and your brain is something we desperately need. What comes after this mission . . . I don't know what it will be. But I know this." Corwin moved toward him, and laid his hand on Darius's arm. The familiar heat of Corwin's presence seeped into Darius's skin even as the power of his gaze seeped into Darius's soul. "I love you, Darius," Corwin whispered. "I need you. I care for Miranda Prosper, and yes, I desire her, as do you, and she feels similarly toward us. Whether this will last . . . We can only hope, Darius, hope and trust and move forward with our task. Can you do this?"

The question stung Darius's pride, but even as he opened his mouth to make a sharp reply, he felt Corwin's fear roll over him like a shock of cold water: fear that if Darius turned away this time, he would never come back, that he, Corwin, had been too careless, that he had lost Darius, lost him forever.

Something loosened inside Darius, whether he wanted it to or not.

All the gods help me.

"Yes, I can do this." Darius gripped Corwin's arm, a hard touch, meant to say so many things, and looked in his eyes, and he knew Corwin understood. "And I will."

Thank you.

Corwin kissed him. It was so sudden Darius barely had time to raise his glamour, but then he gave himself over to it fully. Corwin's strong, ready mouth, his tongue, his hard hands clasping Darius's head to pull him close.

They kissed until breath left them, and Corwin smiled when he pulled away. "You see?"

"Yes." Darius nodded and laced his fingers through Corwin's hair. They stood like that for a long moment before Corwin removed his hand, turned it over and kissed the mottled skin on the inside of Darius's wrist.

"Now, you must continue your investigations. We will meet again tonight, and see what we can do to set Miranda's fears at rest. Are we agreed?"

Darius nodded, and Corwin planted another hard kiss full of promise on his mouth. Then he started off through the bracken with Darius watching.

"Darius?" Corwin looked back over his shoulder

"Yes?"

"You can be as spiteful as you want to me. I know you and nothing you say will alter my feelings toward you, but do not do so to her again. You will break her heart, and I cannot sanction that."

Darius met his gaze for a long time, and then nodded. Corwin nodded in return, turned his back and walked away. Darius stood facing the lake, and it was a long time before he could make himself turn and start off in the opposite direction.

Thirteen

For Miranda, the walk home passed in a storm of shifting emotions. She said not a word to Louise. She could barely see the streets before her, her mind was so filled with the memory of Darius's blue eyes the moment before he turned and strode away into the woods.

What am I going to do?

It was unfair. Darius had neither the right nor the reason to be contemptuous of her. They had come to her. They had led her into this—although she had followed willingly.

Miranda clenched her fists tightly. That was the root of it. She had followed. She had desperately wanted what they had to show her. Now she found that one of her guides on this impossible journey . . . He . . . He what? Disliked her? Distrusted her? Distrusted his feelings for her, certainly.

Which is much the same thing, isn't it?

Did he distrust her enough to leave her and convince Corwin to go with him? Corwin cared something for her—of that Miranda was sure—but his relationship with Darius was one of long standing. He could not possibly abandon the old for the new. If Darius went, Corwin would follow, and she would be alone, not just for an afternoon but for always; stranded on this path before she had even truly started down it.

That thought terrified her, but there was nothing to do but keep walking, and glance over her shoulder yet again, hoping against hope to see Corwin and Darius up the street, coming back to her.

When Miranda reached the house, she had every intention of heading straight to her room. Unfortunately, the sitting room door was open, and Mother was waiting on the other side.

"Miranda, my dear," Mother called. "I would like to speak with you, please."

Miranda hesitated at the foot of the stairs. "I'm sorry, Mother. A sudden headache. I need to lie down."

"But I have something very particular to say to you."

Of course, you do. Miranda sighed and looked longingly up the stairs. She could ignore her mother and continue. But that would lead to recriminations later. Her whole world might have turned upside down in nearly every respect, but this remained constant—she still lived in her mother's house.

Miranda let Louise help her off with her bonnet, and then schooled her face into her habitual attitude of calm and walked into the sitting room.

Mother was sitting on her favorite pink-upholstered chair, where she could see out both the windows and the door without turning her head. Her sharp eyes flickered up and down as Miranda entered the room and sat on the plush sofa.

Looking for flaws, as ever.

"Miranda, I've just had a visit from Lady Thayer."

"Lady Thayer?" Miranda repeated, shocked out of her calm resolve. Lady Thayer had seldom even spoken to her mother, but first they were invited to the end-of-season party, and now she was paying calls? What had happened?

"She wanted to extend us an invitation to her summer house party at Hallowgate. She was most anxious that you should attend."

Miranda opened her mouth and closed it again. She found she had nothing at all to say to that.

"I'm sure you can see this is an excellent opportunity for us both," Mother went on. "So I want you to be careful between now and then not to do anything to . . . call attention to yourself or cause talk."

"Are you referring to my walk this morning with Mr. Rathe?"

"You know what I am referring to."

Miranda straightened her spine. "May I remind you I had your open permission to accompany him. I honestly thought I would find you in here selecting my wedding clothes."

"That's enough, young woman."

"No, I don't believe it is," Miranda snapped back. "For years I have listened to your endless criticisms because I could not attract a man. Now I have done so, and every time I turn around I find you have changed your mind about him!"

In response, Mother stood. She walked over to her writing

desk and pulled out a large, leather-bound book. "Do you know what this is?"

"It's your accounts book," replied Miranda promptly.

Mother slapped it down onto the desk and flipped it open. "Come here."

Frowning, Miranda stepped up beside her. Mother pointed to the neat columns of figures, the majority of which were written in bright red ink. Miranda felt her eyes grow wide as they traveled down the page.

"As you can plainly see, we have nothing left, Miranda. Nothing." Mother's voice was flat and her eyes were hard. "I have done everything I can to find another husband, but I have so far been unable. It is up to you to secure our future."

"But . . . Mr. Quicke left you a fortune."

"On paper, yes. A number of those investments did not prove to be as judicious as they initially appeared."

Miranda blinked at her mother, for a moment feeling like nothing more than a bewildered child. She had known they were economizing. They had done so before, in the period between Mr. Lester and Mr. Quicke. But Mother had never let her near the accounts, and the truth was, Miranda had not asked to see them. She had kept herself as aloof as possible from her mother and her mother's doings, which included the daily running of the household.

"Lady Thayer has a nephew who is interested in meeting you. Unless you can be absolutely certain Mr. Rathe will be making you an offer before the end of the summer, I suggest you make up your mind to be very agreeable at the Hallowgate party." Mother snapped the book shut and returned it to the drawer.

"I see," Miranda said slowly, although in truth she felt as though she had been blind. She had blithely assumed that Mother would find a way to manage, because she always had. She had always taken care of herself, of them, a fact that Miranda, in her distaste for her mother's flirtations and her anger at the criticisms, had never looked at clearly before.

"I hope you do see," replied Mother grimly. "You may go now, Miranda."

Miranda drifted to the door. This latest shift was almost too much. She felt ill. A thousand questions rang through her mind, but she couldn't bring herself to ask any of them.

Except one. Miranda paused in the doorway and laid her hand on the threshold.

"My father was a poor man," she whispered. "Why did you marry him?"

"I thought I had money enough from my first husband," Mother replied. "I thought I could afford to marry for love. I was wrong."

"I see."

Miranda maintained enough pride to walk calmly up the stairs, down the hall and into her room. But as soon as she shut the door, she collapsed into the chair beside her fire and dropped her head into her hands.

What on earth have I been thinking?

The sight of the ledger filled with red ink had been a blow from nowhere. She tried to remember any time when she had stopped to consider money, and she couldn't. Not in any real way. She had her allowance and she managed that. But for the larger finances, Miranda had simply assumed her mother, who loved appearance and luxury, would get by as she always had: by finding another man. She'd believed implicitly in Daphne Quicke's irresistibility. She'd hated all Mother's dazzling flirtation as much as she had hated her mother's constant carping and criticizing, so she'd shut herself away. She who prided herself on being so practical, such a realist, had not even considered the possibility that there might not be enough one day.

But that day had apparently come and gone.

Her blindness had left her without options or recourse. She was supposed to go to Lady Thayer's house party and make herself agreeable to Lady Thayer's nephew, and—what was mother's phrase?—secure their futures?

Why in heaven's name would Lady Thayer's nephew be interested in her when no man had been before? Well, no man save Corwin, and possibly, on some level, Darius, but that was an entirely different set of circumstances. It was hardly likely that Lady Thayer's nephew was a Sorcerer attracted to her because she was a Catalyst.

Was it?

Could it be? Miranda lifted her head and blinked slowly. She had no idea how common Sorcerers were among the haut ton. Corwin's remarks seemed to indicate they were rare, but there were said to be ten thousand members of their class in society. Surely there were more than two among those ten thousand.

What do I do? Miranda rubbed her temples. She needed to talk with Corwin, to find out if he knew Lady Thayer's nephew. But she had no idea how to reach him.

But even as she thought this, she remembered the sound of his voice in her mind. How near did she have to be to reach out to him? He had remarked several times on her strength. Could she call to them, mind-to-mind, and let them know she was in need?

Miranda bit her lip. It was one thing to step into this mode of thought when Corwin and Darius were beside her, but to do so on her own . . . It was as if some final line had been crossed. Once she began to use the magic on her own, she could no longer hold herself apart from it. She could no longer pretend she was in some way safe.

That, she realized, was what she had been doing all this time. It was the deep reasoning at the heart of her contemptuous aloofness from her mother. If she didn't act, if she just let herself be ordered about, she could pretend on some level she wasn't part of what was happening, that she could still leave it behind.

But that is illusion, and always has been.

Miranda crossed to her window. She looked out to the street beyond the garden wall. Several carriages passed by, and a well-dressed couple strolled arm in arm down the walkway. Miranda laid her hand on the cool panes and closed her eyes.

She thought of Corwin. She thought of Darius. She remembered standing between them, feeling so small and yet so strong. She remembered the feeling of their hands in hers as she opened herself to draw the power of the Earth into her. She thought of their eyes, of their mouths, of their bodies, all she could do to conjure in her mind the physical presence of the two men.

Darius. Corwin. She sounded their names in her mind. *I need you.*

Miranda?

It was as if they were standing beside her. The shock of feeling them so completely almost broke her concentration, but Miranda drew a deep breath and forced her mind to remain focused.

Miranda, where are you?

At my home, but . . . something has happened. I . . .

No. Stop. The urgent command clearly came from Darius. *You are not properly shielded. Anyone can hear us. We will come to you.*

Silence descended. Miranda opened her eyes. Darius and Corwin had felt so close inside her mind, it was startling not to see them standing before her. She shook herself and got ready to wait.

The next hour passed at a snail's pace. Fortunately, Louise was ready and willing to bring Mr. Rathe up the back stairs to her apartments, and Miranda trusted that her two lovers could keep Darius from being seen. She paced the confines of her room aimlessly. She thought to write a letter, but what could she possibly have to say to anyone? She tried to read the book she'd begun last week, but she could not seem to make herself care any longer whether Lizzie Bennet ever won the proud Mr. Darcy. She even pulled a piece of fancy work from her sewing basket, only to discard it a heartbeat later and walk back to the window, hoping to see Darius and Corwin walking through the garden.

At long last, Louise's soft knock sounded at the door, which opened a moment later to admit Corwin and, following close behind him, Darius.

"Thank you, Louise," said Corwin fervently. Darius said nothing.

Louise tipped Miranda a knowing wink and laid her finger to her lips as she closed the door. Darius immediately snapped the latch closed and Miranda felt a brief tingle in the air that told her he was bespelling the lock.

Corwin did not give her any time to inquire about it, however. He strode across to her at once and took both her hands. "What's happened, Miranda?"

All at once, Miranda found herself uncertain of what to say. What if she had panicked over nothing? She could hardly tell them Mother was on the verge of bankruptcy and that she had gone running to them like the heroine of a bad novel because she was faced with poverty and an unexpected suitor.

"Stop, stop," barked Darius, pressing his fingers to his temple. "I can't make heads or tails of this."

Miranda stared at him in surprise. "But I didn't say anything."

Darius looked at Corwin and sighed. "You said nothing aloud, but you are communicating a great deal."

Corwin kissed her hand and guided her toward her chair. "And you are obviously very upset. Tell us what the matter is."

Miranda sat, and Corwin drew up the second chair beside her. Darius, as he had the night before, took up his position as sentry at the window. The associations with the last time both men had been in her room were distracting, but Miranda forced herself to set them aside and speak calmly. Despite her misgivings, she told them of her interview with Mother. Not about the money, but about Lady Thayer's visit, and the news that Lady Thayer had a nephew interested in Miranda.

"It sounds ridiculous now," she finished. "But when I heard it, I thought, perhaps, he was a Sorcerer, and I wondered if you knew him and I . . ."

Corwin waved her words away. "When is this party?" he asked. "What are the dates?"

"It begins on the nineteenth, I believe, and lasts the week."

"It passes Midsummer's Eve," said Darius to Corwin, and Corwin nodded.

Miranda frowned. "What does that matter?"

Darius drummed his fingers against the windowpane, hard enough to rattle it in the sash. "Midsummer is one of the days when the barriers between our world and Fae lands are at their thinnest, and the inhabitants may pass back and forth most easily."

"We've been thinking we need to investigate Lady Thayer's guest list," murmured Corwin. "But perhaps we should begin by investigating Lady Thayer herself."

"Investigate Lady Thayer's guest list?" repeated Miranda incredulously. "Why?

Darius looked at Corwin, and Miranda could sense a swirl of thoughts between them, like whispers overheard through a keyhole.

Tell her.

Darius . . .

Tell her, Corwin, or I will!

Corwin's jaw hardened. Darius turned from him and faced Miranda. "Miranda, we came to Lady Thayer's house because Catalysts have been disappearing across the country. No one knows who is accomplishing this, or exactly why it is happening. We are under orders to find the ones responsible, and stop them."

"And to protect any new Catalysts we discover in the course of our investigations," said Corwin. "You."

Miranda didn't know what to say. "How is it possible? There would be a ruckus if women—if anyone—were disappearing! Such a thing can't happen in secret!"

"Can't it?" replied Darius coolly. "Do you know Edwina Hoyt?"

"A little. She's gone on the Grand Tour."

"Barnabas Beauchamp?"

"Yes. He's engaged to Priscilla Wade, and he took them both to India . . ." Her words trailed away. Darius and Corwin both gazed at her unblinking. "But *how!*" she exclaimed. "I know their families. They can't be *lying*. Not about their children having disappeared . . ." But she broke off and answered her own question. "They could have been Persuaded."

Corwin nodded. "No parent wants to know their child is missing or dead. It would be possible for a Sorcerer to Persuade them that nothing was wrong." He hesitated. "They could also have been bribed, or lied to, or coerced by the Fae court. The Fae and their allies have all manner of avenues available to them."

"They are not the only ones, Miranda," said Darius. "But you are less likely to know the others."

Fear gripped Miranda, making her blood run cold and her breath come too shallow. No matter how she tried to swallow, no matter how tightly Corwin gripped her hand, she could not push it aside.

"Why didn't you tell me this at once?" she whispered.

Corwin sighed. "That was my fault. You already had so much to contend with, I didn't want to frighten you further. Can you forgive me?"

The question echoed in her mind, and for a moment, Miranda honestly did not know how to answer. To have concealed such danger from her . . . What else had Corwin concealed?

And what did it mean that it was Darius who had insisted she be told the truth?

"I will consider forgiveness for you," replied Miranda loftily. "If you swear you will be honest with me from now on."

Corwin laid his hand over his heart and bowed slightly. "I do swear."

Miranda turned to Darius, who said nothing, only met her gaze. His blue gaze was closed off, but she could sense a battle going on inside him, a storm of emotion to rival her own. She yearned to reach toward him, to reach inside him, as she now knew she could. She wanted desperately to understand what he was feeling and why he had trusted her in this when he did not seem to trust her in anything else.

But it was because he was trusting her that she pulled back. He would either tell her or he wouldn't. He had trusted her; she would trust him.

As she reined both curiosity and awareness back, Miranda

was ready to swear she felt something new from Darius: surprise. Surprise and gratitude.

Miranda folded her hands on her lap to keep them still. "So," she said to Corwin. "What do we do next?"

Corwin's mouth quirked up. "I admit I find myself wondering what Lady Thayer is doing this evening."

"We should follow her," announced Darius.

"But I am also concerned about the undue amount of interest she is showing in Miranda. She should not be left alone." Corwin got to his feet. "Stay with her, Darius."

Darius jerked himself up straight. *"Me?"*

"Darius?" cried Miranda at almost the same time.

But Corwin just stood, calmly brushing down his coat sleeves and adjusting his cravat. "Unless Lady Thayer plans to spend a quiet evening at home, I may need to insert myself into another household or she may even be at the theater or the opera. Since I was the one at her party, it will be less strange and take less Persuading to convince any staff or companions that I should be where she is." He looked straight at Darius. "And we are very short on time."

Darius's struggle was visible, but Corwin stood firm.

"Very well," Darius muttered.

"I'll be back as soon as I am able."

Before either of them could say another word, Corwin slipped out the door, closing it firmly behind himself, and leaving Miranda and Darius alone.

Fourteen

Miranda looked at Darius. Darius looked at Miranda and swallowed, an emotion crossing his face that Miranda could have sworn was nervousness.

Then he marched over to the door and locked it once more. He stood back, folded his arms, then crossed to the windows and checked that they were soundly latched. He looked out across the garden for a moment and she saw the muscles of his shoulders rippling as he attempted to force his shoulders to relax under his coat of fine green wool.

Miranda knotted her fingers together. If she'd had more time to understand—to sort through this strange arrangement, these previously unimaginable emotions—she might have known what to say. She had shared her body with this man, but nothing else yet. He demonstrated an attraction to her, but it was equally plain he neither wanted nor trusted it.

Neither wants nor trusts me, and he is afraid that Corwin does.

And yet he trusted her to be able to hear what sort of danger she was truly in. Unless he wanted her told the truth so she would be too afraid to act more than once on her attraction to him, to them. Miranda shook her head and tried not to hate the confusion these men sowed inside her.

And here we are stuck with each other in my bedroom until Corwin deigns to return.

It then occurred to her that Corwin might have done this on purpose.

Indignation snapped Miranda's head up so she looked directly into Darius's blue eyes.

"You've guessed it, then." Darius folded his arms once more. "Corwin is hoping you and I will become . . . reconciled to each other."

"And more than that, I expect."

He nodded. "You are a very quick study, Miranda."

"What are we to do, then?" She gestured helplessly.

Darius sighed and looked around. He spotted the book lying discarded on her table. "Do you want to read?"

Miranda thought of attempting to compose herself to concentrate on the book while he watched her with his brooding blue eyes. She shook her head.

Darius sighed and rubbed the back of his neck, and looked out the window again.

"If I had known I was receiving guests this afternoon, I might have thought to acquire a deck of cards, or a chessboard," murmured Miranda.

Darius arched his brows. "Do you play chess?"

"Yes. Although it has been a while."

"For me as well, but perhaps we can make do." He moved a decorative round table from by the window and positioned it between the two chairs.

"Do you remember your lesson in channeling from this afternoon?"

"I think so."

"I'm going to ask you to repeat it, then, but this time, try to modulate the amount of power you draw." He held out his hand.

Miranda took a deep breath. "I will try."

She took his hand. His palm was broad, warm and hard. The touch of it at once brought memories of his hands sliding along her heated skin, of his mouth on her, of his sighs and his fingers wrapped around hers, teaching her how to stroke his cock. Which reminded her forcibly of when Corwin had offered to teach her how to use her mouth on him. To her stunned embarrassment she felt her mouth begin to water, as if she stared at a confectioner's window.

She closed her eyes before she could look into his. She did not want to see evidence of his disdain right now. She had to get herself under control. She had to concentrate.

What are you doing to me?

Her eyes flew open. Darius was looking down at her, his blue eyes wide with a mixture of astonishment and fear. His cheeks had flushed deeply and she was aware her own face burned.

"I'm sorry," he whispered. "I did not mean for that to reach you."

"It's all right." She swallowed. "We are both still learning."

145

Then another dreadfully mortifying thought came to her. "Did you . . . Did I . . . Could you tell what I was thinking?"

"Yes." He reached out with his free hand and stroked the line of her jaw. His gentle touch set her skin tingling from her throat to her breasts, and her nipples began to tighten.

"Miranda."

He leaned down and tentatively kissed her. His mouth was so soft against hers it almost brought tears to Miranda's eyes. He released her hand so he could cradle her head, holding her in place while his tongue stroked her, tasting her lips, then parting them gently. He reached inside, slowly exploring. She could tell he was almost afraid to continue but, like her, he had no wish to stop. His emotion touched her as tenderly as his lips and she strove to open herself, to show him her feeling as he showed her his. He reached deeper. His tongue stroked the side of hers and a shiver of delicious longing ran through her.

Where she found the strength, she did not know, but Miranda wrapped her hands around his wrists and pulled away. He stared at her, and his worry brushed against her mind. *I've gone too far, assumed too much . . .*

"No," she said in answer to the unspoken thought. "But, are you sure, Darius?" she asked softly. "Are you really sure?"

She stared into the depths of his blue eyes and saw the storms there, the scars of old wars waged in his proud and stubborn heart.

"Corwin would say I should ask you if you are sure." He tried to make a jest of it, but Miranda refused to rise to the bait.

"This is not about Corwin," she reminded him. "This is about you and me."

Darius ran the back of his hand down her temple, and the side of her throat. At no time did he cease looking into her eyes. She felt her breath catch. *Say something. Say something, Darius. I cannot bear it much longer.*

"Yes," he said. "I am sure, Miranda."

He pulled her to her feet and once again his mouth claimed hers. But this time was different. This time his kiss was frenzied. His tongue pressed deep inside her, stroking, plundering. She moaned and moved close, her tightly furled nipples rubbing against his hard chest. She was on fire. She could feel his rigid cock against her belly, despite all the layers of fabric and buckskin between them, and she wanted it, wanted him. Now, at once.

Yes. Yes, Miranda.

The touch of his voice in her mind lit an entirely new level of desire within her. The fires of her need blazed painfully bright. She felt hot moisture pooling between her legs as her pussy strained open. She ran her hands down his shoulders, his back, his tautly muscled ass and thighs, around to his bulging cock. He was so hard, so tightly confined. How could he stand it?

"Turn around," Darius ordered.

Miranda obeyed, and turned in the circle of his arms. He laved her neck with his tongue and she groaned and almost lost her balance. He rested both hands on her shoulders for a moment, then ran them down her back, hard and swift, all the way to her ass. Miranda felt the tingling she now recognized as magic, and in a single instant, every hook and lace of her dress came undone. She gasped. Darius's hands shoved underneath the muslin and cambric, finding her breasts and engulfing them.

She groaned and leaned back against him, rubbing her now-bare ass against the ridge of his erection.

"It is good?" he whispered in her ear as he drew one hand down her belly to cup her damp curls. "Do you want more, Miranda? Do you want me?" He turned his hand so the side of it fit into her slit and began to stroke her folds back and forth. The pleasure of it made her tremble.

"Yes! Oh, yes, Darius!"

"I like that you're wet and so hot." His hand moved faster, pressed harder. He bent her forward over the arm he'd wrapped around her waist, so his cock could circle more firmly against her buttocks. "I like it very much. I like that I do this to you."

"Yes," she moaned, letting her knees buckle so she was truly riding his hard, hot hand. It was so good to have him stroking her folds roughly, while his cock sought to nestle itself between the halves of her ass. But it was not enough. It could never be enough just like this.

No. Never enough.

He turned her again, claiming her mouth for another searing kiss while he shoved back the loosened dress and the shift beneath, exposing her skin to him. Miranda found his erection, fumbled with the buttons on his fly, almost weeping in her need to hold his throbbing cock in her hands.

Darius seized her hands, pressing both palms flat against his cock. She felt a wave of pure, heated sensuality pass through her, coming unmistakably and undeniably from him, and the buttons sprang open. She gasped and sighed and reached into his breeches to wrap her fingers around his huge, hard cock.

She stroked him once, and he groaned against her mouth. Delight filled her as she handled him, stroking his shaft with one hand, fondling his tight balls with the other. Boldly she thrust her tongue into his mouth, taking charge of the trembling, shivering kiss.

Oh, no, Miss Prosper. Not yet. He grabbed her hands again and pinned them behind her back with both of his so she was trapped in the circle of his hard arms. *Not until you beg for it.*

With one sudden motion he scooped her into his arms and tossed her down onto the bed. Miranda's breath left her and she gasped, struggling to sit up. By the time she did, Darius was stripping off coat, waistcoat and shirt, and tossing them on top of his boots and breeches. He was magnificent in the daylight, even more so than he had been in the darkness. His eyes glowed with desire, and the head of his massively erect cock gleamed in the sunlight that seeped in around the heavy curtains. She stared at him, utterly mesmerized.

Darius was on top of her in an instant. He spared her none of his weight, but pressed down hard, trapping her beneath him as he claimed more kisses. He felt so good, so hard against her. Miranda moaned and struggled, not to get free, but to rub herself against every inch of him. She could not get enough. The heat of his skin against hers was intoxicating. His cock against her stomach, her thighs, was maddening.

His mouth moved down her throat, to her breasts. He opened wide and licked one ruched nipple before he took her in deeply. Miranda cried out and knotted her fingers in his golden hair. He was merciless, licking and sucking roughly. Then, as if one was not enough, he pushed her breasts together and captured both nipples between his lips at once, dabbing his tongue against each of them.

"Oh, yes!" cried Miranda as he plumped and sipped and sucked. "Yes!"

How hot are you now? He withdrew one of his hands, setting her breasts free, and thrust two fingers into her. *Hot enough to beg?*

Yes. Please. Please. She imagined him inside her, thrusting all the way in with his huge cock. He liked it hard and fast, and he wanted it now. She knew he did; she could feel his desire invading her mind, twining with her own need. *I want you. I want you just like this. Please, Darius.*

Yes, Miranda.

For a single heartbeat he reared back. Then he thrust inside her, hard and deep, right up to the hilt so she felt his balls brush her folds. She cried and wrapped her arms and legs around him, pulling him right down on top of her again so she could thrust her tongue inside his mouth. He opened for her, as hot and willingly as she opened for him.

He began to thrust hard and fast, just as she had imagined, just as she had so desperately desired. Darius filled her, stretched her, gave her no time to draw breath. She could only cling to him, helpless, while his hands cradled her ass, holding her in position while he rode her. She could do nothing but feel him, all of him. Her body was beyond her control. Her pussy tightened and strained open and tightened again in time with his maddening rhythm. Her hips struggled against his hands but that only intensified her pleasure, which only made her writhe harder, kiss harder, cry out.

Come for me, Miranda. Scream my name while you come against my cock.

"Darius!" she cried out. "Darius!"

And he thrust in once more and she did come. Unbearable waves of pleasure poured through her, racking her whole body, but even then Darius did not stop, but fucked her harder and faster, his hips spanking hers, and even that only added to their pleasure. After a searing eternity she felt him tighten inside her and she called his name again and he slammed into her and she arched her hips.

Miranda!

And as he cried her name into her mind she felt his pleasure pour through her, felt the liquid heat of her own body surrounding his cock, felt the power and pleasure of the wild rhythm of his climax and how it drove him mad. That divine madness filled her and she was coming again, soaring on the storm of Darius's pleasure mixed and redoubled with her own pure pleasure of mind, burning pleasure of body, locked in a single ecstatic embrace.

Fifteen

"Where is your wife, Sinjohn?"

Sinjohn Thayer bowed, keeping his eyes averted from the shining figure in front of him. In the darkness the greensward of Hyde Park was a place of shadows and mystery. In the heart of London the unwary could be lost if they trod here at the wrong time. This was one of the thin places of the world, one of the ancient places where the Fae could walk easily because Smith and his fools did not believe that such a place could exist right under their noses.

"Lady Thayer is leading one of Smith's fools through a dance," he said. "It will end with him dead and another Catalyst in our hands as part of our gift to Their Glorious Majesties."

"Well-done." The voice poured into him sweet and strong as heady wine. The figure in front of him was slender and suffused with a beauty that went beyond the merely human. He knew not whether it was male or female, and it didn't matter. All that mattered was that he had done well, that he proved himself to be a true servant of Their Glorious Majesties, unlike his traitorous father.

For generations the Thayers had secretly served the Fae court and held Hallowgate in trust for them. But his father, the previous Lord Sinjohn Thayer, had broken that faith. Sinjohn would never forget the day his father had brought him into the study and tried to tell him that he'd been wrong. The Fae were not worthy of their worship and loyalty. Their immortality, their beauty, their power, were but disguises. He had gone so far as to blame the deaths of Sinjohn's mother and sister on the attentions the Fae knights had condescended to show them.

Sinjohn had not been glad to kill his father. Indeed, had it not been an order from the Fae Queen Herself, he might not have found the nerve. But so severe had been the treason that even kneeling before her with his hands still red with his father's blood had not been enough. She had demanded sacrifice.

Thirteen Catalysts, alive and in good health, to be delivered to her on Midsummer's Eve. Miranda Prosper would be the thirteenth. He and Viola had searched carefully for one as powerful as she was. Miranda would be the brightest jewel in the trove he would lay at Their Majesties' feet.

"And this Miranda Prosper is the lady I am to woo at Hallowgate?" inquired the knight before him.

"If your lordship would deign to offer your assistance, we cannot fail to ensnare her," said Sinjohn humbly.

"Their Majesties are uncertain," drawled the Fae knight. "They argue that it is your sacrifice to make, not ours to aid."

Sinjohn bowed his head. "We are Their Majesties' true servants, and shall do as we are required. This pair of Sorcerers, however, have proved themselves to be deadly to Fae and mortal alike, and it seemed prudent to have a second net in place should they slip the first."

"Yes, we know these two." Anger turned the beautiful voice into a blade, and it slid beneath Sinjohn's skin. "A full dozen of my brethren have they captured or killed, and as many of our allies among your kind. You are wise to be cautious, Sinjohn." The knight's approval went straight to his center. His heart and cock swelled with the pleasure of it.

The Fae took note of his pleasure and smiled, and for a moment Sinjohn could not breathe for the rapturous sight. "Besides, I have not seduced a mortal woman in several of your lifetimes. We shall hope it does not become necessary, but if it does . . ."

As he spoke, the light that shone so gloriously about the Fae dimmed and dwindled. The figure itself shrank and filled at the same time, until a slender man stood in front of Sinjohn. A man with pale hair and green eyes, dressed impeccably in green coat and white breeches. "If it does, she shall find Robin Summerfields quite at her service."

Sinjohn bowed again. "It will be my honor to host you in my home, noble sir."

Amusement flowed from the Fae, but all at once he went very still, like a hunting cat suddenly catching a new scent.

"We are observed," hissed the Fae, outrage filling his mellifluous voice.

Sinjohn lifted his own head, straining his senses. Yes, there.

Two human presences on the very periphery of awareness, detectable only because of the veneer of magic crackling around them.

It worked.

"Forgive me for not informing you before this, noble sir," murmured Sinjohn. "I thought you might enjoy a little entertainment this evening."

The Fae raised one perfect brow. "This is your doing?"

"A Sorcerer and Catalyst. Two of the enemy. I arranged for Lady Thayer to drop a few . . . hints in a literary salon she attends to bring them here tonight."

"A most dangerous plan, Sinjohn," whispered the Fae.

It had in truth been a serious gamble, but if he was truly to regain his family's position in the Fae court, Sinjohn knew he had not only to impress Their Glorious Majesties, but to make friends among the knights and the nobles, most especially those sent to keep watch on him. "I thought only to provide sir with a worthy hunt to pass the time you must walk our dull Earth."

A slow, cruel smile spread across the otherworldly knight's face. "Well, then, since you have taken such pains, how can I refuse? Lead on, Thayer. By all means, lead on."

Thayer bowed once more, and set off down the gravel walk at a stroll. Behind him, he felt the Fae and the Sorcerer follow him more deeply into the dark.

Sixteen

"You love Corwin, don't you?" whispered Miranda. "It's not just . . . just desire for a man's body."

Miranda and Darius lay in each other's arms on Miranda's bed, snug under her sheets and counterpanes. Louise had come in with a tray, which now waited by the window. Miranda had almost panicked then, but Darius had made a small gesture, and Louise had seen only Miranda lying down for an afternoon nap.

Poor Louise. I will have to find some way to tell her the truth as soon as possible.

"Yes, I do love Corwin." Miranda heard the defiance underneath the plain statement. "Does that shock you?"

"No." She drew her fingers down his chest. The touch of his crisp, curling hairs was fascinating. "Once, perhaps, but not now."

His mouth brushed the top of her head. "Are you jealous?" he asked softly.

The question stilled her restless fingers. "I have no right to be."

"That is not what I asked."

Miranda paused, searching her heart to the limit she could sense. All within her had changed, was changing, and would change again, but she still had to find the honest answer.

"No, I'm not jealous," she said, and it was both a relief and a wonder to be able to do so. It also raised the one question she must ask but did not want to. "Are . . . are you?"

"I don't know what I am yet."

"Ah." She thought to pull away then, but Darius held her close.

"I do know this, Miranda," he murmured as his arms tightened around her. "When I am with you it is a feeling I've known in the arms of no other woman. I never have . . . never would permit myself to desire a woman for her own sake, not since I met Corwin."

Abruptly, the vision of the woman she had seen through Darius's eyes while they were in the park filled Miranda's mind; her angry face, the ringing slap. One glance at Darius and she knew he could guess her thoughts.

"Her name was Agnes DeLancey," he said. "She and I were engaged."

"Oh."

Darius smiled grimly and reached across her to tuck the covers around her more securely. "It was something my father arranged. After he dragged me to several whorehouses to attempt to . . . force me into more normal sorts of perversions, he decided to set me up with a wife so there'd at least be some cover if I . . . strayed."

"Darius, you don't have to . . ."

"I do," he said. "You need to know. It turned out for once my father made a good choice for me. She was a widow and she'd used her widow's privileges. She enjoyed . . . an adventurous life but knew how to be discreet, something I'd never bothered to learn. We ran riot together and no one in the drawing room set suspected. I was dazzled the way one is by any beautiful danger. I believed I had at last found the woman I could live with, and perhaps love."

"But she found you with a man. Corwin?"

He nodded. "I was fool enough to think she, who enjoyed such varied exercise, would understand. But I'd assumed too much. She struck me, and she left me flat. Which would have been enough. But she came back, this time with a blackmail threat."

"Oh, Darius." Sodomy in England was a hanging offense. Darius and Corwin could die for what they did with each other. "But, surely, you're a Sorcerer; couldn't you . . ."

"Bespell her? Yes. And we did. But it was not easy, or pleasant." He shook his head. "I was a fool. A careless, raw fool. I had sought to use her, and I deserved what I got."

"No. That's not true."

"It is, Miranda. There is no greater crime than to use another human being for your own ends without their knowledge."

Miranda pushed herself up into a sitting position so she could meet his gaze more easily. "Is that why you wanted Corwin to tell me the truth about the other Catalysts?"

He nodded. "Whatever else I thought, whatever else I felt or did not feel, I wanted you to know the truth. You deserved that much."

Miranda leaned forward and kissed him softly, almost chastely. "Thank you," she breathed.

He smiled and fingered the elfin locks that tumbled about her bare breasts. "You're welcome, Miranda."

Her kiss, his tender and intimate touch, threatened to reignite the fires he had so lately satisfied in her. Miranda reined her desire in ruthlessly. She did not know when Darius would be so disposed to talk again.

"You stayed with Corwin after that. Even though he . . ." She took a deep breath. "Shares his love with others?"

Darius brushed her hair back, his fingers grazing the soft skin of her sloping shoulder. "Corwin has great faith in his own heart. He believes he can apportion his love freely according to the circumstances and feel all the more deeply because of it. I . . . have rather less faith in my own abilities." He kissed her brow once more. "But the moment I took your hand tonight, I wanted you, Miranda Prosper. All of you." He reached beneath the covers and ran his hand across her thigh. Miranda shivered at his touch but it was not entirely with desire. This time that desire raised fresh, unwanted doubt.

"And now you've had me, what do you feel?" she asked.

Darius did not answer, not directly. His hand stilled, resting against her naked thigh, as if waiting permission to move farther. "Do you fear me, Miranda?"

She shivered again. "I fear what I feel for you," Miranda

whispered. She did not want it to be true, but it was. "For both of you. I fear what I'm doing and what I've discovered I am. I am trying not to, but it is all so much and it is happening so quickly."

Darius said nothing but drew her closer into his strong embrace and kissed the top of her head again. She laid her cheek against his chest, letting the warmth of him soak into her skin. His heart beat directly beneath her, strong and steady. She felt safe in the circle of his arms. Safer than she could have imagined just scant hours before. He stroked her hair gently, and the motion of his hand soothed her now as it had excited her before. Her eyes fluttered closed and Miranda slept.

Miranda's dream began slowly. At first, there was only the sensation of motion. This shifted into an understanding that she was walking, quickly, down a narrow street. Every sense strained and gradually she became aware that she was being followed. She couldn't catch any glimpse of her pursuer, and this filled her with cold worry. She should have been able to. She was certain of it.

She slid forward through the shadows, treading carefully on the loose, treacherous cobblestones and skirting pools of mud and muck. If she could get around the corner, there was a doorway on the other side, conveniently located, where she could duck into darkness, and catch her pursuer as he passed by.

But the corner was too far away, and no matter how fast she moved, it got no closer. The pursuer followed, steadily, getting no closer, but getting no farther, and her heart began to hammer in her chest. Why couldn't she see, damn it! Why was it so dark?

There! The corner. She ducked around, and immediately came upon the deep, arched doorway. She pressed into the shadows. For a heartbeat she was safe.

The blow fell sharp on her skull and stars exploded in front of her eyes. She tried to turn, but her legs gave out from under her and her mind reeled. In the manner of dreams, she felt herself falling, then saw herself falling.

But it wasn't herself she saw.

"Corwin!"

Miranda shot bolt upright in bed, clutching the sheets to her. Her eyes darted this way and that, and she half expected to see the cobbled street and the building walls looming close around her, but there were only the familiar confines her own room.

"What is it?" Darius sat up, fully awake, and gripped her arms. "What did you see?"

"A dream." Miranda's shoulders slumped in relief. "Just a dream."

But Darius took her chin and turned her face toward him. His blue eyes stared deep into hers for a long moment, and she could feel him stirring restlessly inside her mind. His eyes widened, and he withdrew, but not before his fear and anger rushed into her.

"No dream," he croaked. "Corwin's been attacked."

Miranda's hand flew to her mouth. "Get dressed," Darius barked as he scrambled out of bed.

Darius threw on breeches and shirt while Miranda struggled with chemise and shift. As he pulled on his coat, he made one impatient gesture and Miranda found herself neatly and completely dressed.

"I am going to draw on your power to try to locate Corwin wherever he is now. We will be linked, so whatever I see, you will see. But you must not let it distract you. You must keep the channel open. Without the magic you can bring, I will soon weaken."

"Yes."

"We shouldn't be attempting this yet," Darius told her with that hard honesty she had come to understand was part of him. "You need much more training than you have had, but I cannot do this alone."

Miranda stiffened her spine. "I am ready."

Darius touched her cheek. "Corwin was right. You are exceedingly brave." He held out his hands and she laid hers into them.

"Now," he said.

It was easier this time, for Miranda knew how it would feel when she opened her spirit to the outer vitality that was the magic of the natural world. Power flowed into her easily. She was able to focus on her palms where they pressed against Darius's, and let the power pass through her into him. She felt him embrace the magic, felt his mind and will impressing form upon its shifting presence, but it was not a form to which she could give any name. It was as if he were spreading it out, both broadening it and sharpening it somehow. She felt him reach for her along the stream of power that flowed between them, and she did not resist. He touched the memory of her nightmare, and it washed over her afresh: the fear, the blindness, the pain. These too were spread out and refined until they merged with the greater magic. Miranda felt Darius tremble. She drew up more power, opening the stream wider, and he steadied.

And in her mind, it was as if a curtain fell away. She could see.

She stared up at a steeply pitched ceiling smeared with dust and cobwebs. A filthy skylight with a rusted latch showed the clouded sky brightening with the slow dawn. She felt pain, and thirst, and Corwin.

Corwin. His wrists and ankles were weighted down with heavy manacles, and their edges cut into his flesh. A cotton cloth had been wadded into his mouth. He was furious, with his situation and himself, and he most definitely did not like the look of those rust-colored smears on the wall.

Then he lifted his head. *Darius?*

Corwin, Darius answered. *Where are you?*

Cut this off. Back away. It's a trap!

Of course it is. But where are you?

Darius, don't do this! Take Miranda to the captain. Tell him what's happening.

Darius ignored him. *Where are you?*

I'm in a goddamned garret! Where do you think I am?

Let me see.

Darius! A wave of fear and fury accompanied the cry, so strong Miranda staggered. But she righted herself and held steady.

I'm not going to stop, Corwin. Darius's reply was implacable. *So you might as well help us see.*

Us? Miranda? Can you hear me? Cut him off!

Miranda understood she would be able to answer and she bolstered her reply with Darius's unyielding strength. *No. Why can't you free yourself?*

They've bound me with cold iron. The metal is impervious to magic. They know what they're doing. You must—

We're wasting time, Darius cut him off.

The stream of invective Corwin released was truly impressive. But Darius did not flinch.

This unleashed another series of oaths. It was so strange for Miranda to see them this way. She had come to think of Corwin as the leader of the two of them, but now she understood their true balance was much deeper and more complex than that.

Can you reach him, Miranda? Darius asked her.

Miranda drew the power into herself as she might draw a deep breath. She stretched through Darius toward the presence that was Corwin in her mind. She stretched until she felt a sick, burning pain rise up in her, and she knew she was in danger of breaking in two, but she still couldn't touch him.

Enough, enough, said Darius. *We'll have to get closer.*

No! cried Corwin. *It's too dangerous!*

But again, Darius ignored him.

"Miranda." He said her name aloud, and it was strange to hear his voice with her ears rather than her mind. "We are going to have to ghostwalk."

"What is that?"

"We are going to quite literally walk through walls. It is not an easy thing . . ."

"I should think not." She gave him a small smile and saw an answering spark of approval in his eyes.

"This is how we found you that first night. It was more difficult then because we had no Catalyst to bring us power, and we were both weak. Your part in this is to keep the channel open and steady, and remain focused on Corwin. The stream of power will link us and him, and I will be able to follow it from here to where he is. Do you understand?"

She didn't really, but she also knew there was no time for questions. "I am ready."

Darius wrapped her arm around his, as if they were to take an afternoon stroll together. Miranda vaguely wondered what would happen if Mother came up to check on her, or if Louise did. But it hardly mattered. Corwin was in danger and she would not let him, let them, down.

Find him, Miranda.

Power swirled and shimmered in her veins. Miranda drew it in through her skin, through her breath, and she poured it forth into Darius. In her mind, she saw Corwin lying bound and in pain. She felt his presence in body and emotion. She knew precisely where he lay, but not what lay between.

Then she felt Darius lay his will against the stream of her power. His intent mingled and merged with the stream. It was equal parts command, plea and prayer to the whole of the universe.

Before Miranda's eyes, the walls of her bedchamber turned

to soft mist. She could see the garden, the street, the next house, and through that to the next, and the next.

All the way to Corwin.

Now.

Darius began to walk, holding her so tightly Miranda had no choice but to walk with him.

Seventeen

It was like dreaming. It was like flying. There was a roaring in Miranda's ears that blotted out all other sounds. People were shadows; objects were fleeting as thoughts. The only real things in the whole world were Corwin, Darius and the stream of magic that stretched like a lifeline, from her and through her, tying them all together. It was current and guide, at once pulling them forward and showing them the way to Corwin. Corwin alone and furious at needing rescue. Corwin praying they were not too late. Wanting them both, and wishing he'd been able to turn them away.

Miranda's skin was cold but her spirit burned hot. She was terrified and she was elated. She forced both emotions away so she could concentrate on drawing down the power, and on Corwin.

Darius moved beside her, his concentration making a stone channel to shape the flow of her power. She felt his arm, felt his mind. Her sense of distance was gone. She had no anchor, no reference point. All things were equidistant, even though she was aware that they moved.

Here!

The word jolted through her, and Miranda slammed her mind and being closed against the power. Pain tore through her and she toppled against a solid, plaster wall. Miranda reeled backward, her slippers skidding on splintered floorboards.

They were back in the normal world, solid, heavy and graceless. Beside her, Darius was bent nearly double with his arm thrown across his stomach like a man with a severe cramp. She tried to move toward him but her body seemed so foreign to her she staggered and sprawled full length onto the floor.

Beside Corwin.

Corwin, who stared up at them both, his face apoplectic as he strained to force words out around the cloth that gagged him.

Miranda reached out one trembling hand, pulled the sodden cloth free and tossed it aside.

"You *idiots!*" roared Corwin. His chains rattled as he squirmed and shifted closer to her. "Miranda! Can you speak?"

"Yes, yes, I'm all right," she said, although she was far from sure. She panted, swallowed, and panted again. She ached and felt weak as a kitten. It was worse than the aftermath of the influenza.

"Darius, you fool! I told you . . ." But Corwin broke off as Darius lifted his head and stared at him with fever-bright eyes.

"Shut it, Corwin," Darius said through gritted teeth. "We're rescuing you. You can call us any name you like afterward."

Darius dropped heavily onto his knees and crawled across to Corwin. "Give me your hands, you ungrateful sod."

"Takes one to know one," muttered Corwin as he rolled onto his side.

"What are you going to do?" Miranda pushed herself back up into a sitting position.

Darius pulled from his coat pocket a delicate loop of copper that looked startlingly like a hairpin. After a couple of tries, he was able to stick the ends into the keyhole of the manacles that bound Corwin's wrists.

"There are some substances like this iron that cannot ever be made to yield to magic," said Corwin. "Therefore, it behooves us all to become good with some more basic tools. Like lockpicks."

Metal scraped softly against metal, and Darius's mouth shaped silent curses. Miranda held her breath. At last, there came a soft *snick*. He hauled the iron cuffs away from Corwin's wrists and tossed them aside with a look of disgust on his face. Then he set to work on the chains at Corwin's ankles.

"Thank you." Corwin sat up. His wrists were swollen and bleeding, and now Miranda could see his face was not just filthy, but pale. "I'm all right, I'm all right," he said as he saw her look of concern. "Iron also interrupts the natural flow of magic in a Sorcerer's body. It is most unhealthy."

The second set of manacles *snick*ed open. Darius yanked them off and sat back on his heels, breathing hard. A sheen of perspiration stood out on his forehead, but his color had returned.

Blood stained Corwin's ruined stockings, and as he leaned forward to try to chafe his ankles, he trembled.

"Can I help?" asked Miranda. Corwin shook his head, but Darius made a face.

Miranda set her jaw and without asking permission seized Corwin's wrist and, shaky as she felt, opened the channel for the magic again.

It was like kissing him, pressing her passion against him before he was ready. But she felt him yield, accept, respond. He opened to her insistence, and she felt the power, the essence, begin to flow once more. It was an effort, for she was so tired, but she could feel the relief in him, feel his health return, and that was all she needed to find her own strength again.

"Enough now, Miranda," murmured Darius.

This time she was able to close the channel slowly. When she came fully back to herself, she felt as if she had just run a great distance, but no worse. Her sight was clear; she could breathe. In front of her, Corwin's color had returned and the skin around his wrists was whole.

"Thank you, Miranda," Corwin whispered. Then he looked to Darius. Miranda's heart swelled to see the love burning in the eyes of the two men as they regarded each other. "Thank you, Darius."

Darius nodded once. "Let's get out of here." He crossed to the door. "More iron." He produced the picklock again.

"Who did this to you?" Miranda asked Corwin as Darius set to work. But Corwin shook his head.

"Never saw the ba— . . . man," he said ruefully. "Our opponents are very clever. This whole time they've been using non-magical means against us. Basic tricks, basic locks, basic violence." He rubbed the back of his skull. "Makes us look like fools, because we're busy looking for grand sorceries and Fae magics, not footpads."

Darius straightened up and tucked the picklock away. He pulled on the handle and the door opened with a long, loud groan. He winced. "Well, if anyone else is in this house, they know we're here now."

Corwin grabbed Miranda's hand. "Straight out the first door we find, then no stopping. For anything."

Before she had a chance to answer, Corwin dragged her out the door into the dingy corridor and started down the narrow stairs, with Darius following close behind them.

It was a servants' stair, she realized, steep, cramped and poorly kept. The advantage was it ought to take them all the way down to the cellar floor of whatever house this was, to its kitchens and back doors. Corwin led them at speed, making no allowances for the awkwardness of her dainty slippers or skirts. Miranda gritted her teeth, gathered her skirts up to her knees and concentrated on staying upright.

They reached the first landing and turned the corner.

Someone screamed.

The sound reverberated through the door to the main house, a woman's scream of pain and fear. Miranda's head jerked up and she immediately dodged toward the door. But Corwin held her in a grip of iron.

"Ignore it," he ordered, and pulled her down the stairs behind him.

"But . . ."

"He's right," said Darius. "Even if it's not a trick, it's a trap."

But the scream came again, and again, piercing straight to Miranda's heart. She tried to believe Darius and Corwin, but how could they be sure? She couldn't leave a woman, a girl maybe, behind in such pain.

They reached the next landing. "Stop!" screamed the unseen woman. "Oh, God, please! Stop! Help me! Someone, help me!"

Miranda couldn't stand it. She wrenched free of Corwin's grip and darted through the door.

She found herself in a long, richly decorated hall.

"Help me, please!"

Miranda snatched up her skirts and ran. Behind her, she heard Darius and Corwin calling her name. She ignored them both and darted through the open door at her right hand.

It was a bedroom, but the furnishings had all been covered with white dust cloths. On a bed that had been stripped of its curtains lay a woman. She was stark naked, her arms spread and tied to the posts with rags. She screamed when she saw Miranda.

"It's all right, it's all right! We're here to help," Miranda cried as she darted forward. "Corwin! Darius!"

"Miranda, no!"

But Miranda's hand was already on the nearest knot. The woman gave one more heart-wrenching shriek, and vanished.

All the bindings went suddenly slack., Miranda stared stupidly at the empty mattress. Corwin's hands seized her shoulders and hauled her backward, just as a strange, shifting shadow fell across her. Miranda lifted her gaze up to the hollow, evil eyes of a monster floating in midair.

172

It was like a woman made out of unraveling strands of yarn. Sharp teeth filled its slavering mouth and its fingers curled into talons.

Miranda had no time to make out more details, because the creature opened its dripping mouth and dove, howling, down at them. Corwin threw himself sideways, dragging Miranda with him so she landed on the floor with him on top of her. Lightning flashed and the creature screamed. Corwin rolled aside, enabling Miranda to shove herself into a sitting position. Darius stood in the doorway, hands upraised, sweat pouring down his face. The creature was back by the curtained windows now, hissing madly. A horrible burning scent choked Miranda and she saw that some of the trailing, ghostly strands that composed the monster's body were burnt black.

"Quick, Miranda!" cried Corwin, hauling her to her feet.

The creature screamed and lunged, this time straight for Miranda. Corwin swung her toward Darius and Darius caught her other hand. The creature missed, caromed off the wall, shrieked its outrage and wheeled in midair to face them.

Miranda grasped both Corwin's and Darius's hands and focused outward, seeking the sense of magic. It was faint, and far below, but she found it. She drew it in, opening herself as wide as she could to the magic and to the men whose hands she held.

Now! Corwin and Darius's voices rang in her mind.

The men threw up their free hands and a massive bolt of blue-edged white whipped through the room. It engulfed the creature, burning so bright Miranda had to squeeze her eyes shut. Still she saw red flame beneath her eyelids.

The monster screamed, but the horrendous shriek was cut off as abruptly as if someone had thrown a switch. The silence was deafening.

Beside her, Darius and Corwin both panted hard. Miranda blinked and slowly her eyes focused.

They were alone in an empty room. The dust covers were not even disturbed. The only evidence of the entire incident was the strips of rag tied to the bedposts, the men struggling to draw breath beside her, and the weakness in her own knees. Miranda desperately wanted to sink down onto the edge of the bed but the idea of touching the place where that . . . monster had rested repulsed her.

Darius gave voice to her feeling. "Let's get out of here."

Without another word, they fled down the hall, and back onto the servants' stair. They clambered down it, not bothering with stealth until they reached the cellar. A quick glance about showed them the tradesman's entrance. Darius worked the latch and held the door while Corwin pushed Miranda through. The street was dark and empty, but they didn't stop. All holding hands, they hurried down the cobbled street until they came to an alley that Corwin must have judged safe, because he drew them both into the shadows. There they all huddled together, trying to catch their breaths.

Even standing so close to Corwin and Darius with their warmth seeping into her skin, Miranda trembled like a leaf in the wind and couldn't seem to stop.

Corwin laid his hand on her shoulder. "Are you all right?"

She nodded and willed herself to stand straighter. "And you?" she asked them both.

Darius ran one shaking hand through his hair. "That was . . . unpleasant."

"What was it?" she asked.

Corwin glanced up the street and grimaced. "Offhand I'd guess it was a wraith. A particularly nasty, though not particularly intelligent, Fae. It does, however, have an unfortunate taste for human flesh."

"That was a *fairy*?" gasped Miranda.

"It was a wraith," said Corwin firmly. "The Fae have many races and many forms. Some are beautiful beyond description. Some are . . ." Corwin gestured toward the alley mouth. "Less so. In many ways it is the beautiful ones who are more dangerous."

"Why?"

Darius raked his fingers through his hair. "If you see a monster, you will run, or fight. If you see something beautiful, you will go closer."

"Oh." Miranda closed her eyes and swallowed. *As you will if you hear a scream and are fool enough not to listen to your friends.*

"You did magnificently back there, Miranda," said Corwin.

Darius nodded in agreement. "Throwing a killing attack takes a great deal from a Sorcerer. I would not have been able to do it a second time on my own. Your power enabled us to throw the second bolt."

"I could have gotten you killed," Miranda whispered. "If not for me . . ."

"You were tricked, Miranda," said Corwin quietly. "As we all have been by these enemies. Darius first, then me, now you.

That is not what's important." He laid his hand on her arm and looked steadily into her eyes. "You kept your head and your nerve. You used your instinct swiftly and surely. This is no small thing, Miranda." He smiled and kissed her hand. "We both owe you our lives."

For a moment she was certain he was exaggerating, but she glanced toward Darius, who nodded in solemn confirmation. It was almost too much to take in, and so she decided she would not think about it just now.

"Somehow I did not imagine victory would leave me feeling . . . ill."

"It is not uncommon after a battle. The body's reaction to suppressing the fear in order to fight. Come, we need to get under cover someplace safe." He glanced up and down the street, checking to see if all was clear.

A fresh panic surged through Miranda. "I need to get home. My mother . . ."

"No," said Corwin flatly. "You need to rest and recover. We all do. I'm not sending you back to your mother's tender mercies in your current condition."

"But . . ."

"But nothing, Miranda Prosper. We're going to my house."

Eighteen

Corwin's large, graceful residence stood on a quiet street in Kensington, not too far from Miranda's own. It seemed terribly strange that this man with all his secrets could have been living less than a mile from her, and she had known nothing of it. It made her wonder what was happening in the other great houses of the London environs, and how many secrets the city held.

The servants were obviously used to their master's abrupt comings and goings because the butler met them in the foyer, utterly unruffled by the disheveled Miranda being propelled through the door between him and Darius.

"Jacobs. We need food for three, hot and plenty."

"Yes, sir," replied the aging man with a bow. "I'll get Cook started at once."

"We'll also need a room for the lady, and hot water for all of us as soon as possible."

"At once, sir."

"We'll be in the library."

"Yes, sir."

Corwin and Darius marched Miranda up the sweeping stairway. Her feet made no noise on the soft carpets that covered the stairs and the dark-paneled hallway. Corwin opened a door on the left and led them inside.

As Miranda saw the room to which she had been led, she stood astonished, forgetting her pique at being so brusquely handled. Corwin's library was like nothing she had ever seen. It was a perfectly round room stretching two stories high. A wooden stairway spiraled up from its center to the second level where a catwalk with an elaborately carved wooden railing circled overhead. The walls were lined entirely with shelves, and the shelves were lined entirely with books. A cheerful fire burned in the deep hearth behind a brass screen. The whole place was furnished with overstuffed sofas and comfortable chairs with convenient tables set between them.

Miranda had always adored books. Her father had taught her to cherish reading and knowledge. But he'd never been able to afford more than a small collection of his own. Such a room in a private home . . . It was beyond anything she'd ever imagined. One could spend hours in such a room. A lifetime even.

"Do you like it?" inquired Corwin as Miranda spun around, craning her neck to try to see the upper level.

Miranda opened her mouth and closed it again.

"Good Lord, Corwin, you've rendered her speechless." Darius selected two glasses from the sideboard and poured a measure of brandy into one and filled the other with sherry. "Sit down before you make yourself giddy, woman."

With a gentle push, Corwin sat her on the nearest leather-covered sofa. Darius handed the sherry to Corwin, who handed it to Miranda, who took it without thinking, or glancing at it.

"You said you were wealthy," she stammered. "But I never imagined . . ."

Corwin chuckled. "Well, perhaps I overextended myself on this room a little." His eyes wandered the polished shelves. "But to me there are few things in this world more precious than good books." Although she could hear the pride he took in his collection, Miranda did not miss the way his gaze traveled to Darius, and to herself.

"Before you start enumerating your worldly possessions, we need to report to the captain." Darius poured a second brandy and set it on the table beside Corwin before dropping into a chair beside the fire and stretching out his long legs.

"Yes, yes. Forgive us a moment, Miranda." Corwin sat across from Darius. Darius pulled a small notebook with a silver pencil attached to it from his coat pocket and handed it over to Corwin.

Miranda nodded and sipped the sherry, which was excellent and a much-needed restorative. Corwin bent over the book, scribbling furiously. Miranda discreetly turned her attention back to the magnificent room around her.

If this is the library, what must the rest of the house be like?

Just as she had never stopped to consider how Corwin had come by his living, she had not stopped to think what his home would be like. She had gotten so used to the strange and the . . .

well . . . *magical* aspects of these men, it felt jarring to see them doing such ordinary things as sitting in front of a fire, sipping brandy, and writing.

After several minutes, Corwin tore a set of pages out of the notebook, folded them into a square and cast them into the fire, and Miranda felt, absurdly, that what she had come to think of as normalcy around these two was restored.

"And now we wait." Corwin snapped the book shut and returned it to Darius. He raised the glass of brandy to them both in silent salute and then downed a healthy measure.

Miranda rallied herself. It would not do to sink any further into the warmth and comfort of the room. "As lovely as it is, I cannot stay here. I've already been gone from the house for hours without explanation."

"Surely that doesn't matter," said Darius.

Visions of the ledger's red ink rose in Miranda's mind. "It does if my mother chooses to turn me out of the house."

Corwin actually looked shocked. "Do you believe I would abandon you, Miranda?"

"That's not the point. My public reputation is in enough jeopardy that Mother may be driven to drastic measures."

Darius lifted his brows to Corwin and set his snifter aside. "Miranda, none of that matters," he said. "You're with us now."

"And what exactly does that mean?" Miranda slammed the sherry glass down on the table so hard its contents sloshed across the brightly polished wood. "What am I to you? Your Catalyst, yes, but what else? Will you make me your mistress? Are we to formalize a contract for my . . . services? Or is one of you going to marry me?" They were both staring at her as if she'd suddenly grown a second head, but now that she had begun to speak so forcefully she couldn't seem to stop. "There's nothing left—do you understand? Nothing! I *have* to get married now and Lady Thayer's nephew is my only suitor, but he might be the enemy and I can't . . . I can't . . ." To her shame, Miranda burst into tears.

All at once Corwin was beside her, wrapping her in his strong arms and pulling her close. "It's all right," he murmured. "It's all right."

She felt Darius sit on the other side of her. A handkerchief was pressed into her hand, and Miranda wiped at her streaming eyes. When she was finished, Corwin folded her fingers around the sherry glass, replenished now, and urged her to drink. She gulped the wine, welcoming the clarifying heat that spread through her.

"Better?" asked Corwin.

Miranda nodded, although she felt her cheeks burning with embarrassment. "I'm sorry. I don't know what came over me."

"Fear and heartache." Corwin reached out and gently tucked one of her tumbled locks behind her ear. "That's enough for anyone." He took her sherry glass from her fingers and set it down, then took her hand in his. "Now, Miranda, I want you to listen very carefully to what I am about to say. I will protect you, Miranda. No matter what happens. I will take care of you."

"We will," said Darius firmly. "*We* will, Miranda."

She looked up at Darius. His eyes were hard, but at the same time utterly open and honest. "Darius?" she whispered.

"You saved my life today. You saved Corwin. You showed a strength and courage . . . I admit I doubted you. I doubted *this*." He gestured to indicate all of them. "But no more." He looked deep into her eyes. "You belong with us, Miranda. As a Catalyst, as a woman, as yourself."

"We are your protectors," said Corwin, and she felt the force of a sacred oath in his words. "Now and forever."

"I want to believe you," whispered Miranda, looking into his dark eyes. "I do, but . . ."

"It doesn't matter what you believe, I'm afraid," said Corwin with a small smile. "It is the truth, and it will not change."

"There is one other consideration," said Darius. "If it were known Miranda's mother had turned her out, Lady Thayer may have a more difficult time inviting her to that house party."

Corwin rubbed his chin. "That is a point."

"But, Lady Thayer . . . She had you kidnapped, Corwin. Didn't she?"

"The fact that I was knocked on the head while following her from the opera strongly suggests it, yes. All the more reason we are going to need the covert entry to their country estate which your invitation will provide."

Miranda swallowed. They were talking openly of sending her into danger a moment after swearing to be her protectors. It was dizzying.

I suppose I should be flattered that they believe I am able to take care of myself. Although, admittedly, they do not seem to be giving me much choice. She frowned.

"None of us has much choice when it comes to our battles,"

said Corwin. "Miranda, do you have someone in the city with whom you could plausibly be staying?"

Miranda considered. She had few relations, and even fewer close friends. The few she'd had as a young girl had drifted away into their own lives once they had married. "Adele Rivers," she said at last. "We were close as girls, and she's always told me I can come to her anytime." The fact that Adele had been a hellion and that Miranda had covered for her more than once wouldn't hurt either.

"Very good." Corwin crossed to a beautifully painted writing desk. "Using the excuse of your row, if you will please to write to your mother explaining you have gone to stay with your friend."

"I should write my maid Louise as well. We'll need her help."

Corwin nodded. "She's a good girl from what I've seen, and devoted to you. I would welcome her assistance."

As Miranda applied pen to paper, the door opened and the butler Jacobs entered and bowed. "Your breakfast is ready, sir."

"Very good. We'll have it in here."

The man bowed again and gestured. In response, a liveried footman entered, pushing a cart laden with covered dishes. The aromas that accompanied them went straight to Miranda's painfully empty stomach.

Jacobs and the footman moved about expertly, clearing one of the square tables and covering it with a white cloth, then laying out plates and cutlery. It was extremely difficult to concentrate on finishing the letters with the appetizing scents filling the air. But she managed, and at last sealed them both.

"Jacobs, see that these letters are delivered at once." Darius handed the missives to the butler. "And you may go now. We'll serve ourselves."

"Very good, sir." The butler handed the letters to the footman, bowed and closed the doors behind them both.

"Now, allow me to escort you to breakfast, Miss Prosper." Corwin held out his arm.

"And me." Darius did likewise.

It was absurd. It was improper. It was wonderful. Miranda took both their arms and permitted them to steer her toward the table. The scents coming from the covered dishes were enough to drive Miranda frantic. Clearly, Corwin employed an excellent cook. There were poached eggs and spiced chops and a fillet of sole in a lovely butter sauce. There was cold ham, which Corwin, as host, carved in thick slices. All was accompanied by toast and marmalade, and a selection of gloriously sweet, buttery, French-style pastries.

Miranda tried to control herself, and take only ladylike helpings, but she was hungrier than she ever had been in her life, and soon found her manners vanishing. Besides, Corwin and Darius kept passing the plates toward her, helping her to this and that. It was almost as if they were enjoying the sight of her stuffing herself.

"Yes, as a matter of fact," said Darius, putting a third pastry on her plate. "It's an unexpectedly intriguing sight."

"I don't know what's so unexpected about it," remarked Corwin as he poured a little more champagne into her glass. "When has it ever been anything but a delight to be with Miranda when she's enjoying herself?"

"An excellent point." Darius raised his own glass to Corwin. Miranda found herself blushing violently.

"You shall have to teach me how to guard against your eavesdropping," she murmured toward her pastry.

"Eventually," said Corwin. "Finish your food. There's a good girl."

Miranda found herself seized by a sudden urge to throw a slice of toast at him. Darius reached out and removed the rack to the other end of the table.

A laugh bubbled up in her. She tried to suppress it, but only for a moment. There was no reason to be quiet. She laughed out loud, and Corwin chuckled, and Darius grinned. It felt wonderful. Had she ever been this at ease? In this beautiful place, with excellent food, a fire and these men. Midnight Corwin. Golden Darius. Both complex, difficult, confusing, overwhelming.

Both magnificent, loyal, courageous, handsome as heroes of Greek legend.

Her protectors. Her lovers.

They both watched her now, and she could feel her heat rising beneath their gazes. Images surfaced in her mind, sensations both remembered and anticipated; of hands on her skin, hot and ready mouths, the cool air as her clothing was removed. A delicious tingle swept through her as she looked from one man to the other.

"Miranda, come here," said Corwin.

Her heart pounding softly, Miranda stood and walked toward him, aware with each motion that Darius watched her. His gaze seared as strong as a passionate caress. It somehow slowed her movements and added a new sway to her hips as she approached Corwin.

Corwin wrapped an arm around her waist and drew her onto his lap. Without a word he kissed her and she gave herself to it completely. She ran her tongue along his lips. He tasted of salt and brandy and sweet desire. His hands circled her waist, cupped her hips and settled her close. Miranda wrapped her arms around his shoulders, savoring the breadth and strength of them.

At last, needing air, she broke the kiss. "We shouldn't," she murmured. "Your man will be back soon to clear away the dishes."

Corwin sighed and put on a perturbed expression.

"You forget, Miranda," he chided. "This is *my* house, and these are my servants. Each one of them voluntarily bound themselves to silence about what happens within these walls, both by inclination and by bespelled oath. I could take you on the floor, right here, and not one of them would say a word."

A teasing contrariness brightened inside Miranda, and she stood. "Do you know, you have this terrible habit of threatening me with a public fucking." She could barely believe she'd used the word, let alone in such a haughty tone, but at the same time, she relished the sense of mischief that had come over her. "I'm beginning to find it rude. And presumptuous."

"Are you, b'gad?" Corwin's eyes narrowed. "Or perhaps you simply want it too much."

"I don't believe I want anything to do with you right now." Miranda flounced over to the sofa and sat. To emphasize her point, she drew in her skirts, and crossed her ankles.

"Really?" Corwin's shoulders slumped. "Heigh-ho. My bad

luck." He stuck his hands in his coat pockets, and let his gaze roam to the other end of the table. "Perhaps Darius?"

"Me?" said Darius, sounding so affronted that for a heartbeat Miranda was afraid he was really angry. "Is this how it's to go on, then? You come to me when she won't have you?"

"Darius, Darius, don't be so cold." Corwin rounded the table and sank to his knees in front of Darius's chair. "I'm in need."

Darius reached out and knotted his fingers in Corwin's dark hair, tipping the other man's face up. "Perhaps you should be left in need a little longer," he whispered. "To remind you not to take me for granted."

But a heartbeat later Darius leaned forward, and they kissed.

And Miranda stared.

They kissed easily, openly, comfortably. They both closed their eyes, savoring. Corwin slid his hand into Darius's golden hair as he stood, drawing Darius up with him. They wrapped their arms around each other, pressing their hard bodies together. Corwin sighed. Darius murmured his name.

Miranda stared.

Corwin ran his hands down Darius's beautifully muscled arms and across the sculpted planes of his chest. In turn, Darius, with expert fingers, undid Corwin's cravat and ran his hand across Corwin's throat, pushing the neck of his shirt open and loosening the collar. Corwin tugged off Darius's coat and tossed it aside. Then he ran greedy palms up Darius's strong thighs, to his ass, and around his hips to his swelling cock. Darius sighed and shifted, leaning himself into Corwin's confident hand.

A riot of feeling surged through Miranda. She was shocked.

She shouldn't have been, but she was. But at the same time, the play between the two of them was beautiful, tender and unabashedly erotic. As she watched Corwin run palms and fingers over the outline of Darius's cock, her skin heated, her lips and breasts seemed to grow heavier and she could feel the sweet sensation of desire rising up from the center of her.

Darius captured Corwin's mouth for another open kiss and his fingers worked the buttons on Corwin's fly, opening the dark-haired Sorcerer's breeches so he could reach inside with both hands. Corwin's shirttail prevented Miranda from seeing his cock, but she could see Darius's hands move beneath the linen, up and down, up and down.

"Mmm . . ." Corwin sighed and gripped Darius's ass, squeezing, and giving it one hard spank. A tiny whimper escaped Miranda.

The men broke off their kiss, and turned their heads to look at her, but neither moved his hands away from the other. Miranda blushed hot, confused to realize her desire could be so swiftly, so hotly, aroused by the sight of these two men pleasuring each other.

"Why, Corwin," said Darius archly. "I believe Miss Prosper has changed her mind." He gestured, and Miranda felt the prickle of magic. In the next heartbeat the two of them were naked in each other's arms, and Miranda could clearly see Darius's hand on Corwin's gorgeously erect cock. Darius ran his fingers almost thoughtfully over the hard length of it. Miranda watched, fascinated. Her mouth was watering again, and her pussy was drenched.

"You may be right." Corwin stroked the curve of Darius's ass appreciatively, almost contemplatively. "Do you know, I promised her a most particular lesson earlier. I think now is the time to make good."

Corwin took Darius's tight balls in his hand, stroking and fondling. Miranda swallowed hard and, without any thought at all, raised one hand to her breast and stroked. She couldn't help it. She didn't want to help it. She had to do something to ease the passion burning inside her.

Corwin smiled, and let his gaze linger on her breast and her restless hand. Darius was looking too. The weight of their gazes only stoked the flames inside her and urged her to gather her hardened nipple and roll it between her fingers. She realized sharply she enjoyed them watching her, knowing the sight of her made them want to touch each other.

"Now, pay close attention, Miranda," Corwin purred. "This is how it's done."

Corwin went down on his knees. Darius ran his fingers through Corwin's dark hair. Corwin took the shaft of Darius's cock in his hand and bent close. He breathed on it and kissed it, as tenderly, as passionately, as he had kissed Darius's mouth. Darius moaned and Miranda brought her other hand up, squeezing both her breasts. Corwin smiled and took Darius fully into his mouth.

The effect on Darius was immediate. He groaned and bucked forward, thrusting himself into Corwin's mouth. Corwin wrapped his lips tight around Darius's shaft, taking the thrusts, letting Darius fuck his mouth. Miranda wondered if Corwin was licking him, running his tongue along that velvet-soft skin. He was fondling Darius's balls and Darius was caressing Corwin, his neck and his shoulders. Miranda shoved one hand between her thighs and pressed her fingers into her drenched slit as if she thought that would somehow stop the throbbing and burning there, but it only inflamed her more. It was maddening, it was wonderful, touching herself while watching Corwin suck so passionately on Darius. Corwin's cock jutted up hard and proud from between his thighs. Her pussy, her mouth, wanted a cock inside, wanted it beyond words, and all she had was her own hands. Darius groaned and arched his hips, his fingers knotting tightly in Corwin's hair.

Slowly, Corwin lifted his head, releasing Darius's gleaming cock. He grinned up at Darius, who fell backward onto the sofa, his legs splayed open, his erection resting on his belly. Corwin sat beside him, wrapped an arm around his shoulder.

"Your turn, Miranda," Corwin said, fondling Darius's cock.

Offering it to her.

She did not need to be told twice. She moved forward and started to drop to her knees, only to be intercepted by Corwin, who kissed her hard and lingeringly. Her body melted at his touch and she sighed against his mouth.

Please. I want to be naked with you.

As my lady desires. Corwin ran his fingers down the lace of her neckline, and her clothes were gone, leaving the whole of her body bared to them.

It was the most perfect freedom.

"Now." Corwin knelt on the carpet and drew her down with

him. He wrapped his arms around her waist, positioning her so she could herself kneel comfortably in front of Darius, whose blue eyes shone with heady desire as he gazed down at her, at them. Corwin's thighs pressed against hers, and she could feel the bulge of his cock against her ass. "Use your hand here." Corwin wrapped her fingers around Darius's shaft. "To control how deeply you take him until you are comfortable with it. It can take a little time, especially with such a monster."

Miranda leaned close over Darius's cock. His musky scent was intoxicating. Darius's hand brushed her hair, her temple and her cheek.

"Suck me, Miranda," said Darius. "Let me feel your mouth around me."

She brushed her lips against Darius's hot, blunt tip. It felt strange and magnificent at once.

"You're *very* big," she murmured.

"Very big," agreed Corwin with a chuckle. He took his hand from hers and cupped her breast, kneading her. "Take him, Miranda. Enjoy him."

She hesitated no longer, but opened her mouth and took Darius in. He was hard and huge, and tantalizing against her tongue. The sensation of his velvety cock sliding deeper into her mouth sent pleasure and desire shooting through her veins. Curious, she licked at him, and he moaned and arched his hips. She squeezed her lips around him; she slid her head up and down, made her tongue busy with the delightful and intriguing contours of him.

"Oh, gods," he gasped. "Oh, Miranda, that's so good."

"Yes." Corwin's hand pressed between her thighs, up into her dripping folds. "Oh, Miranda, I like watching you suck him."

Corwin's fingers were inside her, thrusting and stroking. Darius's cock filled her mouth and any fear she might have had about his size vanished. She wanted nothing but to lick and suck his cock, to feel him throbbing against her tongue and lips.

"I can't stand it. I must have you."

Corwin drew his fingers swiftly out of her sheath and her suddenly empty pussy clenched. She whimpered, but she couldn't pull herself away from Darius's mesmerizing cock. She kissed it, grazed her teeth against it, and every groan he gave pulled her deeper and closer to the new mystery of desire and sensuality.

Corwin was moving behind her, moving her. His hands were on her hips and he raised her up higher on her knees. She felt him at her entrance, his hands splayed across her hips.

Yes. Yes!

With a single motion, Corwin's cock was inside her, the power of his thrust rocking her forward, forcing Darius's shaft as far into her mouth as Corwin's was inside her pussy. She groaned and clamped her lips tight around Darius.

It was amazing, one hard cock in her mouth, one in her pussy. Their four hands stroked her; they caressed her thighs, her head, her breasts and her clit, urging her on, opening her body to all the desire that flooded her so she could take them both deeper inside. Darius groaned and grasped her shoulders, and she dug her fingers into his thighs, urging him to move. She wanted to feel him gliding against her tongue while her hips writhed hard against Corwin, making his cock caress her hot sheath.

"Yes, Miranda." Corwin's fingers found her clit again, and circled there, raising fiery pleasure. "Take him hard; take him deep. We're going to make you come, Miranda." He stroked her clit harder as he thrust. "We're going to make you come so hard with my cock in your pussy and his in your mouth."

Miranda groaned around Darius's cock and he thrust forward, almost to the back of her throat, and as he did, Corwin pressed down against her clit. The twin sensations were maddening and she only wanted more. She gripped Darius's ass, and licked and sucked and moaned.

Conscious thought fled. There was only pure, sensual pleasure. Only the fascination of Darius's cock filling her mouth, and Corwin's inside her sheath. As Corwin drove himself into her, fucking her with his luscious, hard cock, the rhythm caused her to fuck Darius with her mouth and tongue.

"Oh, yes, Miranda. Your mouth feels so good!" Darius speared his fingers into her hair. "Fuck her, Corwin. Fuck her hard!"

Corwin's free hand ran up the crack of her ass until he pressed his thumb against the tight hole there as he obeyed Darius's frantic order and drove himself into her again and again. Slowly, their wild motions worked his thumb into her, stretching her, penetrating her. It hurt, but feeling him inside her in this new way brought a pleasure far deeper than the pain. All at once, she imagined his cock not in her sheath but in *there*. She groaned. She couldn't hold it all; it was too much. Too much luscious, luxurious sensuality, too much delicious skin and heat, too much glorious motion, fast and hard and faster yet.

All at once Corwin roared. His climax drove him into her;

into her pussy, into her anus, and Miranda tumbled over the edge into a whirlwind of ecstasy, screaming her pleasure against Darius's cock. Darius cried out wordlessly and thrust to the back of her throat, and she was caught between the two climaxes, riding them both, crying, flying, floating, falling into their arms, into their eyes and mouths and tender love.

Nineteen

When Corwin awoke amid a nest of blankets and discarded clothing on his library carpet, warmth suffused him as he realized he was also still tangled in a luxurious embrace with Miranda and Darius. It felt . . . right to wake up with them both. Right in a way nothing else ever had.

Corwin was generous with his feelings. "Profligate," Darius called it, but Corwin had always laughed at him. He enjoyed sex, and he enjoyed taking lovers. Darius had been his rock and anchor for many years, but they had both understood that Corwin needed women as well; with Darius and without him, Catalysts and ordinary humans. Corwin was not a complete libertine, however. He had never seduced an innocent, never sought sex where he did not also feel tenderness, and he always did his best to leave no hard feelings behind.

Is one of you going to marry me? Miranda had asked. This was not something Corwin had contemplated before. Love her, yes. Provide for her, certainly. Even if Smith didn't demand that, Corwin's sense of honor did. But marry? He had never truly considered taking a wife. Before this, marriage would have meant either deceiving the woman or breaking with Darius.

But now things were different. Being so much a creature of emotions, Corwin was aware that Miranda was different from the others he had pursued. When he looked at her, something deeper stirred within him. This was not mere tenderness, or even the heat of infatuation he might feel for a new lover. Before meeting her, his heart had moved this way only when he looked at Darius.

Was it possible he had found a woman to complete him? To hold that other side of him that had always remained restless even with Darius's body and heart completely his?

If it's true, how will Darius take it? Darius accepted Miranda and shared in Corwin's vow to protect her. He enjoyed her in their bed—enjoyed her a great deal if last night was any indication. More importantly, Darius now saw Miranda as a trusted comrade in their fight.

But Darius felt deeply, and he held those he loved close. Could he really be open to bringing another heart into the already complex relationship he shared with Corwin? Would he want to?

A flash of white caught Corwin's eye. A freshly sealed letter lay on the table beside the fire. Carefully, he extricated himself from his lovers' embrace. Miranda stirred restlessly, but Darius pulled her closer in his sleep and she sighed and stilled. Corwin smiled and tucked the blankets around them both before he padded to the table and opened Smith's letter. His eyes swept across the boldly written words.

"Damnation!" Corwin crumpled the paper in his fist.

"What!" Darius cried behind him.

"Smith says we've lost another Catalyst." Corwin held the letter toward Darius. "And Andrews is dead."

"Andrews!" Darius leapt to his feet and snatched the message from Corwin. "He was one of our senior . . ."

"He was found in Hyde Park this morning." Corwin dropped into the nearest chair and scrubbed his palms against his face. "The back of his head was bashed in."

"Gods," breathed Darius. "And the Catalyst?"

"Malcolm Hale. Last we knew he was with Andrews. Now . . . he's gone. Like the others."

"Malcolm Hale?" repeated Miranda as she gathered the sheet around her shoulder. "I know him. He . . ." She turned pale and covered her mouth.

"What is it, Miranda?" asked Darius sharply.

"He courted me once," she whispered. "But then Mother decided she fancied him." She waved her hand vaguely. "It didn't last. He wasn't rich enough."

So that's it. Corwin knew Miranda's heart had been broken at least once before. Suppressing a curse against the colossal selfishness of Daphne Quicke, Corwin crossed to Miranda and wrapped his arm around her shoulders. "I'm sorry, Miranda."

But Miranda just shook her head. "It was a long time ago. You say Malcolm is a Catalyst?"

Darius folded the letter, creasing it sharply. "Yes. Andrews was also looking into the Thayer guest list, with Malcolm's help." He paused, frowning. "They're stepping up the attacks."

"The summer solstice is coming," said Corwin. "They may have to."

Darius looked sharply at him. "What are you saying?"

Nothing I want to believe. But we must consider it. "I'm saying what if our Lady Thayer is preparing a formal sacrifice?"

"What is a formal sacrifice?" asked Miranda.

A door in the darkness. A light so bright it cuts into your mind. A voice you cannot ignore saying, "Come with me and you shall have all you could desire." Corwin shook his head. Now was not the time to relive that particular nightmare. "It is a way for a mortal Sorcerer to prove their loyalty to the Fae court. They must give the Queen a gift of lives, preferably either of mortal children or Catalysts."

"Or Sorcerers," added Darius softly. Corwin didn't look at him. He had to control his thoughts before Miranda sensed them.

But Miranda, it seemed, was too distracted to notice. "But . . . you said the Fae are magical beings. What would they need with a . . . person who can channel magic?"

Corwin shot a sideways glance at Darius. He had been hoping to put off this particular discussion a little longer, but now there was no choice. "Miranda, do you remember how you felt after you first drained my magic from me?"

She turned her face away. "Yes."

"Was it good?"

"For a while." She plucked restlessly at the blankets around her shoulders. "But then I thought I was going to die."

"Just so." Corwin nodded. "But what if someone had come to you in your pain and said they could make you feel wonderful again? What would you have done?"

She swallowed, and Corwin watched the play of uncomfortable emotions on her face. "I would have begged for it," she admitted.

"No matter who was offering to give you your relief? Or at what price?"

"I might have."

Darius plucked up his abandoned snifter and downed the remaining brandy. "The Fae know this is what the absorption of magic does to Catalysts when they have no Sorcerer to help channel it, and they find it highly amusing." He gazed into the empty glass, and Corwin could see the effort it was taking for him to speak dispassionately. "This makes them highly prized playthings in the Fae court. The Fae fill them with magic and watch them go through the throes of ecstasy and pain."

"A gift of a dozen Catalysts would surely be acceptable to the Fae." Corwin clenched his fist against his thigh. "All to be delivered at the solstice. Very neat."

"Is that why Lady Thayer invited me to the party? To add to their . . . offering?"

Corwin ran his finger down Miranda's jawline, feeling its smooth perfection. "Their crowning jewel," he said, his voice heavy with sarcasm. "And as a bonus, she made sure your mother would be watching you the whole time, making it impossible for you to move freely."

Darius drummed his fingers on the tabletop. "We'll have to

find some way around her. We need you at that party to get us inside."

"You were able to get inside her house once before without me," she reminded them, her voice taut, and Corwin felt her shoulders tense under his hand.

Oh, Miranda, have we reached your limits? "Yes," agreed Corwin. "But we we were only permitted entry so Lady Thayer could flush us, and you, out into the open. We're all marked now, so I doubt we'll be so cavalierly admitted into the Thayers' home a second time."

"So what do we do?" asked Miranda softly. "We cannot stay away, and if we go, we'll be walking into their trap."

Corwin stared at the fire. He hated this feeling of being hemmed in. He hated the fact that he had been so careless as to allow a common footpad to ambush him and deliver him to his enemies. As a strategy it was brilliant. Lady Thayer was robbing London of its Catalysts without casting a single spell to attract attention. At this point they didn't even know if she was Sorcerer or Catalyst herself, because she'd left them no clues. She simply brought her targets to her parties, flattered them and befriended them. Then, when they trusted her, she had them discreetly removed.

And not one of Smith's people had seen it because, despite their facility with lockpicks and other toys, not one of them truly thought such a great and terrible feat could be accomplished without strong and frequent spell casting.

"Perhaps," murmured Corwin. "We need to give Lady Thayer a dose of her own medicine."

"What do you mean?" asked Miranda.

"They've been attacking us in exactly the way we do not expect." Corwin spoke slowly but he felt the warmth of the strategies taking shape within him. Helplessness fell away. Here at last was the possibility of action. "Why shouldn't we do the same?"

Darius narrowed his eyes. "You have a plan?"

I do, and it could work. Corwin felt his confidence come welling back. "Miranda, you said your mother was near insolvent?"

She frowned at his seeming change of subject. "Yes."

"What would she do to rectify that?"

Miranda drew back, the familiar haughtiness returning to her eyes. "You are not considering *bribing* my mother?"

"I am," replied Corwin.

"To what end?" exclaimed Darius.

"To allow Miranda to move freely. To be an extra pair of eyes and ears in the Thayers' house."

Miranda sat back, clutching the sheets to her. Corwin watched her face shift as she turned the idea over in her mind. Gradually, he felt it settle deeper into her thoughts, then felt her realization spread and grow. "We'd have to tell her . . . everything."

"Not entirely." He smiled and brushed her hair back from her shoulders. "But some things, yes."

Miranda looked down at her hands. Her worry and sorrow were like a cold breeze around his heart. His first instinct was to reach out to offer reassurance, but a glance from Darius stopped him. He was right. She needed to come to terms with this freely, or not at all.

I trust you, Miranda. Trust me.

Miranda lifted her eyes. Whether she'd heard him or not, she'd come to her decision.

"All right." She gave a small smile. "I've hidden myself as far as I could from her for so many years, I think in a way . . . I think it will be a relief to be open with her for once."

"And this time you won't be alone." Corwin took her hand as Darius moved to stand beside them both.

"No." She smiled at him, and at Darius. "Not this time."

"Not ever," said Darius, sinking to his knees before her chair. "Not ever again."

As Darius leaned to kiss Miranda and Miranda opened to receive him, Corwin felt his heart begin to sing with hope. Perhaps they could all of them cleave together. Miranda sighed and shifted closer to Darius, and Darius reached up to cup her beautiful breast. *Yes, oh, yes.*

Miranda fell forward into Darius's willing arms and Corwin could not prevent himself from dropping to his knees so he could wrap his arms around them both, pressing them together, reveling in the touch of their different skins, their different but complementary heats.

Images flashed from mind to mind. Sweet Miranda thought of them lying with her, one on each side, each sucking on one of her gorgeous breasts while she stroked their cocks with her heated hands. Bold Darius thought of Miranda against the wall with Corwin fucking her hard and fast the way she liked best, while Darius's own cock fit snugly inside Corwin's anus. His lovers' erotic imaginings woke his own, and Corwin thought of the pair of them licking his rapidly hardening cock, tongues and hands teasing and tantalizing each other even as they pleasured him.

Vision and longing became heat, and heat became fire and lust flowing freely among them all. Corwin lay back, bringing Miranda and Darius with him.

He would see them all through this. If he had concerns about the future, the first of them should be to make damn well certain he *had* a future.

Twenty

O f all the strange things that had happened to Miranda, surely sitting in her mother's sunny morning room speaking of magic and the Fae was the strangest of them all.

Miranda was willing to swear her mother did not even blink as Corwin explained to her the bare facts of the case: that Miranda was a Catalyst, that her aid was required in the war against an unearthly foe, that Lady Thayer was quite probably an enemy of humanity itself, and that she, Daphne Quicke, was being asked to aid the fight.

When Corwin at last fell silent, Mother's hard gaze went from him to Miranda. Miranda met her mother's eyes proud and unafraid. She'd been right. It was a relief for her to know the truth at last.

Slowly, Mother got to her feet. She staggered, and Corwin reflexively held out his hand. But she cut him off with a sharp gesture and walked to the window. She stood with her back to them, staring out at the garden for a long time. So long that Miranda shifted in her chair and glanced up at Corwin, who stood on her left. Darius, from his position to her right, shrugged, and she felt the mild confusion running between them.

At last, Mother turned back around, her face and stance utterly composed. "I recognize that the proper form at this moment is to ask if you have all gone quite mad," she said. "I'm afraid you'll have to forgive me if I don't follow the formalities."

"You believe us?" The words burst out of Miranda in something close to a squeak.

"It is not the first time I have heard of such things." She returned to her chair, sitting smoothly, folding her hands on her lap, just so, as if perfection of deportment could shield her from her own words.

Corwin frowned. "May I ask, madame . . ."

"My second husband," she replied coolly. "Miranda's father."

"Father?" breathed Miranda. "Father knew of the Fae?"

"He knew of magic. He knew he was . . . different from other men. It was the root of all his scientific inquiries. He did not believe in the supernatural, as you well remember, Miranda. He believed all observable phenomena could eventually be explained. He wanted to understand himself, so that he could explain your own nature to you."

Miranda sat stunned. Her father . . . Her father had known what she was?

"Do you know, madame, if he was Sorcerer or Catalyst?"

"If I have understood your explanations correctly, I believe he was what you call a Catalyst."

How did the captain miss this? Miranda sensed the thought flash through Corwin's mind.

I don't think he did, returned Darius. *Perhaps it was no coincidence we were sent to the party where Miranda was.*

But this was not what concerned her, not now. "Why didn't you ever tell me?"

"I didn't believe him!" cried Mother. "How could I? He was such a dreamer, so deep into his philosophies. I thought this was just one more of his mad notions. I didn't know. I had no idea until now." She closed her eyes. "I'm sorry," she whispered. And Miranda knew the apology was not to her, but to the place her father still occupied inside her mother's heart. "I'm so sorry."

"If you believed him so mad, why did you marry him?" Miranda felt herself trembling. Her mind was reshaping years of understanding, and it was almost too much. Her mother and her understanding of her mother had been a fixed point in her universe. To discover that Daphne Quicke had been keeping secrets from her all these years and that it was not Miranda who had been hiding. It was too much. It was as bad as the revelation of the household accounts. Miranda's anger blazed, more at herself than at her mother even. *If only I had asked. If only I had not been so closed off . . .*

"You've been in society, Miranda," said her mother. "You should be able to imagine how wonderful it was among all that glitter and greed to find a man who cared what one thought, what one believed, whose demands were of the mildest kind . . ." The sentence broke off abruptly. "He worshipped me as his perfect goddess, and that's what I wanted to be for him. I wanted to shelter him, to free him to pursue whatever path his intellect took. In turn he would free me from the loneliness and dependency society forces on a woman." Her mouth trembled for a moment. "Then he died. He died and there you were, and my investments failed. I had to go back into that mill." Mother drew a deep breath, bringing her body back under her ruthless control.

"I didn't know," whispered Miranda. "I never realized . . ."

"No," said Mother heavily. "And you never asked either."

"And you never offered."

They stared at each other, neither blinking, neither breaking. At last, Mother looked away. "Very well. We are both at fault."

Miranda opened her mouth to make a cutting remark, but Corwin's hand fell heavily on her shoulder, restraining her and reminding her there were other issues at stake here than these very personal wounds.

"Will you aid us?" asked Darius flatly.

Mother drew another deep breath. "No," she said. "Whatever she may be, I cannot afford to make an enemy of Lady Thayer. Miranda may not have told you this, but we are a fair way to being destitute." She spoke the words with her frosty practicality. "If Miranda chooses to go with you . . . I suppose I cannot stop her but I hope you . . . gentlemen"—her gaze shifted from Corwin to Darius and back again—"are prepared to take over her maintenance, because I have nothing left for her."

The words were coldly spoken, and Miranda felt her cheeks flush with anger, but only for a moment, for she became aware of something else, a crushing tide of sorrow. But it came not from Corwin or Darius. This sorrow was Mother's, and it was so deep as to be all-consuming. Mother had failed, failed supremely, failed the man she had loved above all others, failed his child. She had permitted herself to become as hard and petty as the worst of the society wolves her husband had so pitied, and now she had nothing, nothing at all.

Corwin squeezed Miranda's shoulder. He felt it too, whether on his own or through her, and he understood.

"You would not be expected to give your aid for nothing," said Darius.

Mother tilted her head ever so slightly.

"Miranda is one of our number now, and she will be amply provided for," said Corwin. "This extends to her family as well."

"Why would you make me such an offer?"

"Because it is necessary to our efforts that Miranda maintain her position in society," replied Corwin. "This means that nothing can be seen to change in your life or hers, or there will be talk that is best avoided. Rest assured, Mrs. Quicke, if you play your part in this, you will be doing the work of your country and you will be paid accordingly."

Mother rose once more from her chair. She walked three paces across the room to the mantel. A square box of lacquered wood waited there. She opened it and drew out a golden locket. It was a small thing, and much plainer than any jewels Miranda was accustomed to her mother wearing. Mother opened it and stared at the contents for a long moment before she snapped it shut.

"Miranda, is this what you want?" She clutched the locket tight in her fist and Miranda was certain it contained her father's miniature. "You join this . . . situation of your own free will?"

"Yes," Miranda answered. "For a host of reasons, but let this suffice: this situation, as you term it, permits me to be who and what I wish to be."

"Very well." Mother nodded, but her fingers did not loosen their grasp on the locket at all. "What must I do?"

Twenty-one

Under other circumstances Miranda might have permitted herself to enjoy the drive through Hallowgate. The estate was beautiful in the thoroughly grand, thoroughly English style. Nestled under green windswept hills, its rolling grounds had been meticulously maintained by generations of dedicated gardeners. The main avenue lined with stately oaks was truly breathtaking. But the awareness that she was in enemy territory with her mother as a most unlikely ally robbed Miranda of any ability to relax. Nothing was made easier by the fact that neither Corwin nor Darius was with them.

"One of our men has been out to the estate already to scout the territory," Corwin had said the day before they left. "There are wards in place—magical shields that can prevent a Sorcerer from entering the grounds, or at least give warning that he's there. There are ways to breach such shields, but they are most easily done from inside." He'd kissed her hand. "And that, my dear, is where you and your mother come in."

Inside Mother's bag was a small silver amulet. They'd been given strict instructions on how it was to be placed, and when. Supposedly, it would create a breach in the wards to allow Corwin and Darius to slip through.

For the thousandth time Miranda wished it was she who had charge of the amulet. If she had hoped for an immediate change in her feelings toward her mother, it had not happened. The habits of so many years would not break so soon, and despite a new intellectual understanding of all Mother had been through, Miranda found none of it could erase the old angers. Not yet anyway.

But as Darius pointed out so bluntly, Miranda was the one who would be watched. Whether any of them liked it or not, this party was a trap for her. Lady Thayer would be taking a keen interest in Miranda's movements. It was Mother who would be able to move freely.

Miranda understood, as she understood the necessity of sleeping alone in her own bed for the remaining nights before the party in order to keep up the illusion that she was being confined under her mother's watchful eye. She did not like that either.

"You can stop looking at me like that," Mother said. "This is no easier for me than it is for you."

Miranda shook herself. She truly had not realized she was communicating so much in her glance. "I'm sorry. I just . . ."

"You don't trust me." The carriage jounced as it rolled over a loose stone and Mother smoothed her skirts. "I suppose I have only myself to blame for that. Perhaps after all these years I have thought too much on survival and too little on . . ." She broke off, staring out the carriage window. "But no matter. You may be assured I will play my part, Miranda."

And what then? Miranda bit her lip. *If we all come through these next few days, what then?*

It was a terrible thing to feel her old doubts returning. Miranda found her new-won intimacy and confidence was not so strong as she would have liked to believe. When Corwin and Darius were with her, it was easy to trust them utterly. The brief time they had spent together in Corwin's house . . . It had been as if they existed on another plane. They could all be free and open with one another, as one was supposed to be in one's home. Being forced to exist again in the real world . . . It was difficult.

Their carriage halted on the wide gravel courtyard, joining a line of others waiting in front of the low Tudor-era sprawl of Hallowgate House. Servants scurried to and fro with bags and bundles, and members of society in their bright summer clothes stood about giving orders and exchanging greetings.

"Smile, my dear," said Mother. "The show's about to begin."

A liveried groom opened the carriage door, and helped Mother out. She cast a radiant smile around her, rising into her element as easily and naturally as ever.

"Phoebe, my dear! That pelisse is simply charming! I must have the name of your dressmaker . . . Why, good afternoon, Lord Tapscott. I declare, it *has* been an age! How marvelous to see you looking so well . . . Mr. Beale, how delightful. I was hoping to run into you . . . Caroline! I've just heard the most delicious story . . . Oh, not here; later. Do you know my daughter, Miranda?"

Miranda smiled politely, made her curtsies and gradually faded away from conscious regard as the other arrivals circulated around her mother. It was a familiar role and she welcomed it with a sense of relief that sparked more than a little worry deep in her mind. How, after all that had happened, could she still be most comfortable when no one noticed her at all?

No one except Lady Thayer.

Perfectly turned out in a deep green morning dress trimmed with antique lace, the mistress of Hallowgate sailed out of the carved doors straight toward Miranda.

"My dear Miranda!" she exclaimed, taking both of Miranda's hands. "I do so want to welcome you personally to my home."

"Thank you, Lady Thayer." The by-now-familiar tingle ran up Miranda's arms. She met Lady Thayer's eyes, and a sensation of déjà vu swept over her. *You're like me. You're a Catalyst.* "It was very kind of you to invite us."

"Not at all, not at all!" Lady Thayer waved Miranda's words away. "I'm sure your delightful mother told you I had a most particular reason for asking you to come down." Lady Thayer smiled, but the smile did not reach her eyes. Curious, Miranda tried to sense some emotion from her, but the woman in front of her was like glass, hard and slick and impossible to grasp.

"Now, we shall get you installed in your rooms so you can rest and refresh yourself. We've the welcoming ball tonight, and I'm sure your mother will want you to look your best. Isn't that so, Daphne?" Lady Thayer turned to her mother, who had come up behind Miranda.

"To be sure," Mother purred. "In fact, my dear, I think it

would be advisable for you to remain in your room until dinner. You've been so tired lately."

Miranda met her mother's gaze and held it for a count of three, and then dropped her eyes. "Yes, Mother."

"There's my good girl." Mother patted her hand in her usual patronizing manner. "Now, for myself, Lady Thayer, I think a stroll in your *lovely* grounds before dinner would be just the thing."

"Did someone say a stroll in the gardens?" Lord Tapscott stepped up. He was a big, bluff man with gray hair, a gray mustache, a large inheritance and an inconvenient wife. "Just the thing after all that dashed road dust." He smiled broadly at Mother. "Daphne, have you seen the folly? Splendid view of the lake, don't you know."

"Why, Lord Tapscott, that sounds delightful." The smile she flashed was calculated to dazzle, and even Miranda could see she succeeded. "Will Lady Tapscott join us?"

"Alas, no." Miranda noticed the man's regret was completely feigned. "Headache, you see. Poor thing has had to lie down."

"Oh, dear." Mother laid her fingertips delicately against her perfectly rouged lips "A headache is *such* a nuisance. Still. I'd hate to waste this lovely weather. But I'd better see Miranda settled first."

"Oh, no need, Daphne, dear," Lady Thayer said at once. "I'll see to her."

Lord Tapscott held his arm out for Mother to take, and off she went with a light tread, and just the barest hint of a wink at Miranda.

Miranda stared after her mother, half in disbelief, half in blatant admiration. She'd spent so long disdaining her for being a shameless intriguer, she hadn't stopped to think of the level of acting skill Mother had cultivated over the years.

I certainly never would have believed I'd be making use of those skills.

"Well, come along, Miranda." Lady Thayer took her arm as if they were intimates. "I want to show you your room."

Miranda let herself be led away. She kept in mind the parting advice Darius had given her and concentrated on the way in front of her, on the broad, low steps and the arched doorway. The whole house was low and filled with dark wood, from the heavy beams to the linen-fold paneling to the steep staircases. Miranda forced herself to wonder about the history of the ancient hall, if Queen Elizabeth had ever stayed here, and how much it had cost to increase the number of fireplaces and chimneys to make the place habitable in winter.

It was difficult. Her thoughts kept drifting to Lady Thayer, who was chattering away about who had arrived so far and who was expected, and everybody's clothes. It was all so bland, so ordinary. Could this woman truly be involved in abduction, murder and intrigue with the mysterious Fae? Walking up the heavily carved wooden stair and down the narrow halls of a Tudor country house, it seemed quite ridiculous.

Concentrate, concentrate, Miranda chided herself, noting the oak paneling, the miles of turkey carpet covering the ancient floorboards, and the stained glass of the window at the corridor's end.

"I do so hope you'll be comfortable here." Lady Thayer opened a door in the left-hand side of the hall. Miranda glanced through to see a low-ceilinged room furnished in quite the modern style in shades of green. There was a clean bed and a comfortable chaise in front of the diamond-paned windows, as well as a marquetry writing desk and everything else that could make a guest feel at home. "I've put your mother next door." Lady Thayer indicated the connecting door.

"It's lovely, thank you." Mindful of her role, Miranda made herself hesitate. "But I really don't feel like a rest right now. I'm sure a turn around the grounds would be just what I need."

Steel flashed in Lady Thayer's gray eyes. "Oh, no, my dear. Forgive me, but I must agree with your mother. You look quite tired. And you want to be at your best tonight." She patted Miranda's cheek.

Miranda drew upon the skills she had so recently discovered, and sent a wave of frustration out into the air. "Of course," she murmured. "Then I shall bid you good afternoon, Lady Thayer."

Miranda went into the room and closed the door. But standing where she was, she was certain she detected an air of smug satisfaction before she heard the whisper of Lady Thayer's skirts as the woman moved away to attend to her other guests.

The rest of the afternoon was maddening. Miranda had to remind herself over and over again that this was a good thing. If she was being watched by Lady Thayer, having a genuine and growing air of frustration about her was only helping the cause.

And there was now no doubt at all that she was being watched. Twice, Miranda left her room, once by the front stair and once by the back. Both times, Lady Thayer just *happened* to be by the door with her hospitable smile and her "Oh, Miranda, *dear*."

Which was just what they wanted to happen. It was all going according to plan. Except the shadows were lengthening outside, and Mother had not returned. Miranda's suspicions began to deepen into alarm. Yes, Mother had agreed to do this thing; yes, she seemed to believe in it on the strength of Father's apparent confirmation. In the yard, she had played her part to perfection, but she'd always been so flighty, so scattered and intent only on the next party, the next man, the next meal ticket.

Does Mother really understand that there is something greater at stake here? Miranda asked herself as she stared in vain across the empty gardens. *How can she when I can only half believe it sometimes and I've been living it for days?*

Just as the clock was chiming six, and just as Miranda was certain she would begin tearing her hair out, she heard a door open and close.

Miranda flew across her room and pounded on the connecting door.

"Good heavens, Miranda!" exclaimed Mother from the other side. "What is the matter?"

Miranda stood there panting as if she'd just run a mile. A lock rattled and snapped, and Mother pulled the door open. But there was Mother, perfectly composed, except for the tiny vertical line between her brows.

"I was afraid . . ." Miranda gulped air, suddenly ashamed of being so dramatic. "I thought . . ."

"Well, you needn't have." Mother turned away and settled at her dressing table. "The deed is done."

"But you were gone so long." Miranda stepped into Mother's room. Its furnishings were nearly identical to her own, except done in shades of rose rather than green, and the bed was larger. A subtle gibe at Daphne Quicke's reputation?

"Lord Tapscott was most interested in showing me every inch of the gardens." Mother studied her face in the mirror. Miranda couldn't help looking as well, and for the first time in her life, she noted how tired her mother looked. "I had a time keeping him from doing something Lady Tapscott would make him regret. Still." She drew herself up. "We are here, it is done, and now, my dear, I must ask you to withdraw. If I don't have a nap before the festivities this evening, I will be quite useless."

"Of course," murmured Miranda. "And . . . thank you."

Her mother smiled, an oddly wistful expression. "When all this is over, Miranda, I think you and I are going to have a very long talk."

"I think I'd like that."

Again Mother smiled, and unfamiliar emotion squeezed Miranda's heart. "Now, get along. You also need to look your best tonight."

Miranda closed the door softly and drifted into her room. She sat on the edge of the chair by the window and stared out at the darkening gardens until Louise knocked at the door.

"Excuse me, miss," said her maid as she bustled into the room. "But it's time to get you ready for the party."

"Yes, of course." Miranda got to her feet. "The show's about to begin."

Twenty-two

Twilight was just deepening to full dark when Darius and Corwin arrived at the stout hedge that marked the boundary of Hallowgate Park. The ward slid against Darius's skin like the flat of a knife, telling him plainly that if he turned the wrong way, he would be cut open.

"Here's the gap." Corwin was crouched well down beside the hedge. They were both dressed as countrymen, in tweed trousers and stout boots with rough caps on their heads. Anyone seeing them now would take them for gardeners.

Or poachers. Darius knelt beside Corwin, who was eyeing the low tunnel in the living wall. They could have made themselves invisible with ease, of course, but not without risking detection by Lady Thayer and her accomplices. There was also the question of the effort. Until they rejoined Miranda, he and Corwin had only the reserves they carried within them, and they needed to husband those against genuine need.

"Can you sense the breach?" he asked Corwin.

"Give me a minute," muttered Corwin.

Darius sat back on his haunches and tried to rein in his impatience. He did not like having to depend on Daphne Quicke. The woman was a mercenary, pure and simple, and her treatment of Miranda was reprehensible. Certainly, Corwin had offered to permanently end her financial worries, but a person who could be bribed by one side could be bribed by the other, and they had absolutely no assurance that Mrs. Quicke truly understood the seriousness of situation.

"There," murmured Corwin, extending his hand into the tunnel. Darius felt the ward ripple briefly and still.

Without a moment's pause, Corwin dropped to his belly and slithered through the low gap. Darius followed after as quickly as he could. Twigs poked and scratched his face and knocked his hat askew. But he came out unscathed on the other side. He could sense the ward behind him now, as solid and menacing as it had been just moments before.

Corwin rooted around in the grass for a moment and came up with Smith's silver disk. "Well-done, Mrs. Quicke." He grinned as he slipped the amulet into his pocket.

"Strange," said a low voice. "That's just what I was thinking."

Corwin and Darius were on their feet in a flash. In front of their startled gazes, a dark-cloaked figure stepped out of a grove of trees. The deep hood and voluminous folds of cloth made it impossible to tell whether it was a man or a woman. The only details that could be seen were a gleam of white teeth and a dangerous flash in dark eyes.

Two gigantic wolves flanked the figure, as patient as trained hounds, their attention fully focused on Darius and Corwin.

The cloaked figure's mouth curled into a cruel smile. "And this is England's final defense, the pride of her hidden powers: two little men, sneaking through hedges in the dark."

"Who are you?" demanded Corwin.

The figure shook its head. "Oh, no. You'll have no name to work on me with. I just came to decide what I should do with you, since I find you here without your so charming Catalyst."

Anger flooded Darius, throwing open the doors inside him. Power surged into his blood and he leapt forward. His limbs and back lengthened, his head dropped, the bones of his face re-formed and, before he had moved a yard, he was man no longer, but a charging stag, his sharp crown of antlers lowered toward the stranger who threatened his own.

The right-hand wolf sprang toward him. Darius did not slow at all, but met the creature head-on. The wolf's belly caught on his powerful antlers and, with a single flick of his head, Darius tossed it aside.

"That was mine!" cried the figure.

As Darius wheeled, the figure raised a gloved hand. Power glowed from the palm. Darius lowered his head, and prepared to charge again.

A human roar split the night and a pale figure launched itself against the cloaked figure, knocking it to the ground. Darius reared up, his forelegs pawing at the darkness, and Corwin rolled, and came up onto his knees, clutching nothing but an empty cloak.

The figure, and the wolves, had vanished.

Corwin stared up at Darius, trembling. Darius felt his anger and focus melt away. His form shortened and softened, becoming human once more. They faced each other, silenced by shock. Then Darius's legs gave way and Corwin dove forward, catching him the instant before he hit the ground. They stayed like that for a moment, chests pressed together, supporting each other.

"Can you stand?" whispered Corwin. Darius tried to get a leg under him, but his knee buckled and fell, and he cursed. Corwin took a deep breath and, bracing himself against the tree trunk, tried to climb to his feet, but he too fell back. "Damn." He coughed.

"She betrayed us," grated Darius. "That witch!"

Corwin said nothing. He just clenched his jaw shut and tried once more to haul himself upright. This time he made it, although the effort left him breathless.

"Come on." He extended his hand to Darius. "We've got to get to Miranda."

B y the time Lady Thayer's servants threw open the doors to Hallowgate's great hall, Miranda was well and truly worried.

She'd managed to sit still while Louise dressed her and fussed over her hair. She wore her most dramatic gown: silver silk covered with emerald green netting and gold embroidery, and tied with a gold-and-emerald sash. With pearls at her throat and white plumes in the emerald band in her hair, Miranda was aware she looked quite fine, but she couldn't bring herself to take any pride in it.

Her attention kept turning outward, straining to sense Corwin and Darius.

But there was nothing.

They should have been here by now. They should have been here hours ago. She'd wanted to go in search of them, but they'd played their cards too well. Lady Thayer seemed to be everywhere. Probably she had a servant watching Miranda's room. Miranda did not know the house well enough to find a back way out without a great deal of wandering around. She had no choice but to wait.

They'll be fine. They are fine. They know what they're doing. She all but chanted the words to herself as she followed Mother down the corridor.

"Don't frown so, Miranda; you'll give yourself a crease," said her mother as they started down the stairs.

Miranda sighed with exasperation. But halfway down she reflected there was something comforting in the fact that Mother hadn't really changed. She made a kind of anchor in a rapidly shifting world, and right now Miranda was glad to have her.

Lady Thayer's glittering ballroom was about half-full when Miranda and her mother arrived. Green and blue hangings lent dramatic color to the ancient carved paneling. Huge vases of fresh flowers stood at regular intervals, filling the room with the scents of midsummer. The musicians poured the lively strains of country tunes down from the gallery.

As usual, Mother had many acquaintances to greet, and many

men who came up to claim dances or to try to steal her away for a bit of private conversation. Usually, this was Miranda's cue to fade discreetly into the background. But not tonight. Tonight, Mother wrapped her arm around Miranda's, and would not let go. This was part of the facade they were maintaining for Lady Thayer, and Miranda affected an expression of weary tolerance as she strolled the room at Mother's side. She needed to make it seem as if she was only just enduring the annoyed glances of the men and the suspicious looks of the women, not to mention the peeping of the girls from behind their feathered fans, something inevitably followed by bouts of whispering and giggles, which Miranda was meant to be able to notice.

By the time they completed a full circuit of the hall, Miranda found herself wondering if her newly discovered powers extended to being able to make time stand still so she could run outside without being observed. Again and again she glanced toward the door, hoping in vain that Corwin or Darius would appear. Each time they didn't, she felt her heart sink a little further. She didn't dare use her thoughts to try to reach them. Darius had been very clear. They had no idea who would be listening. She had nothing but trust and hope, and Miranda was running short of both.

"Look, there's our hostess." Mother tugged on her arm. "And who is that *handsome* young man with her?"

Lady Thayer was indeed making her way through the crowd toward them. At her side walked a tall, lean man who looked to be about Miranda's own age.

"Daphne!" exclaimed Lady Thayer as she reached them. "I've

been looking *everywhere* for you. Mrs. Daphne Quicke, may I present my nephew the Honorable Mr. Robin Summerfields?"

"How do you do, Mr. Summerfields?" Mother dropped her best curtsy. "This is my daughter, Miranda Prosper."

"Very pleased to make your acquaintance, Miss Prosper." Mr. Summerfields bowed low. His light, melodious voice made Miranda look at him more closely. Mr. Summerfields was a striking gentleman; slender and tall with wide-set eyes above high cheekbones. He wore his chestnut hair long enough to brush his collar, but it was refreshingly free of the macassar oil popular with so many of the young blades who affected that style. His coat was a very fine green silk, his linen spotless and his waistcoat figured in silver.

"Mr. Summerfields." Miranda made her own curtsy.

"They are forming up the allemande, Miss Prosper." Mr. Summerfields gestured toward the dance floor. "I would deem it a very great favor if you would agree to dance with me." His full mouth relaxed into an easy smile as he offered her his hand.

Lady Thayer smirked meaningfully at Miranda, and Mother mimicked the expression. The air around Lady Thayer positively crackled. She wanted this, wanted it so badly that Miranda could feel the need beating against her skin. But why?

Miranda swallowed. She could refuse, say she was not dancing. But the whole gathering was watching, and if she turned away now, she might lose her chance to find out anything useful about Lady Thayer, and this convenient nephew she had developed.

"Thank you, Mr. Summerfields." Miranda laid her hand in his. "That would be lovely."

Mr. Summerfields bowed over her hand, and led her to the

foot of the growing line of couples. He placed her across from him. As he did, she saw that his eyes were the exact shade of green as his coat. The effect was arresting, and Miranda became aware she was close to staring.

Then the musicians struck up their first notes. Miranda dipped a curtsy to honor her partner, and the dance began.

Miranda had to give Mr. Summerfields his due; he was an excellent dancer. He was more slender than Corwin, and a little taller, but he moved through the figures with a rare, confident grace. When they came together so he might take her hands to turn her, or lead her to her corner, his grace seemed to pass into her. Her feet grew lighter as they tripped along the line, and the music felt positively infectious. Mr. Summerfields's smile lit his eyes when he came close to her, and it was plain to see he was genuinely enjoying himself.

It seemed almost no time at all before the dance was finished and they were applauding the music.

"Thank you, Mr. Summerfields," said Miranda. "I enjoyed that very much." The words were out of her mouth before she could stop them. What was even more shocking was that they were absolutely true.

"As did I, Miss Prosper." Mr. Summerfields bowed again and glanced toward the musician's gallery. "I believe they are about to play a waltz. I would ask if you might care to dance it with me, if you would not deem that too presumptuous? Or would you prefer to be escorted you back to your mother?"

Miranda's gaze strayed around the ballroom. Still there was no sign of Corwin.

Mr. Summerfields cocked his head. "Or perhaps you are already engaged?"

Guilt nagged at Miranda, and worry. She still desperately wanted to know where Corwin and Darius were. But surely they were all right. They always had been. They were powerful and well schooled in magic, things that she was not. Surely they were delayed only because they had discovered something useful and had to report it into their mysterious captain. The dance with Mr. Summerfields had been most pleasant. Far more pleasant than squiring Mother about the room would be. One more dance would help her pass the time. It would be only a few minutes, and surely Corwin would arrive by the time it ended.

Miranda turned her attention back to Mr. Summerfields. "I am not engaged at present."

"Excellent." Mr. Summerfields's green eyes glowed with pleasure as he took her hand in his. "Then shall we?"

Miranda had heard girls talk of soaring when they waltzed, but she had always dismissed this as pure exaggeration. Now, however, with Mr. Summerfields guiding her about the floor, she understood it absolutely. With him she flew. Movement was perfection. There was no separation between the dance, the music and herself. It was not the sensual heat she'd felt when she'd allowed Corwin to take her in his arms. This was something different, something clearer and purer, but equally intense. It was amazing. It was intoxicating.

When at last the music ended, she could still feel it thrumming across her skin as she gazed breathlessly into Mr. Summerfields's eyes.

"May I compliment you, Miss Prosper, on your excellent dancing?" He smiled and Miranda felt her breath catch in her throat.

"Thank you, Mr. Summerfields." Her breathlessness raised a blush in her cheeks. "But I'm sure it is because I've never had such a fine partner."

"You flatter me," he said modestly but his eyes gleamed. "Come, let me take you back."

He gave her his arm and she took it, but she had to admit her feet lagged a little as they left the dance floor. Already she was wondering if he would ask her to dance again. As they crossed to the edge of the hall, she felt oddly leaden, as if something vital had drained from her.

"There!" exclaimed Mother. "I was afraid you were going to claim her all night, Mr. Summerfields!" The words were delighted, but there was something brittle underneath them that Miranda couldn't understand, although she was aware on some level she should.

"Which would be entirely my pleasure, I assure you." Mr. Summerfields smiled and Mother laughed brightly, and Miranda was aware she should say something, but her mind was suddenly blurry, as if filled with cotton wool.

"I'm sorry." Miranda opened her fan and tried to raise a breeze for herself. "It is rather warm in here, don't you agree?"

"Perhaps a glass of punch?" suggested Mr. Summerfields.

Which made Miranda aware of how very thirsty she was. It was as if she'd been dancing for hours rather than just a few minutes. "Thank you, yes. That would be most welcome." There

was something wrong, something she had forgotten, or had been
warned about. But she couldn't seize on it. The music was playing again. She didn't really want the punch. She wanted to dance.

"I have my orders, then." Mr. Summerfields stood up straight
and clicked his heels in the German style. "And I will return as
soon as may be."

"Well!" Mother opened her own fan. "I can hardly blame
you for feeling overheated, Miranda, my dear. Such a charming
man!" She was glancing around the room, her eyes hard and
calculating. Miranda felt Mother willing her to take the hint, but
she couldn't understand what hint or why. There was something
in the way . . .

"You said he *asked* to be introduced to me?" Miranda tried to
focus on the main doors, and on the wide windows and French
doors, flung open to admit the night breeze from the garden. But
the music was playing again and her attention kept straying to the
dance floor, and as she watched the couples moving through the
figures she was acutely aware of a feeling like envy smoldering
below her thoughts.

*How can I be thinking of dances when there might be real
trouble?* Miranda tried to muster some of the urgency of feeling that she had carried all the way down to the ballroom,
but the music was filling her mind and there was no room to
think of anything else. She would drink her punch, she would
smile, and perhaps he would take her onto the floor just once
more . . .

"Apparently he saw you at Lady Featherstone's party last De-
cember," Mother was saying.

"Strange." Miranda watched Mr. Summerfields's straight green back as he maneuvered through the crowd. "I would have thought I'd remember seeing . . . someone like him."

"Well, I've always told you that you need to pay more attention. Still, my dear, I have to say I am truly proud of the way you're conducting yourself this evening. Every inch the lady." Mother chucked her under the chin and for once Miranda did not feel the urge to flinch. "I always knew something of my lessons must have sunk in somewhere."

"Thank you, Mother," Miranda murmured. *You're laying it on a bit thick, aren't you?*

As she thought this, she saw Mr. Summerfields crossing the ballroom again, bearing with him two cups of ruby red punch. Miranda did not remember seeing the beverage on the buffet, but the sight of it reminded her how intensely thirsty she was. Mr. Summerfields handed one cup to her mother and one to Miranda with a bow and his bright smile.

"And perhaps when you're finished, Miss Prosper, you might favor me with another dance?" he inquired.

"Well! What do you say to that, Miranda?" Mother took a healthy gulp of punch and then held up her cup as if to examine it closer. "This truly is delicious. I must go compliment Lady Thayer." And she sailed away.

Mr. Summerfields smiled indulgently after her. "Your mother is an . . . exceptional woman."

"That she is."

"But perhaps a bit much all at once?" he added softly.

Miranda met his twinkling eyes and gave one very small nod

as she raised the punch cup to her lips. She smelled cherries and something stronger. Brandy?

"Miranda!"

Corwin! Miranda turned, but too fast. The brimming cup of punch sloshed, splashing onto the floor and across her sweeping skirts.

"Clumsy fool!" shouted Mr. Summerfields, and rage twisted his face horribly. Miranda shrank back, but it was gone in an eyeblink, and he was himself again.

Corwin was at her side. "Oh, I am sorry! This is my fault, Miranda. I do apologize. You must get to the retiring room. I'll send Louise to you at once. There may still be something that can be done."

Miranda, get out of here. Get away from him.

Miranda felt the blood drain from her cheeks. "Yes, yes, thank you." She batted ineffectually at her stained skirts. "Mr. Summerfields, if you will excuse me?"

"Of course, Miss Prosper," Mr. Summerfields said, but his attention was entirely on Corwin. "I do hope there is no permanent damage."

"So do I," she said. But neither man was listening to her.

What is it? Where have you been? She sent the thought toward Corwin.

Go!

Miranda bunched her skirts up and shouldered her way through the staring crowd. Mother, Heaven help her! Mother detached herself from Lady Thayer and hurried up behind her just as she entered the old parlor that had been set aside as a lady's retiring room.

"What have you done?" she demanded, seizing Miranda's skirts. "Oh, for Heaven's sake! Couldn't you manage one night, just one night, without making a fiasco of everything?"

"I was startled; the cup was full . . ."

"That is Lady Thayer's *nephew* out there paying court to you, you silly thing!" shouted Mother, not caring that all the maids in the room turned to look. Her cheeks were flushed and her eyes seemed oddly bright. "That is more future than you have the right to expect and you throw it away!"

"It was an accident!" cried Miranda. "A spilled punch! It's not as if I slapped him."

"You permitted that Mr. Rathe to speak with you!"

"Mr. Rathe and I . . . !" began Miranda.

But Mother cut her off. "Stupid girl, he's an Honorable! What is a fur trader's son compared with that!"

Words failed Miranda and she was relieved that at that moment Louise bustled in with a basin and a sponge. Mother clamped her mouth shut and contented herself with tapping her foot impatiently.

"Well?" she demanded of Louise.

Louise sat back on her heels. "I'm sorry, madame; there's nothing I can do. If I didn't know better, I'd swear this was blood . . ."

"For Heaven's sake, get up to your room and change, Miranda, before Mr. Summerfields's attention wanders! I'll do my best to hold him for you, but you must hurry!"

Mother bustled out of the room, and Miranda stared after her. Then she shook herself.

"Come, Louise. I'm going to need your help."

Louise got up and followed obediently as Miranda retreated in haste, clinging to the edge of the great hall and then hurrying up the stairs as fast as her ruined skirts would permit.

What just happened? The question echoed over and over in her mind. They were supposed to be playing their parts, yes, but it was as if Mother had all of a sudden forgotten it was a *game*. If Miranda hadn't known any better, she'd have sworn Mother's outrage was in utter earnest.

Her mind reeling, Miranda opened the door to her room, and there, just out of the threshold, she saw Corwin and Darius.

Twenty-three

"I've changed my mind, Louise." Miranda turned, blocking the entrance to the room. "Please tell my mother I've developed a headache and have decided to lie down."

Louise frowned. "If you're sure, miss?"

"Perfectly."

"Yes, miss." Her maid curtsied, but Miranda could tell she didn't believe a word that was said. It didn't matter, as long as she left.

As soon as Louise started down the hall, Miranda slipped into her room and closed the door.

Corwin was across the room in three strides, seizing her shoulders roughly. "Did you drink any?" His face was gray as ashes and his eyes were frantic.

"What?" cried Miranda.

"The punch he gave you. Did you drink any, any at all? Even one drop?"

"No! I spilled it before I had a chance. Let go of me!"

Corwin did, and ran a shaking hand through his hair. "Thank all the gods," he whispered hoarsely.

"What is the matter?" Miranda adjusted her sleeves. Corwin sank into the chair beside the fire. "What is it?"

It was Darius who answered. "You were with a Fae."

"*What?*" cried Miranda again, staring from one of them to the other. "Who?"

"The man in the green coat, the one who gave you that drink."

"He was a fairy?"

"And if Corwin had been a moment later, you would have been his."

Miranda's blood ran cold. She could sense the utter seriousness in both men and it banished any doubts she might have had. "How?" she whispered.

"The drink. It came from the Fae country. Surely you've heard the old stories, how you should never eat or drink what you're given in fairyland or you'll never be able to leave." Darius swallowed. "That much of the fairy tales is absolutely true."

Miranda's hand flew to her mouth. She remembered thinking she hadn't seen that particular punch on the buffet. It had smelled so appetizing and she'd been so thirsty . . .

And I danced with him and I wanted to keep dancing. Isn't that in the stories too? The fairies dancing their victims to death . . .

"Yes," Darius answered her thought grimly. "Now you begin to understand."

Realization hit Miranda and her stomach knotted so violently that for a moment she thought she'd vomit.

"Mother," she croaked as she wrapped her arms around herself. "She drank the punch. When she was in the retiring room, she was . . . behaving strangely. It was as if she couldn't remember we were just acting a part with Mr. Summerfields."

"Is that what he's calling himself?" snorted Darius. "Hardly subtle."

"Darius, please," whispered Corwin.

He was still shaking. Miranda stared. Darius too seemed unsteady. The golden Sorcerer leaned against the mantel, and despite his gruff voice, he had no color at all in his cheeks.

"What happened to you?" breathed Miranda.

"I'm beginning to suspect your Mr. Summerfields did," said Corwin. "We were met when we crossed the barrier."

"By a Fae," said Darius. "No one else could have been so strong, or vanished so quickly."

"We suspected your mother had betrayed us," continued Corwin. "But if she was already one of their creatures, they would not have needed their potions to enthrall her." He winced.

"We must warn her!" Miranda remembered the fond look in her mother's eyes. She had come so close to understanding the woman. She had begun to hope that perhaps, just perhaps, there might be something more for them besides contempt on one side and disappointment on the other . . . To have Mother endangered because she had agreed to help Miranda . . . Miranda's throat closed tightly and she could barely breathe.

"We can do nothing if you do not help us, Miranda," Darius reminded her harshly. "You must be able to focus."

"Yes, yes, of course. Forgive me."

Miranda stepped between them and took their hands. She closed her eyes and forced herself to concentrate, but it was slow and difficult. The vitality that had come to her so easily before seemed almost beyond reach. She could not banish thoughts of Mr. Summerfields's green eyes as he danced, as he urged her to drink. She saw again the red stain on her mother's mouth as she lowered the punch cup from her lips. In memory it seemed to glow as if in warning. And despite all, Miranda could not forget the way she had flown in the dance, the way the music had thrummed through her blood, and some treacherous, terrible part of her yearned to feel that way again.

The connection shattered and Miranda's hands fell to her sides.

"I'm sorry," she whispered. "I'm sorry. I can't . . . I . . ."

"It will do." He looked to Darius. "As long as we stay together, we can try again . . ."

"There's no time," said Darius flatly. "We must find your mother now."

We don't know what he's doing to her. We don't know where he's taken her. Darius had no need to say anything aloud. Miranda was already imagining the worst.

Corwin caught up her hand again and looked deeply into her eyes. "You're her blood kindred, Miranda. It will be very difficult to hide her from you if you open your mind."

Miranda took a deep breath and held out her other hand for Darius to take. Standing between her lovers, Miranda braced herself once again and she opened her mind.

Mother . . . She stretched her awareness out. *Mother . . .*

A thousand memories: Mother chiding her, Mother in black beside her father's grave, Mother dancing and laughing in the ballroom, the most beautiful woman in the throng, the bitterness of seeing Mother on Malcolm's arm, not caring that her actions broke her daughter's heart in two . . . Mother promising they should talk, Mother's eyes oddly deep as they sat in the carriage waiting to begin this new and most unlikely stage of their relationship . . .

A vision leapt into Miranda's mind. Mother on a man's arm. Awareness filled in like details in a dream; Robin Summerfields walked Mother down the low-ceilinged corridor. Mother was laughing. She felt filled with all the brightness and beauty of the girl she had once been, and Mr. Summerfields smiled at her. That smile filled Miranda with dread, as if she saw Mr. Summerfields holding a sword to her mother's side.

Then Summerfields bent and whispered, "I know a place we can be alone, Daphne. Say you'll come with me."

"I'll come with you," Mother answered immediately. In Miranda's vision, she felt hollow—no, blocked. Isolated. Miranda had felt just that way after leaving the dance floor. She had known something was wrong but could not understand what it was.

Stay with her, Miranda, Darius's voice sounded in her mind. *The way you stayed with Corwin when he was taken.*

Yes.

Miranda reached. This time the vitality, the magic, answered her command. Corwin and Darius were both with her, and she felt their essences meld with hers, reaching inside, shaping and binding. She felt the shining thread stretch out toward her mother, as if unraveling from her hem.

Let's go.

Corwin led them. Miranda couldn't see clearly. Her mind was filled with the vision of her mother tripping lightly down deserted corridors on Mr. Summerfields's arm. It was early. Everyone was at the dance. The house might as well have been empty.

She felt herself being lead forward by Corwin and Darius, felt carpets beneath her feet and walked forward by reflex. Mr. Summerfields drew her mother into a darkly paneled sitting room. It must have belonged to Lord Thayer, decorated as it was with books and stuffed heads. He backed her up against the wall and Mother tipped her head back to receive his kiss, and Miranda's stomach clenched with nausea as she felt a wash of greed and hunger flow from Mr. Summerfields.

Leave her alone!

The thought went out utterly unbidden. Mr. Summerfields's head snapped up, and his smile grew sharp as a knife.

And the vision was gone.

It was like being struck blind, and Miranda cried out, and fell, toppling sideways. Corwin barely caught her before she fell headlong down the stairs.

"Damnation, woman!" cried Darius. "What did you do that for!"

"I'm sorry!" Miranda covered her face with her hands. "Oh, God. I'm so sorry . . ."

"No time for that," Darius snapped. "We need to find that room. Can you do that much?"

"Darius . . ." began Corwin. But Darius ignored him.

"Well?" he demanded.

Miranda lowered her hands. "Yes," she said, but her voice was hollow. "Yes. This way."

She gave no thought to subtlety or maintaining appearances. She just snatched up her skirts and ran. This was not a modern house. The corridors were a maze of turns and little side passages and little stairs up and little stairs down again. But she knew her way now, through the door on the left, down the four stairs to the blue-carpeted hallway, past the main stair, into the east wing.

"Here." Miranda stopped in front of one particular door.

"I'll check farther down," said Darius. "You search here." And he hurried on before either Miranda or Corwin could say anything.

Corwin laid his hand on the door. "Empty," he announced. He tried the knob and the door came open. He and Miranda hurried inside, and he locked it behind them.

The room was dark. Corwin snapped his fingers and a waiting candle flared into life. The sudden light glimmered on the glass eyes of bison and antelopes, and, terribly, the snarling head of a Siberian tiger.

Miranda circled the room, straining, trying to sense something, anything. But there was nothing. Nothing at all. It was as if Mother and Summerfields had vanished off the face of the Earth.

"Not yet, not yet," murmured Corwin. "It's too soon, and they don't have all they need . . ."

A soft scratching sounded at the door, and Miranda knew it was Darius. Corwin let him in.

"Nothing," he reported as Corwin again locked the door. "Damn it! What do we do now?"

Miranda's mind was awhirl with a thousand thoughts, none of them to any purpose.

"Call your maid," said Corwin suddenly.

"What?"

"Your maid. These grand houses are warrens of back passages for the servants. Your maid will have been shown at least some of them by the house staff. Summerfields might have taken your mother down one of those."

"Yes. Yes, of course." Miranda ran to the bellpull and tugged hard. After a long, anxious moment a knock sounded on the door. Darius and Corwin both pressed themselves against the wall so that the door hid them as it opened to reveal the liveried footman.

Miranda drew herself up straight, remembering one never explained oneself to servants. "I need my maid, Louise," she said. "Send her here."

The man bowed and retired. Miranda knotted her fingers together and began to pace. Darius prowled the edges of the room, running his hands over the paneling, stretching his awareness, even as she had stretched hers.

"Where is it?" he muttered. "Where?"

"Stop it, both of you," commanded Corwin. "You're doing no one any good."

Darius clenched his fist against the wall. "There must be *something.*"

But it wasn't just the frustration of inaction Miranda felt from him. It was something more, something worse. It was distrust. Distrust of her mother, and distrust of her.

Her eyes widened and she stared at him. Darius did not flinch. He let her see. He wanted her to see. He wanted her to be aware of the question that flickered through his mind.

If her mother had so easily betrayed them, what might Miranda do when pressed?

"Darius!" snapped Corwin. "That is beneath you!"

There was no chance to say anything else, for good or ill. There came another knock, and Miranda recognized it as Louise's.

Miranda went to the door. The men did not bother to hide themselves, and as Louise dropped her curtsy, her eyes slid sideways to Mr. Rathe and the golden stranger.

Miranda took her maid's hand. "Louise, are you my friend?"

Louise blinked, and her gaze drifted to the men once more. "Always, miss. You know that."

"I have to ask something very important and very strange. I swear when this is over I'll give you a full explanation, but right now there's no time. My mother's been abducted."

"Abducted!" gasped Louise.

Miranda nodded. "By Lady Thayer's nephew, Mr. Summerfields."

"But . . . such a gentleman . . ."

"Oh, come, girl," snapped Darius. "You know perfectly well gentlemen are capable of all sorts of crimes."

Louise lifted her chin. "Maybe I do; maybe I don't. It's not your place to ask what I know."

Darius straightened, his eyes flaring dangerously.

"Louise, we think they went down the servants' stairs some-where. Is there a back passage from this room, do you know?"

Louise's gaze swept the room. "Could be. We were told by the housekeeper to look for the Hallowgate arms. The white rose would open most doors."

"The white rose." Corwin smiled grimly. "They were Yorkists once upon a time, then."

Darius said nothing. He just strode over to the fireplace. A coat of arms had been worked into the center of the decorations on the front of the hearth, its paint now faded and chipped. He pushed the white rose in the lower-right corner of the shield.

Click.

Slowly, a panel beside the hearth slid open. Darius touched it, and winced.

"Cold iron. That's why we couldn't tell where they went."

Louise was drawing breath to ask another question, but Miranda cut her off. "Thank you, Louise. You should go."

For once, her maid failed to obey. "I'd rather not, miss."

"Go. I am well looked after," said Miranda with more certainty than she felt. "I promise I'll tell you all when I get back."

Louise didn't budge. "We were warned not to go through any of the black doors, miss. We were told they were family business . . ."

"I'm sure you were," said Corwin. "Go, Louise. If we don't have your ladies back by midnight, you may summon the police."

For a moment Miranda thought Louise was going to refuse, but the mention of police seemed to convince her that Mr. Rathe took the matter seriously enough. "Yes, sir." Louise curtsied and left them there.

"What will the police be able to do?" asked Miranda as Darius took two more candles from the mantel and lit them.

"Nothing." Corwin took a candle from Darius. "But it will get her out of the house if things go badly for us."

Miranda clamped her mind closed against the fear that boiled up from her heart. She took her candle, hiked up her skirts once more and followed Corwin and Darius through the black iron door.

Twenty-four

"There's iron here too," said Corwin, laying his hand on the rail that ran along the side of the descending stair. "I suppose it's some small consolation that this must have been an extremely uncomfortable walk for our Mr. Summerfields."

Miranda didn't answer. She had no ability to make light of this. It was her fault they were all in this danger. She should have recognized that her sudden affinity for Mr. Summerfields was not right. She had seen and felt enough of magic by now. She knew the touch of it, inside and out.

She had been careless, and now others would pay for it.

Whatever Mother had done, whatever Miranda had felt about her treatment in the past, she did not deserve to be so enchanted and lured away.

The stair was narrow and splintered. The only light came from their flickering candles as they hurried down deeper. The walls were unfinished here, and the rail was furred with cobwebs and dust. Corwin went first, Darius followed after, and Miranda was caught between them, wishing desperately that they would go faster.

"We will find her, Miranda," said Corwin. "With this much iron about, he cannot have spirited her away."

"Why would a Fae bring his captive into an iron cage?" murmured Darius.

Corwin didn't answer out loud, but Miranda felt him closing a kind of door between them, shutting his fear away from her.

The walls around them changed from splintered wood to stone. Miranda could tell by the damp weight of the air that they were descending into the Earth. She should have been glad. It meant she was that much closer to the source from which she drew the power she would need to meet any challenge, but instead her unease intensified. The walls seemed to draw close around her. The darkness gained weight and substance from the damp air and threatened to smother her puny candle.

"Careful. We're at the end of the steps," said Corwin.

He was right. The splintering staircase ended abruptly at a narrow corridor with a flagstone floor. Miranda lifted her candle. The walls were old, undressed stone, but there were narrow rectangles of newer brick set at regular intervals along the whole length of the cramped hall. The pale, flickering light also showed that the edges of the floor sloped toward the center where a narrow channel led to an ancient, rusted drain.

"Gods," whispered Corwin.

"It was a dungeon," muttered Darius, kicking at the channel.

"It still is." Corwin nodded ahead of them. At the end of the hall waited a door. No inviting portal, it was old and scarred and heavily banded by black iron.

Miranda tried to breathe, but the cold air choked her.

"We need to get out of here," said Darius. "It's a trap."

Miranda clung grimly to the end of the rail. "I will not leave my mother here."

Corwin turned to face her. "Miranda, it's what they want," he said. "They took her to draw us down here, among all this iron. We cannot use our magic to any great effect here."

"They took her, or she went with them," muttered Darius.

"Stop it," snapped Miranda. "My mother is many things, but a traitor to her own kind she is not."

Darius just cocked his head and looked at her. The whole strange, sordid scene of Corwin's holding out a bribe to her mother came rushing back.

Is that all you're worried about? Mother's loyalty? Or do you think I'm part of this as well?

Darius's jaw clenched, but he said nothing, and Miranda drew herself up to her full height.

"I am going forward," she told him quietly. "What you choose to do is your own affair."

Gathering up the trailing skirts of her ball gown, Miranda Prosper started down the dungeon corridor.

Damnation. The curse came from both Corwin and Darius. She did not need to look back to know that they both followed her.

The corridor was ice-cold and suffocating. Even her dancing shoes made echoes ring against the walls. It was quite plain now that the bricks filled what had once been doorways. Doorways to cells. Nightmare flashes tugged at the edges of Miranda's mind, of men and women slumped in the dark, too exhausted to even rattle their chains, all of them weeping as the last brick was pushed into place.

No, no. That is fancy only. Nightmare only.

It took forever to reach the end of the corridor. It took no time at all. The door was black and pitted with age and Miranda could see the bolts for the bar that had once been laid across it to prevent anyone from leaving the chamber beyond. Since then, a modern lock had been fitted to the ancient wood, and warm firelight gleamed through the keyhole.

Miranda's nerve faltered and she stopped in front of the door. She was smothered, cut off, alone. Not even the awareness of Corwin and Darius at her back alleviated her sense of isolation. It was as if she had somehow been blinded.

"It's the iron," Corwin told her. "It's affecting us the same way."

"There is no time to stand here. We've come this far. We finish it." Darius reached past her, grabbed the iron handle and heaved the door open.

Light and heat tumbled over her, blinding Miranda momentarily.

"Ah! Miranda, there you are!" cried a man's voice happily. "I was wondering how much longer you'd keep us waiting."

Miranda blinked hard to clear her eyes, and looked into a gaudily decorated Hell.

It was a large room, its low ceiling striped with beams of black oak. A fire blazed cheerily in the hearth. Mother, blessedly unharmed, sat in a comfortable wing-backed chair with

Mr. Summerfields standing sentry on one side and Lord Sinjohn Thayer on the other.

But the rest of the place . . . Miranda's stomach turned over. It was obscene.

Every article of furniture was in the shape of a naked human being. But these were not beautiful nudes in bronze or marble. These were scenes of torture. The floor sconces were women and men with their hands bound cruelly behind their backs and their heads tipped back so candelabras could be thrust into their distended mouths. The low tea table was supported by a man thrusting hard into a woman on her knees, both of them weeping in anguish. The far wall was hidden by a carved screen, its frame made of men and women. They were all blindfolded with their hands chained, and their clothing in shreds. *Things* protruded from their anuses and vaginas while tears ran down their faces and their mouths were open to scream or to plead.

The screen itself held the implements of torture so vividly depicted in the vile statuary; chains and knives, cruel leather gags and blindfolds, rods of rough clay and iron, the sight of which filled Miranda with horror. But none of this was as bad as the bare bedframe with its dangling chains and stained and splintered planks.

"Mr. Summerfields was growing quite impatient waiting for you," Mother said, clearly and terribly oblivious to the sort of room she occupied. "Weren't you, dear Mr. Summerfields?" She smiled up at the fair man, the Fae creature.

"That I was," Mr. Summerfields replied. "I was hoping to beg one more dance from you, Miranda."

His voice caressed her skin and Miranda shivered. Despite

the horror around her, her mind flashed back to the dance floor, to the sensation of being borne aloft on the music, the pure, effortless freedom . . .

Miranda!

Corwin's voice rang in her mind as clear as a bell. The other memory shattered and Miranda could see again.

"Ah, the gallant Mr. Rathe." Lord Thayer sauntered forward to one of the vile candleholders. Quite deliberately he reached out and stroked the carved breast. "I've so been looking forward to meeting you personally. You and your friend." The glance Thayer cast at Darius was slow and so filled with unmistakable lascivious meaning that Miranda felt her skin crawl.

"How long have you been an agent for the Fae, Thayer?" inquired Corwin calmly.

"Ah, well that's rather a long story." Thayer folded his arms and leaned against the room's central pillar. "My family served Their Glorious Majesties going back seven generations, right to Bastard Elizabeth's time. But my father, well, he was the first in all that time to fail in his duty."

"To remember he was human and owed his duty to humanity, you mean," growled Darius.

Thayer ignored him. "So, it came to me to reestablish my family's allegiances with Their Glorious Majesties. And now that you are here, I will have completed my task."

"What task, Thayer?" said Corwin, keeping his voice mild. "How many Catalysts did she demand from you?"

"Thirteen," he answered without hesitation. "For the amusement and glory of her court. Miss Prosper here is the last."

"I will die before I go with you," said Miranda grimly.

"Miranda!" cried her mother. "Such ingratitude!"

Miranda stared at her. Mother looked back, her posture the same queenly demeanor Miranda had known all her life. But there was something wrong with her eyes, something distracted, as if she were not looking at quite the same scene the rest of them were.

"It will not come to that, I think," said Mr. Summerfields calmly. "Daphne, my dear, I have dropped my ring into the fire. Would you be so kind as to get it for me?"

"Of course, Mr. Summerfields." Mother at once slipped to her knees and reached her hand, unhesitating, toward the flames.

"Stop!" screamed Miranda.

"Sorry, Daphne; here it is," said Mr. Summerfields calmly.

"Oh." Mother stood and brushed her skirts down. "I don't wish to criticize, Mr. Summerfields, but you should be more careful."

"You are quite right. In future I shall be." Summerfields kissed Mother's hand so that she beamed and settled back into her chair, gazing up at him as if he were the most splendid thing in the whole of the world.

Miranda felt as if she were going to be sick.

"You begin to understand, don't you, Miranda?" Lord Thayer smiled. "Sir Robin here could command your mother to do anything. Anything at all." He ran his hand over the statue's unyielding breast again to emphasize his point. "And she will do it without hesitation, whether it is to lay herself down to be fucked by myself until I tire of her, or to take one of my knives and cut her own throat."

Miranda held rigidly on to her composure. She could not let

these vile creatures see any more of her fear or outrage. "What do you want?" she demanded coldly.

"I thought I had made that plain enough," said Thayer. "I want the three of you. Your three lives for hers, Miranda." He smiled. "Thirteen Catalysts and two great enemies. Their Majesties will reward me well."

"You may depend on it." Mr. Summerfields smiled.

"You're taking the word of a Fae knight?" Darius shook his head. "Thayer, you're a bigger fool than I thought."

"You understand nothing," snapped Thayer. "What do you know of their glory, their purity? If you understood the least thing, you would know you are not fit to kiss the foot of the lowest of them, and yet you stand here defying . . . !"

"Enough, Thayer," said Summerfields coolly before he turned his green eyes on Miranda. "Well, Miss Prosper, which shall it be? Your life, or your mother's? Choose carefully." He laid his hand on Mother's shoulder, and she patted him indulgently. "It need not be unpleasant, you know," he went on. "I can make your submission very good for you, as you already know."

She felt it again, that pure, freeing joy. It was stronger now, creating an ache of happiness inside her. This was not passion or lust, nothing she would have to dare or defy or regret. It was simple, innocent joy, as if all bad things had fallen away, and she was made new.

"Come to me, Miranda," murmured Mr. Summerfields. "Take my hand."

Miranda took two steps forward, wavered, and then took another.

"Yes, that's right." His voice sounded so sweet. "Closer, Miranda."

A roar split the room. The light of magic flared high and hard. Miranda felt Darius's and Corwin's powers lash out. A sheet of blue-tinged flame leapt up around Lord Thayer and Mr. Summerfields.

"Don't be ridiculous," snapped Thayer.

And Miranda felt new power, straight from the Earth, straight from the air. It ran through Thayer and the flames were doused in an instant. Before Corwin or Darius could rally, Thayer sent out another bolt. It struck the Sorcerers like an iron bar so they flew backward, and slammed against the wall, sliding stunned to the floor.

All at once Miranda understood the truth about the terrible statues around her. She knew how Lord Thayer—doubtlessly helped by the power of Mr. Summerfields—had been able to conceal the Catalysts, and now was able to draw on them as they stood helpless all around him.

Thayer saw realization dawn on her, and smiled cold and cruel.

"The fate of the other Catalysts is not your concern, Miranda," said Mr. Summerfields. "Her Glorious Majesty has other uses for your strength. Come here."

Miranda stood alone. She stared at Corwin and Darius, collapsed doll-like and drained against the wall. She stared at Mother, made witless, sitting calmly beside Summerfields.

Miranda.

Corwin's thought was so soft at first, Miranda assumed she imagined the touch of it.

Remember that first night. Remember all that happened. All of it.

"Silence!" barked Thayer. Power again shot through the room. Corwin's whole body arched as the pain took him and he collapsed again. A thin thread of blood trickled out of the corner of his mouth. Darius gasped and lifted his arm, only to fall back a moment later.

"You can stop this anytime," said Mr. Summerfields to Miranda. "Her Majesty does not need them. It's you she wants." His voice grew soft. "It's you *I* want."

It felt so good, the touch of his voice. So close to the pure freedom she'd felt that first night, when she'd been filled with the power she'd unwittingly stolen from Corwin.

Remember that first night. Remember all that happened.

Mr. Summerfields held out his hand. "You can save them, and you can have all you want. Come now, Miranda."

Miranda moved forward. One step. Two.

"Stop, Miranda!" cried Darius harshly. "Don't!"

Three. She laid her hand in Mr. Summerfields's.

"Good, Miranda," he breathed. "Very good."

The joy flooded her. Now, touching him, she recognized it for what it was. It was the pure vitality of magical power, such as she drew from the Earth. But this came from Mr. Summerfields himself, and he poured it freely into her, and without anywhere to channel it, it filled her with its potential and its terrible beauty.

I remember. I remember everything.

With all the strength she possessed, Miranda forced herself to open wide to the Fae knight, and to the Earth; the infinite, vital Earth from which her own power sprang, and to which this power could be made to return.

"What . . ." began Summerfields. He began to pull away, but Miranda gripped his hand tightly. "What are you doing?"

Miranda was fully open to Summerfields now, drawing down the terrible, beautiful flood of his magic. She drank it down greedily, reveling in the power as it flowed into her, and through her, down into the stone, down into the Earth, which was not troubled at all. She stretched out her free hand, and her delirious mind and the power flowed also into Darius, and into Corwin.

Summerfields struggled against her, but he was a weak thing, a puny thing; a creature made of dreams and illusion. She was a sturdy human woman and he had opened himself to her. She had hold of him now and she could drink and drink the heady nectar of his power and never be full.

"Stop!" Miranda heard Thayer roar. Distantly, she saw him leap toward her.

But Darius was there, grappling with the smaller, older man. Power crackled and sang between them. She saw Corwin leap past them and snatch a set of chains from out of the terrible collection. He dove in, crying out in pain as he drove his hands into the glowing barrier of Thayer's power, to wrap the iron around Thayer's waist. The light vanished; the buffeting power vanished. Thayer's head fell back as he howled.

Through it all Miranda drank. Now Summerfields screamed and in front of her dazzled eyes, his form began to dwindle and darken. The handsome golden man was gone. His hand slipped from hers, as he toppled to the stones. Now there was only a tiny pale thing with twiglike limbs huddled on the floor at her feet.

Then there was nothing at all.

The power shut off so abruptly Miranda staggered and nearly fell, but Darius's strong arms caught her. He held her so close she could feel the rapid drumming of his heart. In her chair by the fire, Mother blinked, shook her head, looked around her and began to scream.

Miranda broke from Darius's embrace and ran forward.

"It's all right!" she cried, wrapping her arms around her mother's shoulders, blocking her line of sight with her body. "It's over. It's all right."

As if her words had been some kind of signal, Miranda heard the pounding of boots from the hallway outside. Corwin lurched to his feet from his position beside the collapsed Lord Thayer and opened the door.

A crowd of people charged into the room, led by a small, rotund, bald man in a black coat and white stockings and trailed, improbably, by Louise.

The black-coated man drew himself up and raised a hand. The crowd with him halted, panting and staring about themselves.

"Mr. Rathe?" the man said in a stately, educated voice. "Mr. Marlowe? Would you care to explain why you no longer seem to be in need of rescue?"

Twenty-five

The rest of the night passed in a blur. Miranda and her mother were escorted out into the gardens where they shivered on stone benches surrounded by a crowd of serious men whom Miranda gradually understood to be a combination of military officers and Bow Street Runners, very far off their usual patch. Hallowgate was being turned upside down, very much over the loud protestations of the guests. The black-coated man, whose name seemed to be Smith, paid no attention to any of them. From the men's talk, she gathered Smith was searching for Lady Thayer, and Lady Thayer was nowhere to be found.

None of this touched Miranda much. She could not shake the cold that filled her, and she could not shake the memory of what she had done. She had not just failed in her duty; she had killed a . . . a . . . fairy. An enemy to be sure, and she had done it to save Corwin and Darius and Mother. She could live with that. But it had felt so good. It had felt like Heaven.

That, she would never be rid of.

And worse—oh, so much worse—she knew some dark, damned part of herself would always long to feel the sweet sensation of drinking living magic down once more.

They said power corrupted. It was true. And when corruption felt like blessing, how could that urge fail to return?

So when Corwin and Darius finally emerged from the crowd, and Corwin knelt beside her, Miranda turned from him. How could she look at him, knowing what she was and what she truly longed for?

"Miranda . . ." he began.

She shook her head. "I want to go home," she said. "You will have someone take us home, please."

Corwin stood. She was aware of him breathing heavily, of his hands dangling loose at his sides. She was aware of Darius coming up beside him, of him reaching for her. She drew away, huddling closer to Mother, and he let his hand fall.

"As you wish," breathed Corwin.

And that had been that. Two of the Bow Street Runners had escorted them back to Mother's house, and there they had remained. London was deserted and quiet. They had no callers, no visitors of any kind. They moved through the rooms almost like sleepwalkers, going through the mechanics of living, but at a remove. Days passed behind a shield of mental isolation Miranda found herself afraid to break.

But even so, news filtered into them that Lord Thayer had been found guilty of smuggling, spying and white slavery. At first, Miranda thought it was nonsense. But then she realized it was not, because that was what he had been doing, but with the Fae rather than with the French, as the accusations read. In idle moments, Miranda imagined the shocked talk buzzing around the summer ballrooms at this development, but never for long. She seemed to lack the strength for such musings.

Miranda was not surprised that Mother began to recover before she did. Daphne Quicke's restless nature would not allow her to remain cut off from the world for very long. Mother was soon leaving the house to stroll through the summer parks, or to shop in the high street, although Miranda noticed no parcels were ever delivered after these trips.

They still had no money, and Miranda had heard nothing from Corwin or Darius. That was good. She wanted nothing to do with them. If they were gone, she would not know the touch of magic again. She would not be tempted to drink too deep, to drain them dry for her unnatural pleasures.

So June faded into July, and July began to shade into sultry August. Mother discovered she had a certain notoriety, having been brought out of Lord Thayer's "secret den," and concocted a story that went well with the public charges. Or maybe it was what she actually believed. Whichever it was, Mother began to be invited out to the country to tell her tales to the fascinated, horrified and extremely diverted ladies. At first she pressed Miranda to come with her. But Miranda just shook her head. To show she was not entirely the same as she had been, Daphne Quicke just laid her hand on her daughter's shoulder, and left her alone.

It was while Mother was away on one of these visits that a

knock came at the door. Miranda was in the sitting room staring at the garden and did not bother to stir herself. But a moment later, Louise pushed open the sitting room door to admit a tall man in red and gold livery with a powered and curled wig on his head.

The man bowed and held out a folded letter sealed in red wax. "From Her Royal Highness, Princess Augusta Sophia," he announced.

Princess Augusta Sophia! With numb fingers, Miranda took the heavy envelope, broke the seal and opened the paper. The handwriting underneath was flawless but it took a moment for Miranda to be able to make out the words, she was so shaken. Gradually it sank in that she held in her hands a royal summons from one of the reclusive princesses, a daughter of King George III, who was currently confined to his summer palace for his "health" while his son ruled in splendor and debauchery in his stead. The letter announced that she, Miranda Prosper, was expected at Buckingham House at four of the clock on the day mentioned.

It was signed *HRH The Princess Augusta Sophia.*

The day mentioned was today.

Today! Miranda stared up at the liveried servant.

"I am to wait for an answer, ma'am," he informed her stiffly.

"Yes, of course." Miranda moved to her writing desk to take out paper and ink, but her hands were shaking so she could barely hold the quill.

At last she was able to scrape out a reply, fold it and seal it, and hand it to the footman, who received it with another perfect bow.

"I am charged to inform ma'am that this visit is strictly private. A carriage will be sent at three of the clock." He bowed once more and made his exit, leaving Miranda staring at Louise.

"What does it mean, Miss Miranda?" cried her maid.

"I don't know, Louise," whispered Miranda. "I don't know."

Three of the clock found Miranda dressed in her best white gown and pearls, ready and waiting when the unadorned carriage arrived. It was a well-sprung and well-appointed conveyance and Miranda had what was probably the most comfortable ride of her life. They crossed London to the very edges of the great royal parklands and the square brick edifice that was Buckingham House. Once inside the great doors, the footman turned her over to a thin, no-nonsense woman dressed in sober black and white. She introduced herself to Miranda as Lady Winslow, chief lady-in-waiting to the Princess Augusta Sophia, but had nothing else to say at all as she led Miranda through a dizzying array of corridors and up a host of broad staircases to a door, which another footman opened, and which led into a sitting room filled with glass cases of delicately painted china and fans.

An aging woman with a careworn face sat beside a fire, despite the fact that it was August and sweltering in the little room. She wore the heavy skirts and low-cut bodice of another era and the cap on her head made her look oddly like a market wife. She was not alone, however. The black-coated man, the one called Smith, stood behind her chair, eyeing Miranda calmly as she entered.

"Miss Miranda Prosper," announced Lady Winslow. Miranda, who had never been presented at court and had never expected to be, dropped into the deepest curtsy she had ever made.

"Thank you, Lady Winslow," said Princess Augusta Sophia. "You may go. Stand up, Miss Prosper. I'd like a look at you."

Miranda stood, but kept her gaze on the rose-patterned carpet, folding her hands in front of her.

"Yes, yes," she murmured. "There's spirit there, despite all. You may sit."

"Thank you, Your Highness." Miranda bobbed another curtsy, wondered if that was the right thing to do, and all but groped for the little Queen Anne chair behind her so she could sit.

"I understand we are in your debt, Miss Prosper," said the princess crisply. "You helped unearth a traitor who has eluded capture for many years, and you destroyed a powerful enemy agent."

"I . . . did what I had to, Your Highness."

"As do we all," replied the princess wearily. "Nonetheless, I am grateful for your service and you will not find me ungenerous. As an acting agent of the crown, you are entitled to four hundred pounds a year. Mr. Smith will see to it."

Miranda's head jerked up. "Acting agent of the crown . . . ma'am?"

"Yes," replied the princess. "As of today, you may consider yourself in the charge and employ of Mr. Smith." She waved at the bald man in his plain black coat.

"But . . . but . . ." began Miranda.

"This is not a request, Miss Prosper," snapped Princess Augusta Sophia. "You know full well what a deadly serious matter we are involved in."

"Yes, Your Highness." Miranda dropped her gaze again.

"It has been the fate of the rulers of this island from time to time to have to repel invasion both open and subtle." The princess's voice grew hard. "Unfortunately, ours is not an unbroken line, and neither are the lines of command or defense. My father's . . . illness . . . helped create a breach that has allowed the enemy to infiltrate once more. My brother, who should have taken charge, is interested in nothing beyond his pleasures. All his efforts are directed toward grabbing the throne while our father yet lives so he can pay for his palaces and his mistress. My sisters have enlightened themselves to the point where they cannot see what is plainly before them. So it is left to me to do what can be done. I require all hands to the defense of our island and our people."

The princess's words were so strong and so steady, Miranda felt shaken at her own selfishness. Mired in her fear and misery, she had allowed herself to lose sight of the greater stakes being fought for.

"Yes, Your Highness." Miranda forced some strength into her voice.

"We are at a low ebb now," the princess went on. "But it will not always be the case. By his arts, Mr. Smith has uncovered a prophecy that gives us great cause for hope." Miranda risked a glance up, and saw Mr. Smith nod. "A new queen will soon take the throne, the greatest our land has yet seen. She will lead a decisive battle against the Fae court, possibly the final battle. We must hold the line for her coming. I trust, Miss Prosper, we may count on you?"

Miranda stood, and dropped into another curtsy. "You have my word, Your Highness."

The princess reached out and touched her shoulder, in blessing and in acceptance of her service. "Thank you, Miss Prosper."

A t the princess's command, Mr. Smith was to escort her home. Miranda sat awkwardly in the carriage with the little man. She had no idea what to say.

But Mr. Smith did. "They are fine."

"I beg your pardon?"

"Mr. Rathe and Mr. Marlowe. They are fine. They have been helping chase down the last of Lord Thayer's confederates, and, of course, hunting for Lady Thayer."

The memory of that terrible night came flooding back and Miranda's mouth went dry. "Have they found her?" she croaked.

"Unfortunately, no. We think she may have escaped abroad." Smith looked grimly out the window. "However, should that be the case, certain measures are being set in place to make it . . . difficult for her to enter the country again." He paused and then said, "You will not be required to work with them if you do not wish to."

Miranda almost begged his pardon again, but she realized quickly what he meant. He meant she would not be required to work with Corwin and Darius.

"Thank you," she murmured.

"Although I will not order it, I wish you would consider the matter carefully," he went on. "First of all, you are clearly a powerful and effective grouping of the sort we are in desperate need of. Secondly, agents pining themselves sick for love are of a limited value to me."

Miranda started at this. Mr. Smith regarded her mildly. "Yes," he said. "They are and have been. They hide it badly, and make themselves so generally unpleasant that if you do not take them back soon, I shall be forced to exile them to the north of Scotland."

Miranda's hands began to tremble. She was glad she was sitting, because all the strength had drained out of her in an instant. "I can't," she whispered.

Mr. Smith's sigh was nothing short of exasperated. "Really, Miss Prosper. After all I have seen and heard of you, I did not expect to find you a coward."

The words stung, but Miranda had no answer and she and Mr. Smith rode on in silence. At last, the carriage dropped her off at the door of her house, and Louise let her inside. Miranda drifted into the empty sitting room and stood at the window, staring out at the garden and the street beyond.

I did not expect to find you a coward. Mr. Smith's words echoed in her memory.

Is that it? Cowardice? No. I am a danger. I will hurt them. I will kill them and I will glory in it.

But Corwin and Darius didn't know this. They hadn't shared what had happened to her; they'd only seen her defeat the Fae knight. Mr. Smith was right about this much: Corwin and Dar-ius deserved an explanation so they could forget her and move on. They had each other, after all; they would soon heal from whatever wounds she had dealt them.

Yes. It will be better that way. Miranda straightened her shoulders and tried to ignore the fact that her heart was breaking.

Corwin's house was even more imposing the second time than it had been the first, not in the least because the sight of it reminded Miranda of all that had passed inside. For a day and a night she had been happy. More than happy. She had been free. For the first time in her adult life, she had not had to guard her words or her actions. She could be wholly herself with two men who would neither judge nor condemn.

Two men who loved her, and whom she loved.

It was a long time before Miranda could make herself climb the steps and ring the bell.

The span of time she waited after that was probably quite brief. Nonetheless it gave her plenty of time to regret coming, and to wonder how quickly she could retreat back to the waiting carriage. But before she could do more than edge away, Jacobs opened the door.

"Good evening, Miss Prosper." He stood back to admit her. Miranda stepped into the foyer. The setting sun shone through the stained glass fanlight, spreading colored patterns across the marble floor.

"Good evening, Jacobs. Is Mr. Rathe at home?"

"Not at present, miss." Relief flooded Miranda. She did not have to face them today. She could go. "But I expect him and Mr. Marlowe shortly," the butler went on. "Would you care to wait?"

Miranda hesitated, but then replied, "Yes, thank you." *Get it done. Then you never have to come back. Then you can mourn what might have been and begin again.*

Jacobs led her up the stairs and into Corwin's magnificent library. Miranda's eyes prickled as the scent of paper and leather bindings again enveloped her.

Miranda drifted into the middle of the room, and this time it was Jacobs who hesitated. "Is there anything you'd care for, miss? Some tea, perhaps?"

"Thank you, Jacobs. That would be most welcome."

"Very good, miss. And, miss . . ."

"Yes?" she said without turning around.

"I'm glad to see you have returned. I believe the master has missed you very much."

Miranda was thankful she had kept her back to him. It would not do to let the man see the tears that welled up in her eyes. "You may go, Jacobs."

"Yes, miss."

When she heard the door close, Miranda collapsed into the nearest chair and hid her face in her hands. *I never should have come back here.* She had thought she could stand to see the room. She had even fancied that it might even do her good to visit the place this last time so she could say farewell. But the memories were too strong for her. It was not possible to look about and not be reminded of the passion she had shared with Corwin and Darius here. The touch of their hands and their mouths, the glory of their heated bodies against hers, and under her hands, and their magnificent cocks inside her pussy, inside her mouth. Paradise for a few short hours. And now she was like Eve, ashamed of her nakedness and weakness, and Paradise was closed to her.

The sound of boots thundering up the stairs made her start to her feet. In the next heartbeat the door burst open and Corwin and Darius both dashed inside.

"Miranda!"

She was in Corwin's arms before she could protest and he was kissing her and crushing her to him, and she melted. She could not resist the touch of his mouth and she opened hers at once so he could slide his tongue inside, caressing, tasting, devouring.

Then Darius spun her into his arms and captured her mouth in his. His body was so hard, so hot, as he pulled her to him, grinding his hips against hers while he rained kisses down on her mouth and throat. How had she stayed away so long? How had she forgotten the fire these two men lit in her body and her soul?

But even as she thought it, she remembered the Fae knight, and how it had felt to drink away his sustaining magic, how she had watched him dwindle and die, and felt nothing but pleasure.

She remembered how Darius had thought her mother had betrayed her humanity for gain, and how he had wondered if Miranda was a traitor not just to the nation but the whole world.

Miranda threw herself backward, breaking Darius's embrace. "I'm sorry." She stumbled backward. "I'm sorry!"

"No, I understand." Darius's hands fell to his sides. "I promised to stand by you, and then I failed you."

Miranda stared. Corwin walked up to Darius and laid his hand on the other man's shoulder. "It was no one's fault. We were all afraid and filled with suspicion."

Darius lifted his head, his eyes filled with hope and sorrow. "Could you forgive me, Miranda?"

Miranda had thought her heart could not break any more. But the sight of Darius pleading for understanding undid her completely. "Of course I forgive you," she whispered.

"There! You see!" Corwin slapped Darius's shoulder. "I've been telling you all these weeks! A little faith in our Miranda was all that was needed—"

"No," she whispered. "No. I'm not your Miranda."

Corwin stopped, his mouth frozen in a smile from which the mirth drained rapidly.

"I came to say farewell," she went on. "I cannot see you . . . I cannot be with you anymore. But you deserved to hear that directly. I'm sorry. I'm so sorry."

Corwin reeled backward, and it was only Darius's hand on his back that steadied him. "Why, Miranda?" Darius croaked. "What have we done?"

"It's not you!" she cried. "It's me! It's what I am!"

"You are Miranda Prosper," said Corwin. "You are our beloved."

Beloved. Oh, God help her, how sweet that word sounded

coming from him! "I am a monster! I kill with my touch and I delight in it! I almost betrayed everything, everyone, because being with Mr. Summerfields felt so good that I couldn't even think of anything else!" Tears flowed freely down her cheeks as the words tumbled out of her. "I am a disgusting, licentious creature! I will not risk your lives with my presence!"

"Gods all," whispered Corwin. "Miranda, you cannot truly believe this."

"What else is there to believe?" she demanded. "I know what I am! I know it! I wish I had died in that house! I—"

But before she could say anything more, Darius strode across the room and gripped her shoulders. "Stop this!" he roared.

Stunned, Miranda stared up at him.

"Stop this," he repeated, more softly but no less sternly. "By all the gods, if I had known this was festering inside you, I never would have left you alone."

"Don't touch me, Darius," she whispered.

"I will not let you go until you have heard me." His blue eyes bored into hers, and she felt his will pressing against the edges of her mind, demanding entry.

"No. Please." She closed her eyes. "It's hard enough as it is."

"Miranda Prosper, look at me!" he barked.

"Look at us."

Corwin was beside Darius, and she felt his second warmth against her skin, and his softer, subtler, but no less persistent presence against her mind.

"Look deep, Miranda," Corwin urged. "See what we have seen."

She was so exhausted, so miserable, she could not hold her own against them. Slowly, her mind began to yield to their pressure.

And she saw.

She saw herself. She saw the chamber of horrors she had led them into. She saw Robin Summerfields the Fae knight and Lord Thayer the traitor. She felt the Sorcerer's twinned weakness and their fear that they had failed. She saw herself walking forward, and, in reliving the ordeal from their point of view, saw herself as the shield between them and death. She drank in the knight's power. She bought Corwin and Darius time to struggle to their feet. She fed them the power they needed to strike back and strike hard.

She felt their triumph, felt their gratitude, felt their grim satisfaction at the death of their enemy.

You did what was needful, Miranda. No more. You have been wounded, love, but wounds heal.

But . . .

You did what was needful, and no more. You could have turned on Thayer then, as flush with power as you were. You could have turned on us. But you didn't. You stopped when the fight was over. You thought to bring your mother out of that dreadful place, and to protect us, although no danger truly existed. Are these the actions of a monster?

But I almost gave in. The Fae, he almost took me . . .

Almost. Almost. Miranda, Corwin's hand was holding hers, and she felt his warmth envelop her soul. *We have both seen strong men fall to the glamour that the Fae project, Catalysts and Sorcerers alike. It is what they do, Miranda. That pleasure, that beauty, is their ultimate weapon.*

Miranda felt her spirit tremble. *How can you stand against it?*

Love. Their voices in unison rang in her mind, in her soul. *Human love with all its passion and its frailty, its earthy lust and its high-flown spirit. No illusion of perfection can stand against that.*

"I love you, Miranda," whispered Corwin.

"I love you, Miranda," said Darius.

Miranda's eyes opened. They stood with her, their arms around her. She could feel their breath, inhale their scents, feel their hearts beating. She looked into their eyes, into Corwin's warm brown and Darius's piercing blue. Midnight and dawnlight, they were the two halves of a great whole. One love joyous and open, one complex and hard, but no less true. Both offered to her. Both accepting her, trusting her, desiring her.

Loving her.

"I love you," she breathed. "I love you!" she cried.

"Miranda!" Corwin swept her into his arms, spinning them both around and laughing.

"I love you!" she cried again because it felt so magnificent to say it aloud. "I love you!"

And all at once she was on her feet again and staring into Corwin's dark eyes. "And I you, Miranda Prosper," he said.

His mouth fell upon hers and this time Miranda did not hesitate at all. She opened wide to admit his tongue, sliding her own along it, invading his mouth deeply, reveling in the heat she found there. Corwin leaned her backward, one hand on the small of her back, the other gripping her ass possessively, sensuously.

Darius's hands reached up for her, and Corwin lowered her down into her other lover's arms. She rolled over, stretching herself full length against his taut and ready body. It was so delicious to rub her whole self against him as she kissed him, hot and openly. His cock was already gorgeously erect, as hard as she was wet, and the realization made her moan.

Above them Corwin chuckled, and she felt his hands on her back. But no magic removed her clothing. There were only Corwin's clever fingers at her hooks and laces, slowly undoing her, while Darius's commanding hands spread her legs. He caressed her thighs and gripped her ass so her pussy slid right against the ridge of his swollen cock. It was wonderful. It was what she had been longing for. It was agony, because it was not nearly enough to answer the passion raging through her.

"Oh, please," she whispered. She could not stand that there was so much cloth between them. She needed their skin against hers. Needed it now before she burst into flame. "Corwin, hurry!"

"Now, why would I do that?" Corwin planted a teasing kiss on the back of her neck. "When it is so lovely to hear you beg like this?" He knelt behind her close enough that she could feel his cock swelling beneath his breeches. He reached beneath her loosened dress, cupping both her breasts through her chemise. His fingers sought her hardened nipples and began to pinch and to play. At the same time, Darius gripped her thighs and thrust his hips up against her, forcing her to rub him, to ride him. His heated palms ran up her naked thighs until his thumbs found her dripping pussy and her swollen, throbbing clit.

"Yes!" cried Miranda as he stroked her there. "Oh, yes!"

"Yes what, Miranda?" asked Corwin as he massaged her breasts, plumping and stroking in ceaseless, maddening rhythm. "Yes what?" He pressed his erection hard against her ass, settling her more firmly against Darius's questing fingers.

"Yes, make me come!" she cried. "Please make me come!"

"Oh, yes." He rolled her nipples between his fingers. Just as Darius pressed deep into her slit, arcing underneath her, Corwin dragged one hand swiftly down her body until it too found her pussy and her clit, and they were both stroking her there, both teasing her clit, both pressing their cocks against her.

"Ah!" she cried out wordlessly as she came, rocking and bucking against their hands and their hard bodies and they laughed and stroked her and called her name.

"Yes, Miranda, yes!"

"Come for us! Come hard, Miranda!"

And she laughed and wept as her shudders played themselves out so deliciously until she collapsed back against Corwin.

"That's it, Miranda," murmured Darius as he stroked her thighs. "That's what we like to see."

"You are so beautiful when you come." Corwin kissed her mouth. "And there are so very many pleasures yet to teach you."

"Oh, yes." Darius's fingers lazily stroked her loose, heated pussy.

"I want you," she murmured, although she lacked the strength to do anything about it. As much as she wanted them naked, as much as she wanted their cocks, it felt so good to be held this way with their hands wandering over her body.

"Do you know what I want, Miranda?" murmured Corwin. "Do you know what I have wanted from the first?"

"What?"

"I want to be in your ass with Darius in your pussy."

Surprise stiffened Miranda for an instant. "Both of you?"

"Oh, yes," said Darius, stroking her folds. "Would you like that, Miranda?"

Miranda tried to imagine it, both of their hard cocks, one in her pussy and one . . . *back there*, and imagination failed. "Is that even *possible*?"

"It is." Corwin nibbled her ear. "If the men are willing and the lady is just a little patient."

A vision seared in her and she couldn't tell whether it came from Darius or Corwin: of their cocks filling her together, their rhythms merging as they fucked her and each felt the heated passion of the other thrusting hard within her.

"Oh!" She arced her back, all languor burned away by fresh desire. "Oh, yes!"

Darius pulled her down again, and again plundered her mouth while Corwin pulled down her dress and chemise, leaving her naked except for shoes and stockings. He gripped her ass, massaging and playing just as he had with her breasts, and this felt even better, because it rolled her pussy against Darius's erection. Darius stroked her back and crushed her breasts against his chest. Magic prickled across them, and he was naked. The sudden sensation of his hot, rigid cock against her pussy made her gasp and moan. Corwin chuckled deep in his throat and pressed his hand against her soaked pussy, stoking her labia and lifting Darius's tight balls so they rubbed against her.

"Ah, God, yes!" groaned Darius as Corwin stroked them both together. "That's good!"

"Not as good as it will be." Corwin pushed Miranda up and forward, and reached between her and Darius, to grasp Darius's swollen cock. He stroked Darius, and the same motion rubbed Miranda's pulsing clit, making her grind down with her hips and kiss Darius deep and hard. Darius gripped her head, holding her in place as he took control of the kiss. And while his tongue plunged into her, Corwin's hands worked, opening her folds, guiding Darius's hot, hard cock inside her.

"There," Corwin whispered, circling Miranda's hips with his hands, settling her farther down onto Darius's cock. "Is he deep, Miranda? Is it good?"

But she couldn't answer, because Darius would not release her mouth. He continued to kiss her, to stroke and fuck her mouth with his tongue. Miranda could only sigh and writhe against him, delighting in how his cock stroked her sheath when she moved.

"I'll take that as a yes." Corwin massaged her ass slowly, moving her up and down on Darius's hard, eager cock. Pleasure melted Miranda's body and carried away all volition. She could do nothing but feel, Darius's body and Corwin's hands.

Corwin's finger pressed against her folds, then drew itself up the split to rest against her second tight, sensitive entrance. Slowly he pressed a damp finger inside, pressed and breached and probed, stretching her wider than she would have believed possible. It hurt, it burned, but oh, it was sweet pain, especially as Darius gripped her thighs, holding her in place for his cock and Corwin's fingers. He eased a second finger inside her, pressing her so tightly against Darius's cock she cried out with the delight of it. Darius moaned and writhed beneath her. "Now, Corwin," he begged. "Now."

"Hold her tightly, Darius," murmured Corwin. "Miranda, press outward as I press in."

Miranda felt the blunt tip of Corwin's cock press against her. Uncertainty stiffened her, but Darius held her close, kissing her, stroking her back and breasts, suffusing her with pleasure, heightening her eagerness for new sensation. Corwin pressed forward, slowly, his hot cock stretching her as his fingers had, easing into her. There was pain as her muscles strained, but she remembered to press outward, and that pain was not greater than the pleasure of the two men, above her and below her, and both inside her.

"Yes." She arched her back. "Yes!"

She could hold still no longer. She had to move. Had to feel them moving inside her. She strained, her thighs clasping Darius, Corwin's clasping them both. She moved as they had taught her, and cried out again for the pleasure of it. They throbbed inside her. She held the hearts, the heat, the glorious strength of them both.

"Now!" cried Corwin.

And Darius arched below her and Corwin bucked forward, and both their cocks drove into her.

"Yes!" she screamed. "Corwin! Darius! Yes!"

After that there were no more words. There was only them inside her, driving themselves into her, stroking each other roughly and sweetly as they fucked her. Pleasure spilled from their separate minds and souls and bodies, twining together into a new and absolute passion.

I'm coming! I'm coming! The cry rang from them all and through them all.

The storm broke, wild beyond description, beautiful beyond compare. Her men bucked, gone past all possible restraint, and Miranda rode them, transformed from woman to pagan goddess by the strength of their glorious passion.

And in the heart of the storm she knew that none of them would ever leave, ever doubt, again. She knew and accepted for now and forever the strength and the safety of love.

Keep reading for a preview of
the next novel by Marissa Day

The Surrender of Lady Jane

Coming soon from Heat Books

One

I'm here, Jane. The urgent male voice sent a hot shiver of longing down Lady Jane's spine. *I'm waiting.*

Jane was dreaming. She knew she was dreaming, and in the dream, she opened her eyes.

As she had every night for the past three weeks, Jane found herself standing in a dark corridor carpeted with deep plush. Some nights she had been clad in only a white silk robe. Some nights she was dressed in a fantastic concoction of velvets like a medieval lady. Tonight, she was dressed for dancing in pale blue silk with three tiers of silver lace and rosettes. She felt the weight of plumes decorating her hair. But what truly mattered was the voice. Calling to her. Longing for her.

I'm here, Jane.

Jane began to run.

Doors flashed past her shoulders. Hints of movement caught

at the corners of her eyes, but she did not stop. *He* was waiting, and she must find him.

Breathless and flushed, she stopped before one of the identical closed doors, knowing, in the way of dreams, that it was the right one. She laid her gloved hand upon the surface, anticipation quickening her pulse. This was where the dream would change and become new. The only thing that would be the same after this was the waiting man, and the feelings he aroused in her.

Jane opened the door.

Warm candlelight filled a chamber as spacious as any royal apartment. The room was an Oriental fantasy furnished with all manner of velvet couches and lounges, some big enough to accommodate four or five persons at once. Silken hangings adorned the walls and green velvet draperies hid the windows.

A man stood in the center of the room. Like her, he was dressed for dancing. Tight, white knee breeches encased his muscled legs and he wore a gray silk waistcoat embroidered in silver over a spotless white linen shirt. His coat was shimmering emerald green with more silver at the cuffs and throat.

But the beauty of his attire was nothing when compared to the beauty of the man. He was not too tall, only topping Jane by six inches or so. He wore his blond hair long, and tied back in a sailor's queue. Neither was he too broad, but built in good proportion with himself. Everything about his form spoke of active living. His face was magnificent, with high cheekbones and a strong jawline. Jane's breath caught in her throat as she met his bright green eyes. They slanted dramatically but were saved from being too feminine by his heavy brows.

"Sweet Jane." He opened his arms. "You are very welcome here."

Jane ran at once into her dream lover's embrace. His mouth fastened on hers in a strong kiss. His tongue pressed against her lips and she opened eagerly, ready for the strange, sweet sensation of his tongue stroking hers while his hands caressed her shoulders and her back, gliding down to the curve of her derriere, around her hips and up again to brush the sides of her breasts. Jane shivered again, and felt him smile against her mouth.

"Are you glad to be here, Jane?" he whispered as he drew his lips along the curve of her jaw.

"Very." She sighed. His mouth brushed her throat, as if seeking to learn its every line, while his strong, capable hands caressed her waist and the curve of her belly through the layers of silk and muslin that clad her. For all he was a compactly formed man, he enfolded her completely in his embrace in a way her late husband never had. She liked that. She was no petite miss and had no wish to be treated as if she might break. Her mother had more than once despaired over Jane's curves, which were of the sort much more suited to pannier skirts and cinched waists than this time of high-waisted gowns and minimal foundation garments. But her dream lover appreciated the whole of her body. As he claimed her mouth again, he took her derriere in both hands.

"Such a beautiful ass," he murmured as he squeezed and kneaded, clearly relishing the softness of her flesh. He pressed her even closer to him, until her breasts rubbed his chest and her belly circled the ridge of his erection. Jane groaned with pleasure and tilted her hips against him. He smiled and took her hand, kissing the palm.

"Do you feel that?" He laid her hand against the outline of his cock, drawing her palm up and down its length. "This is yours. This is what you do to me."

"I want you," she whispered hoarsely. "I want to give myself to you."

"Do you?" He smiled mischievously and leaned in to graze her lower lip with his teeth. "How would you give yourself to me?" He released her hand, turning her as he spoke, until he stood behind her, one strong arm wrapped around her waist to pin her against his hips. His cock was so hard and so strong that she could feel it pressing between the halves of her ass, despite the layers of her skirts and petticoats. His other hand closed possessively over her breast, making her gasp. "What would you do when you give yourself to me?"

She meant to answer, but he began to plump and pet her breast, and Jane found she could do nothing but groan. His fingers found her pebbled nipple and rolled it. It felt delicious and wicked, and all she could think was how much better these caresses would be without the barrier of their clothing between them.

"Tell me what you would do, Jane." His breath was hot against her ear, his body a wall behind her. She had no strength. He supported her entirely.

"I would lay myself bare for you. I would open my thighs . . ."

"These thighs?" Without ceasing to play with her breast, he ran his other hand down her hip, his fingers knotting into the fabric of her skirt. "These luscious, smooth thighs?" He drew her skirt up as he lovingly spoke each word. Cold air touched the heated skin of her legs, sending fresh shivers rippling through her.

"Yes," she said. "The whole of my body would be yours."

"Would you touch yourself for me?" Now his hand traveled up the soft skin of her thigh, caressing her, slowly, possessively, almost reaching her straining center, but not quite. "Would you let me see how beautiful you are when you play with your breasts and this sweet pussy?" He cupped his hot palm over her damp curls and she sighed with relief and pleasure. "Would you do that for me?"

"Whatever you would want."

"And if I should want to play games of desire?" His mouth was on her shoulder now, kissing soft, sensual trails down her bared skin. "If I should wish to hold you helpless to our pleasure while I worked my will upon you?" Skilled and infinitely wicked, his fingers played with her folds, sending flashes of desire through her body.

"Yes, anything."

"Anything, as long as I do not stop," He laughed, but he did not stop. He stroked her and cupped her. His knowing fingers found her damp slit and pressed into it, and she writhed with delight. He caressed and massaged her breasts roughly even while his arms made sure she remained tight against the length of his body so the halves of her ass rubbed hard against his cock.

"Yes, please." She did not think on what she said. She only thought of his hand on her breast and his fingers in her slit, for he had found the hot and swollen center of her pleasure and was rubbing it in earnest now.

"Such a sensitive little clit. So eager to be pleased," he crooned, and the fire in her roared higher. Jane felt her whole self begin to slip away into the glorious current of pleasure.

"That's it, Jane. Come for me. I want you to come for me."

"I want you!"

"You shall have me soon, but you must obey your lover, and come for me now."

He thrust his fingers deeply into her, pressing hard, stroking fast until the sensation of that decadent friction became too much to contain. Pleasure broke from her in long, simmering pulses, rocking her buttocks against his cock and wringing wordless cries from her.

"That's it, Jane. That is so very good." His breath hitched in his throat as he cradled her body made limp by the force of her satisfied desire. "Every moment brings you closer to me, my beautiful Jane. Soon I will hold you in truth, and then you will have all that you desire."

And he was gone.

Jane woke with a start, the aftermath of pleasure still coursing through her veins. But the essential vitality had vanished along with the dream, and now she felt deflated. Jane lay curled in a truckle bed with a lumpy straw mattress at the feet of her new and profoundly pregnant mistress: Her Royal Highness Princess Victorie of Saxe-Coburg-Saalfeld, now Duchess of Kent and wife of Prince Edward, Duke of Kent and Strathern. The sounds of the sea rippled through the open window along with the salt breeze. Slow hooves thudded on the dirt lane, and a bird twittered tentatively. Calais was beginning to wake.

Sweet Jane was as far gone as her dream lover, and she was only Lady Jane DeWitte once more. Biting her lip against a groan of fatigue and disappointment, Jane curled her knees tighter to her chest. How much longer could these sweet, torturous dreams continue? Each night of the journey across the Germanies and France, her nameless lover had called to her in her sleep. Each night his urgent voice had led her to a scene of sensuous luxury. There, his words and intoxicating caresses sent her hurtling over the crest of pleasure. But each time when she woke, she was only restless and bereft.

Because despite all she had been given, Jane wanted more. During the daytime as the carriages bumped over the country roads, she had found plenty of time to imagine what that "more" might involve. She had yet to see her dream lover naked, had yet to bare herself fully to him. They had not performed the marital act. Widowed as she was, Jane was familiar with the feeling of a man inside her. But Lord Octavius had never touched her as her dream lover did. She had never before been aware there existed such a dizzying height where she could ride delicious waves of feeling. Surely, having her dream lover inside her would be similarly intense. That idea regularly robbed her of her breath, until she had to reach for her violet water to calm herself.

Women dreamed of men. Jane knew that. As a girl on the threshold of marriage, she'd often dreamed of being held and being touched. But to have such dreams occupy so much of her waking thought now that she was full grown and much more experienced was ridiculous. No, it was insupportable, and possibly a sign she had somehow become unbalanced.

But even that did not frighten her as much as the possibility that this new plaguing restlessness of her body might drive her to risk her reputation and position by entering into a liaison with a man.

Tomorrow the ducal party would all board the royal yacht and return to London for the birth of the child her mistress carried. That child might very well one day wear the crown of England. To have secured a place in the household of the royal family was no small feat for a woman who had been left without family or money. To have such a place in the household of the heir presumptive was nothing short of miraculous. Jane could not do anything to jeopardize her standing.

The dreams will eventually end. Jane knotted her fists in the inn's stiff bedsheet. *I will simply have to bear it until they do.* Jane squeezed her eyes shut, shuddering against the sense of loss that accompanied the thought.

Mad. The word whispered itself in her mind. *I am going mad.*

Two

"Jane! My dear Jane!"

A familiar, and very welcome voice cut through the glitter and elegance of Lady Darnley's ball. Jane turned to see Georgiana Martins—who had lately become Lady Hibbert-Jones—make her way through the crush of London's finest, all invited to welcome the Duke of Kent home.

"Georgiana! How good to see you!" Jane stretched out her hand, deeply relieved. The ducal party had only arrived in London that afternoon. Her maid, Tilly, had not even finished unpacking the trunks, and yet the duchess had insisted Jane be here.

"You are to pay particular attention to what the ladies say," the duchess had told her earnestly. "I know the prince regent would rather we had stayed in Saxe-Coburg. It is vital to know if the lords of England think the same. Their ladies can tell us that."

So, here Jane was, turned out in her finest ice blue satin

with its gold netting and scallops. She smiled and made small talk, and was ready to fall asleep on her feet. She reached out to Georgiana as she would to a lifeline.

"You're looking very well," said Jane to her friend as they clasped hands. Georgiana's second marriage evidently agreed with her. Her brown eyes sparkled with good humor and she carried herself with pride and energy. Her gray gown, trimmed with freshwater pearls and ivory rosettes, set off her black hair very well.

"But you, my dear, look positively exhausted." Georgiana tucked her arm in Jane's and steered her closer to the wall and the blessed breeze allowed by the open French doors. "Tell me, was the journey very tedious?"

"The weather was awful." Jane flapped her fan and peered over its edge to locate the Duke of Kent. Plain-faced, portly, flushed with wine and exertion, he stood with a group of exquisitely tailored men who all laughed heartily at some bon mot. He appeared to be in a better humor than he had been upon their arrival at Kensington House. As soon as they'd walked in, he'd pronounced the place "dim and pokey, begahd!" This despite its silk-clad walls, painted ceilings and many beautiful windows.

"The duke insisted on driving the duchess the entire distance to Calais himself, in an open landau of all things," Jane murmured to Georgie. "It was . . . most difficult."

"And how does our new duchess?"

Jane thought on her mistress, sitting in her wingback chair behind the great curve of her belly. Much younger than her husband, the new duchess of Kent was plump and sturdy rather than pretty. The journey of over four hundred miles in the seventh month of her pregnancy had worn on her, but had not damped her spirits in the least. She'd had a ready answer for the duke as he barged about the parlor, complaining of Lord Darnley holding a welcome ball the very night of their arrival.

"Lord Darnley could not have foreseen the delay in our crossing," the duchess reminded him firmly in her idiosyncratic mixture of German and French. "Otherwise I'm sure he would have moved the date. But his lordship has done so much for us, we must not neglect what he does in our honor."

"If I tell you anything of the duchess, Georgiana, I am relying on you to spread the word," said Jane seriously. "It is the only subject anyone wishes to converse on, and I am worn out repeating myself."

"Jane!" Georgie hid her mock astonishment behind her ostrich plume fan. "What sort of gossipmonger do you take me for?"

"One of the best I know."

Georgiana stared at her for a moment of genuine astonishment and then laughed heartily. Jane joined in. It felt so good to relax with a friend after spending so many months abroad and alone, not to mention spending so many nights teased and plagued by her wicked dreams.

Don't think on those right now. Her mind had been wandering too much as it was. If she should start dwelling on imagined pleasures, she would quickly become useless.

"Of course I'll tell everyone whatever you like," Georgiana was saying. "They'll all be asking me anyway."

"And I need to hear all the news."

Georgiana eyed Jane shrewdly. "You do, or your patrons do?"

"Georgie . . ."

"All right, all right, I won't press. But I will tell you, Jane, it's going to be hard going. The regent wants nothing to do with either of them. Any of them."

"Yes, we'd heard." In fact, the prince regent had refused to advance a single penny to help his brother return to England. The duke, who was perpetually in debt, had been obliged to turn to friends to raise the needed cash—Lord Darnley among them. Jane opened and closed her fan restlessly, eyeing the glittering crowd. It was impossible not to notice how many gentlemen and ladies stood talking confidently to each other as their eyes sought out the various members of the ducal party; His Highness, his private secretary Captain Conroy, herself.

"But the prince regent . . . can be persuaded, can't he? He has proved willing to change his mind on other matters." This in particular was a point the duchess asked her to sound out. The Prince of Wales could be as changeable as the spring weather, especially when he sensed the opportunity for love or money.

Georgiana paused as she considered her words. "All the little birds tell me the regent complains the Duke of Kent is claiming too much privilege too soon. After all, his child is not yet born, much less been declared heir apparent. He says he is insulted. I suspect much of this springs from his feelings after the death of the Princess Charlotte."

The reminder of that tragedy silenced them both for a moment. Jane had met the princess a few times, and formed a good impression. Compared to her luxury-loving father, the lone child of the prince and princess of Wales had seemed remarkably sensible. But Princess Charlotte had been both married and buried two years since, and her stillborn son with her.

Jane fingered her fan for a moment. She did not want to ask her next question. Her interest was purely mercenary, and it shamed her. "At the risk of sounding terribly indelicate, what is the state of . . ."

"Hymen's War Triumphant?"

"Georgiana!"

"Tush, Jane! It's only what the papers are all calling it. Truly, it is shocking." Georgiana sighed, and her bright manner faded to expose the sharp and observant woman underneath. "Twelve princes and princesses, who among them have brought forth near fifty children, but not one both alive and legitimate." She rolled her eyes heavenward looking for explanations. "The regent still hopes he might sire another legitimate child, but that will require a new, legitimate wife. My husband says Parliament is not in the mood to grant a divorce, no matter how many Italians our Princess Caroline is caught with. Of course, any potential Princess of Wales will have to be willing to overlook the fact that the regent is already married to Mrs. Fitzherbert and is carrying on with Lady . . . Let me see, I think it's Lady Jersey this week." She tapped her fan against her palm. "So that's the first in line. Second, the Duchess of York is past child bearing. This leaves the Duke of Clarence and his new duchess as the closest competition for your patrons."

"Have you seen her yet?" Jane asked.

"I have. I don't speak German so well as you, but she seems to me both healthy and pleasant. The greatest shock is that she and Clarence appear devoted to one another. I would be most surprised if there was not an announcement from that quarter shortly."

Jane's fingers closed a little too tightly around her fan. The Duke of Kent lived beyond his means. Everyone knew it. If Parliament could not be persuaded to extend him an additional income as father to England's heir, accommodations might have to be made. The first of these would be the dismissal of some members of the household. At which point, Jane would find herself with nowhere to go.

"Perhaps that's for the best," murmured Jane, struggling for disinterest. "It cannot be a good thing for the future of the nation to rest on a single unborn child."

"I'm sure you're right." Georgiana's face and voice both hardened. "Look at us. We spend our days talking of fripperies and scandal. In the meantime, there are riots in the streets and the king runs mad. His sons think of nothing but how to get their hands on the public purse strings, his daughters have been made into a flock of nuns, and none of us knows what is coming next. Is it a wonder we dance all night? If we stopped to think, we would drop dead of terror."

Hearing the anger and the warning in her friend's voice, Jane laid a hand on Georgiana's arm. "I'm sorry, Georgie, I'm not good company right now and I'm spoiling your night."

"You are the best of company, Jane." Georgiana patted her hand. "You are only tired from your travels." They smiled, each understanding the other saw past their *politesse*, but each silently agreeing it would be best to move back to conversation more proper for a ballroom.

Just then, movement caught Jane's eye.

"Oh, no," Georgiana muttered. "It is our *dear* Mrs. Fortesque."

A woman with a square jaw and square brow overshadowed by a forest of dyed ostrich plumes strode straight toward them through the crowd. Claret crepe encased thin shoulders and an improbably full bosom.

"I'll distract her, Jane. You make your escape." Georgiana fixed on a brilliant smile and sailed directly into Mrs. Fortesque's path. "Agnes! I was so hoping I'd find you here!"

Jane did not wait to hear what Mrs. Fortesque replied. She slid out the nearest French door and onto the balcony, and dodged sideways where she would not be immediately visible from either door nor window. The fresh night air that enfolded her was chill but exceedingly welcome. Jane closed her eyes and raised her chin, relishing the cool breeze as it swept across her skin, and tried not to wish herself elsewhere.

The dinner had been excellent. The music was very fine. The whole of fashionable London, dressed in their finest, swarmed a ballroom hung with French blue, said to be the prince regent's current favorite color. This was diplomatic of Lady Darnley, Jane thought. In a pinch, either of the Darnleys could argue they had chosen the color to remind the royal duke where their ultimate loyalties lay.

And this was only the beginning. Hymen's War Triumphant, indeed. Should the Duke of Kent's babe be born whole and healthy, the nobility would begin jockeying for position in earnest, and Jane, as the duchess's attendant and presumed confidant, would be hauled into the thick of it, whether she wanted to be there or not.

Jane sighed and forced her eyes open. The gorgeously illuminated formal gardens spread out beyond the balcony. Couples strolled to and fro, enjoying the evening. As she watched, melancholy dug its claws into her. No such activity awaited her this night or any other. She was the eyes and ears of the Duchess of Kent, and she was the sole survivor of a family that had fallen up to its hips debt. Love and desire were nothing but the stuff of dreams for Lady Jane, and, she must find a way to make her peace with that.

"A pleasant night, isn't it?" inquired a man's deep voice.

Jane's straightened at once, snapping open her fan to cover the shock on her face. She glanced wildly about, but saw no one.

"Down here, and I'm sorry if I startled you."

Cautiously, Jane advanced to the balcony's carved stone rail. There, she looked down onto the shadowed figure of her dream lover.